# BLEEDING OF THE SHADOWS
## A Nurse's Tale of Loss & Hope

# A Debut Novel

## Inspired by True Events
# J. Pierce

Paperback ISBN: 978-1-64719-568-7
Hardcover ISBN: 978-1-64719-569-4
eBook ISBN: 978-1-64719-570-0

Published by BookLocker.com, Inc., St. Petersburg, Florida.

This fictional novel was inspired by true events. Names, locations, and specific details have been changed to protect the identities of those involved. The description of any nursing procedures, medical or mental health information is intended for literary purposes only. It is not intended for the cure or treatment of any ailment, injury, or disease. If you are not feeling well, please contact an appropriate, licensed, healthcare provider.

Library of Congress Cataloging in Publication Data
Pierce, J.
BLEEDING OF THE SHADOWS: A Nurse's Tale of Loss & Hope by J. Pierce
Library of Congress Control Number: 2021907070

Printed on acid-free paper.

BookLocker.com, Inc.
2021

For my precious mother.

# ACKNOWLEDGMENTS

Many thanks to my family and friends for their insights and support during my sixteen-year journey in writing this book. I am especially grateful to my wife and kids for their putting up with my dialoguing with characters both on and off the keyboard as well as for their never denying me time to complete this novel. A special thanks to my editorial team David Aretha, Emily Drabek, and my original editor and brother, Greg. Their time, talent, and dedication are truly appreciated more than words can express. I am likewise grateful to Angela Hoy and the publishing team at Booklocker for their time, persistence, and expertise in getting this book to market.

Finally, profound thanks to my dear friend and mentor, Phillip V. Benevento, Jr., for decades of friendship and support as well as for his inspiring me with a love of creative writing at an early age.

# THE CAST OF CLINICAL CHARACTERS

Wanda: Schizophrenic patient who aspired to become an Olympic archer in her youth

Richard Goldmann: Schizophrenic patient who was a former research scientist

Phil Morgan: Depressed patient with PTSD and paranoid tendencies who was a New York state trooper during 9/11

Sally Waterman: Borderline mentally challenged patient with schizophrenia who suffers abuse from her sadistic brother, Walter

Mike: Traumatic brain-injured patient and aspiring young landscaper

Lucinda Rosado: Sexy schizophrenic patient with anger and family issues

Nick Fain: Schizophrenic patient with extreme antisocial personality disorder, delusions of grandeur, and religious hyper-zealotry

Rob Reilly: Cross-dressing schizophrenic patient with a split personality issue

Jim Greene: U.S. Army Veteran and visiting nurse with depression

# AUTHOR'S NOTE

Welcome, readers! Before you delve into *Bleeding of the Shadows*, I want to mention some fun facts that should maximize your reading experience. First, in this book an unconventional technique is used to advance the plot. Unlike traditional novels in which a protagonist rides the crest of a story arc, this book is more episodic in nature. Also, some of the chapters are shorter and faster than those in a traditional novel. Each chapter has a short story flavor to it because of the episodic style of this novel. Like an intricate mosaic coming together, the recurrent episodes do relate to one another and create a unified tale in which each character's story comes to an intriguing yet logical conclusion.

The main protagonist, Jim, is a visiting nurse, and most chapters capture him visiting his group of patients in their homes. It was purposely written in this episodic fashion to accurately depict a day in the life of a visiting psychiatric nurse and each of his patients.

Although this book is based upon some of my past experiences as a visiting nurse, certain clinical sacrifices had to be made to keep the story focused. The biggest one is that Jim doesn't acquire any new patients during the six months he worked with Harmony Healthcare. This is not truly representative of the shifting caseloads that visiting nurses have.

Finally, this story is set in 2005 because, well, that's when the original draft was written. There are figures in the book that had a different public image in 2005 than they do today. For example, in 2005 Chief Wahoo was still the logo on the Cleveland Indians ball cap and Donald Trump was a popular reality TV star. Although times have changed, I have kept such figures and references in the book for the historical authenticity of the time period.

I hope you gain insight into mentally ill patients, understanding their day-to-day struggles, and realizing that we are all very much the same. In my experience, I have seen mental illness cut across all cultural, educational, gender, religious and socio-economic boundaries. Mental illness does not discriminate. Unfortunately, some of those who suffer from it still face discrimination. I hope that in some small way that this book will change that.

The mentally ill patients that I worked with had aspirations, trials, disappointments, and heartaches that are all part of the shared human experience. My patients were often loving, funny, angry, endearing, and inspirational. I hope you cherish your relationships with these characters as I did my time with my patients.

*Who knows what is good for a person in life, during the few*
*and meaningless days that they pass through like a shadow?*
*—Ecclesiastes 6:12*

# CHAPTER ONE

As Jim unsteadily sat up in bed, his feet and toes landed on the hideous shag carpet beneath him. Sitting there and trying to wake up, Jim wished that that his feet were firmly ensconced within cold leather and that he was preparing to jump from the belly of a metal beast. This beast was the iconic and herculean Army C-130 plane that Jim thought he would never miss as much as he did now.

Focusing was difficult for Jim because of his hangover. Too many beers at Yankee Stadium. He groped clumsily for a cigarette from the pack on his bedside table and for his chrome Zippo. Jim struggled to ignite the cigarette because his lighter was low on fluid and his hands were a bit shaky. Soon he inhaled fresh tobacco while regretting his behavior from the night before.

Jim was usually jovial whenever he got drunk, but last night's game was different. He quickly got hammered during the early innings and hardly spoke to anyone. The event had been planned several weeks earlier by some of his coworkers, but shortly after the tickets were acquired, Jim received his pink slip. Jim Greene had worked for Acme Insurance Company as a nurse case manager for about a year. It was the most lucrative and least demanding job that he'd ever had. He liked the job and most of his coworkers; however, he intensely disliked the one person whom he needed to impress: the new boss. Not wanting to seem like a poor sport, he decided not to skip out on the game even though he knew that he'd probably never see any of his colleagues again. His last day of work, April 15, 2005, coincided with the ballgame.

Jim had a vague recollection of constellations swirling on Grand Central's ceiling after the game before he departed for his drunken trip back to the Valley. From the Valley train station, he took a cab back to his modest South Ashton apartment. South Ashton was one of the southernmost towns in the seemingly dead-end and blue-collar Valley. It was about ninety minutes, and several decades, removed from the excitement of New York City.

At noontime, Jim noticed the blinking light on his answering machine on his bedside table. He hit the play button.

"Hello, Mr. Greene, this is Rose Coppola from Harmony Healthcare. I was wondering if we could meet today at 3:00 p.m. instead of tomorrow. Please call me at 203-555-2351."

Jim cleared his throat. Then he dialed the number but got her answering machine. He left an awkward message confirming the change for his job interview, killed his cigarette, and lumbered into the bathroom to get cleaned up.

He was taken aback by what he saw in the mirror—his wavy black hair was completely disheveled, and his face was thick and rough with dark stubble. He looked like the 9/11 terror mastermind, Khalid Sheikh Mohammed, when he was captured. Jim had inherited the features of his Sicilian mother, instead of those of his Anglo-American father. Features that seemed more Arabic whenever Jim had any facial hair or a tan. He deliberately avoided having either one since 9/11. Quickly, he shaved, then entered the shower.

Jim's left hip felt acutely painful as the hot water cascaded over his body. It hurt like hell from being crammed into a small folding seat at the stadium. The hip pain was a frustrating reminder of a promising career as an Army nurse that had been thwarted by a bad jump during his first skydive as a civilian following his enlistment. Shortly Afterward, he and his friend, Chris Roberts, began nursing school at a small Catholic college just outside the Valley. Jim hoped that his hip would recover while he was in nursing school. It didn't. After graduating from school, he failed his physical fitness test and was denied a commission in the Army Nurse Corps. Chris passed and was currently serving as a nurse in Iraq.

After drying off from the scalding shower, Jim stumbled back to his bedroom and was surprised to see the light blinking again on his answering machine. He plopped down on the bed and played it. It was a voice that he hadn't heard in many months. It was Holly's.

"Hey, Jimmy boy, how ya doing? It's Holly—just callin' to say 'hi' and let you know that—well—I've been dating this guy, Miles, Miles Upton—and he like—he just proposed to me. So, I said yes. Well, I just wanna tell you before you heard from someone else. Anyhow, hope you're doin' good and to talk to you some time."

Jim had dated Holly off and on since they met online while he was in nursing school, although he hadn't seen her since their last date during the previous summer. He recognized Upton's name, as his father owned the largest funeral home in Ashton. Jim was a bit jealous but knew that his relationship with her wouldn't have worked out because he couldn't handle her bipolar disorder. She was downright Goth whenever she was in one of her black moods. Perhaps her undertaker fiancé could better deal with her dark side.

Before his interview with Nurse Coppola, Jim stopped at Gus' Diner. Even though it was 1:30 p.m., Jim was in the mood for breakfast food. While waiting for his food, Jim nervously flipped through a newspaper that someone had left behind. His waitress suddenly plopped a steaming dish of eggs with bacon and toast in front of him.

"Do you want anything else, honey?"

"No, thanks."

Soon he finished the meal. He sipped his coffee, as he still had plenty of time before the interview. He broke out a copy of his resume from his leather binder. His credentials seemed pretty good to him on paper, but he worried about how to explain why he had left a lucrative job in New York City and now wanted to work with psychiatric patients. He decided to describe his departure as due to downsizing, rather than telling the truth. Jim felt a surge of self-confidence as he looked at his sheet of references. It included an old nursing professor and two of his former Army buddies, Captain Chris Roberts and paramedic Jake Gianni. Chris and Jake were like brothers to Jim, and he looked forward to seeing them whenever he could, which hadn't been much lately. Chris was still in Iraq, and even though Jake lived right in the Valley, he was a lot less accessible, as his wife was very pregnant with triplets.

Although Jim didn't particularly want to go to work for Rose Coppola and Harmony Healthcare, he couldn't work in a hospital or nursing home anymore because his hip hurt too much after standing for more than an hour or two. The pain had forced him out of a job at a local nursing home, but he ended up with the better-paying nurse case manager job in New York. Now he'd settle for a way to pay his rent while he tried to make sense out of a once-promising professional life.

Jim found a quaint, brick Victorian house at the address that Ms. Coppola had given him. He straightened his tie, adjusted his jacket, and rang the bell. Suddenly, a tall, broad-shouldered and middle-aged lady opened the door.

"Hi, you must be Jim. I'm Rose," she said, extending her hand.

Jim shook her hand. "Pleased to meet you."

Rose led him to a nearby office and took a seat behind a large oak desk as Jim sat in an overstuffed leather chair facing her.

She looked down at his resume on her desk and said, "Very impressive clinical experience. Have you ever worked with psych patients before?"

"Not really," Jim admitted. "Once in a while at Valley Memorial Hospital we'd get a psych patient who also had some sort of medical problem. The psych ward shunned medical patients, and whenever any of their patients developed a medical problem, the head nurse would transfer them to a medical floor."

Rose nodded and made note of it. "Looks like you have solid geriatric experience from working at Sunny Meadows. Why'd you leave that nursing home?"

"I heard about a great opportunity to work at Acme Insurance as a nurse case manager in their workers' compensation unit."

"Sounds interesting. And did you leave that job?"

"I was downsized," Jim replied.

"Are you currently working?"

"No, ma'am. I'm in between positions."

"Have you ever worked with violent patients before?"

"No, but the Army taught me how to defend myself."

"If you come to work for me, where do you see yourself in five years?"

*Damned if I know! Five years ago, I thought I'd be an Army nurse. Seven years before that I thought I'd be married to Maria and working on her family's ranch.*

Jim began to cough uncontrollably in response to her question.

"Here, take some water." Rose poured him a glass from a ceramic pitcher that was on the corner of her desk. "Look, I know that's a tough question to answer. That's why I ask it. If someone asked me that question at your age, I would've said, 'In five years I'll be a happy housewife with twin girls in grade school.' But then my husband died in a car accident without enough insurance, so my whole concept of what I'd be doing in five years radically changed. I busted my ass working as a waitress and went to nursing school part-time at night. My mother-in-law was around to care for my twins. Finally, I graduated and worked at a couple of different hospitals before getting into home care. Then I had to take out a second mortgage on this house when I started my own agency."

Jim nodded with interest and was a bit more at ease by her unexpected revelation.

"Let me tell you my management philosophy: If you work hard, do what I tell you to do and how I tell you to do it, then you'll do very nicely for yourself in the next five years. Most importantly, you should always treat my patients the same way that you want me to treat you."

"Sounds fair."

"So, are you interested in joining Harmony Healthcare?"

"Sure, sounds good to me." *Yeah, why not take another bullshit Plan B job instead of pursuing something that I really want,* Jim agonized to himself.

"Good. Meet me a week from today at 5:00 p.m. to start your orientation," Rose said. "Better yet, make it 4:30 p.m., so you can fill out your W-4 and other forms before we head out to see patients. And wear street clothes. If anybody sees you in nursing attire, they'll presume that you have drugs."

Jim headed back to his car, thinking it would be best to keep a low profile around this lady, as she would surely sense any hint of nonsense and probably not tolerate it.

Jim didn't do much the following week except eat, sleep, and watch TV.

Soon the time had passed, however, and he found himself back at Rose's, filling out the mandatory paperwork. They then departed for their first patient, not too far from Rose's home office.

Jim followed Rose onto the porch of a rundown, two-family apartment building and waited while Rose grasped the knocker and rapped on the faded, warped door three distinct times.

"If you don't knock three times, Wanda will think that you're a solicitor and not open the door."

The door was suddenly pulled open about three inches, yanking taut the thick chain attached to the jamb. Wanda, a diminutive and disheveled-looking woman, peered through the crack, allowing cigarette smoke to waft out of the darkened living room.

"Good evening, Rosie. You're a bit early today."

"Yeah, I'm orienting a new nurse. This is Jim. Do you mind if he comes in?"

"Oh, he's a big one! I don't mind at all," Wanda replied mischievously.

She closed the door for a moment, then swung it wide open, revealing a large and cluttered living room.

Wanda walked toward the far side of the room, and Rose asked her, "How's your sugar been over the weekend?"

"Up and down. The cotton candy at the Valley Festival kinda did me in on Saturday."

"Wanda, you know better than to eat something like that. Why don't you get started with the blood glucose meter while we get your pills set up?"

As the three of them began walking to Wanda's kitchen, a wild shriek startled Jim, and he jumped back slightly.

"Ah, don't worry about him, son. That's just Bubba. He's harmless," Wanda said.

"Bubba's an Amazonian parrot," Rose explained.

"Jimbo, do you want to see him up close?" Wanda asked.

18

Jim reluctantly agreed. Wanda approached the large wire cage suspended from the dingy, peeling ceiling. She undid the metal clasp, then thrust her hand in toward the bird's rough talons. Bubba reflexively grasped Wanda's wrist, and then she rotated toward Jim, presenting the bird mere inches from his face.

Bubba cooed quietly, his eyes quickly dilating to take in the new visitor, then he crowed, *"Live like you were dying!"*

Wanda and Rose laughed hysterically, but Jim didn't quite know what to make of this strange bird.

"Bubba is a country music aficionado. He absolutely loves Tim McGraw," Rose told Jim.

Wanda added, "Yeah, I bought him in Texas after an archery meet years ago. You should see him with his tiny cowboy hat on—it's a real hoot."

After Wanda returned Bubba to his cage, she walked to the kitchen adjoining the living room. The living room was very dark and flanked on all but one side by tall stacks of numerous newspapers and magazines. The remaining side, which bordered the kitchen, had an old TV ensconced in a credenza made of cheap particle board. The only windows in the living room were blocked by the bundled periodicals. The far side of that room held a partially inflated air mattress covered by nicotine-tinged sheets.

"Do you need any more test strips yet, Wanda?" Rose asked as Wanda pricked her finger at the kitchen table and squeezed it to produce enough blood for a blood glucose meter reading.

"No, thanks. I should be good for about another week or so."

Jim tried to be discreet as he studied Wanda's appearance. She looked to be about fifty-five, but he knew from Rose that Wanda was actually forty-three. She wore badly faded jeans with an oversized sweatshirt that hung loosely from her slightly hunched shoulders. Her skin was dry, and her teeth and nails were stained brown from her incessant cigarette smoking. Her hair was like how Gwen Stefani wore hers at times, with tufts sticking out in all directions. Her eyes were slightly bloodshot and surrounded by dark, wrinkled lids.

"Rosie, you got any Milk of Magnesia? I haven't pooped in five days," Wanda said as the blood glucose meter beeped and displayed a normal reading.

"Let me see," she said, searching through her satchel. "Sorry, Wanda. I don't have any with me. Why don't you get some prune juice, and I'll tell Cindy to bring you some milk of mag tomorrow?"

Rose tore off the top of a small coin envelope from her nursing bag and dumped the pills into her palm to check them.

"Here you go, Wanda—the usual."

Wanda nodded, took the pills, and swallowed them. She then reached for a new cigarette and lit it with a cheap plastic lighter.

After taking a deep drag, she extended her hand to Jim. "Pleasure meeting you, young man. Am I going to see you often?"

"As often as Rose sends me out here," he replied, feeling awkward.

"Jim should be seeing you on the nights that Vicky doesn't," Rose added. She then slid the MAR (Medication Administration Record) across the table for Wanda's signature.

After they left Wanda and returned to Rose's black Cadillac SUV, Rose told him, "Wanda's situation is very sad. As a young lady, she was an award-winning archer, even had Olympic aspirations, but then she was diagnosed with schizophrenia at twenty-five.

The psychotropic medication caused her extrapyramidal symptoms, mostly fine hand tremors. The tremors ended her archery career. She then moved up here from Texas to live with an aunt. When her aunt got admitted to a nursing home a few years ago, Wanda moved into this state-subsidized apartment. Her schizophrenia has worsened over the years, so she started on clozapine about three years ago. Two years ago, she tested positive for diabetes. Unfortunately, some antipsychotics either induce or aggravate diabetes."

On the way to their next patient, Richard Goldmann, Jim learned about the Valley's odd history. In the mid-nineteenth century, captains of industry decided to expand the area's steel mill business. To maximize profits, they wanted the cheapest workforce available. The inmates at the Valley Asylum were freed from the institution and worked like peasants in the mills. Eventually, they married and bred—sometimes interbred. Even some of the normal people in the Valley just didn't look right.

Jim sat quietly, taking in the information, all the while missing his former cubicle at Acme Insurance Company.

"Richard Goldmann lives in the most unusual home you've ever seen," Rose said. "He lived with his father until their house burned down. Then Richard's father replaced it with an old railroad passenger car that he'd gotten free from his brother, who was a railroad executive. They remodeled the car and made it very habitable. It worked out fine until it blew over during a bad hurricane. So, Richard's uncle brought in a slightly rusted tanker car, which he split in half. He anchored the passenger car between the tanker halves, which were positioned with their rounded ends facing up."

"Was that safe?" Jim asked.

Rose shrugged and smiled. "The halves of the tanker car looked like towers flanking the passenger train car—kinda like a castle. So, they decided to expand upon it by adding two more passenger cars. They planned to add another passenger car with two more towers to complete a four-sided castle with an enclosed courtyard."

"Why didn't they?"

"Well, when Rich's uncle and father died, the money and surplus railroad supplies dried up. Not having the fourth side has always been a sore spot with Richard. He got in trouble with the DEP a few years back when a moat that he had dug on the fourth side flooded a few houses downhill from him."

Rose continued, "Richard has had schizophrenia since about his thirties and came down with diabetes after being on meds for a couple of years. He was a very successful research scientist for a large drug company, but then he started seeing pink pills dancing a conga line in the lab. He lost his job and spent nearly a year in the VMI (Valley Mental Institute) before moving in with his dad."

Rose pulled into a narrow driveway. Jim was astounded at Richard's castle—it was even odder than Rose's description had led him to expect. The front door was on the side of the original passenger car that faced the street. Richard answered the doorbell wearing a white lab coat over semi-casual clothes.

"Good afternoon, Rose. Who's this fine gentleman with you?"

"Richard, this is Jim. He is going to be working evenings."

With the scrutiny of a disgruntled drill sergeant, Richard examined Jim, starting with his face and working down to his shoes. Richard looked like a cross between LBJ and Larry Bud Melman. He had slick dark hair and thick black BCGs (Birth Control Glasses) anchored behind his enormous ears. Jim had worn BCGs when he was in the service; they were reputedly so ugly that anyone who wore them was guaranteed not to get laid.

Richard extended his pale, bony hand and with a broad smile, said, "Sir Richard Goldmann, gentleman and scholar. A pleasure to make your acquaintance."

Jim was amused by this unusual introduction and heartily shook his hand.

"Let us retire to the laboratory. I believe that I am finally on the verge of discovering the missing link of all matter. I call it Paramatter."

Rose nodded as if he'd offered fries with her Happy Meal. Rose then explained, "Jim, Richard has a dual PhD in both physics and biochemistry. He did some pioneering work with antineoplastics when he was younger."

Richard said, "I found cancer and antineoplastics to be somewhat mundane and depressing after a while. Paramatter, on the other hand, holds the promise to cure all diseases and maladies. Conceptually, it's the blueprint of all matter—the stem cells of the entire universe."

"How long have you been working on it?" Jim asked.

"Since I was five. But I didn't understand its true implications until nine years ago when the flame from my Bunsen burner whispered to me that Paramatter was the only worthy scientific pursuit."

"Have you been hearing any strange voices or seeing anything unusual this week, Richard?" Rose asked.

"Just my moronic neighbors at the zoning hearing last Tuesday night."

"Are they still giving you a hard time about wanting to build up that brick wall?"

"Yes, they're afraid of a fatal rock slide if the Valley gets socked with a massive earthquake—the Valley has not had any sizeable earthquakes since prehistoric times. Any imbecile knows that a properly cemented brick wall isn't going anywhere in the absence of an earthquake."

"I guess they just don't appreciate that better fences make better neighbors," Rose said with a wink.

After she gave Richard his meds and supervised his blood glucose meter reading, Richard signed the MAR. Jim and Rose then got back on the road.

"Phillip Morgan lives in Ashton, about fifteen minutes from here. He's not schizophrenic but has profound depression, PTSD, and paranoid tendencies. Years ago, he worked as a security guard at the World Trade Center, where he met his wife,

Debbie, who was a successful businesswoman. In the mid-'90s, Phil left that job to become a New York State Trooper. On 9/11 Debbie was eight and a half months pregnant with their first child. The Friday of that week was supposed to be her last day before going out on maternity leave. After the Towers fell, Phil spent several weeks at Ground Zero, sifting through tons of flesh-strewn rubble and circulating flyers with Debbie's picture on them. No trace of her was ever found."

*Damn, this guy has the worst 9/11 story I've ever heard,* Jim thought. "How did he end up here?"

"After his search failed, he just couldn't do much anymore. He surrendered his badge and gun, lost his home, and then drifted from shelter to shelter. Eventually, he was found almost dead on the street and was admitted to the VMI (Valley Mental Institute). From there he moved to the Ashton YMCA."

"What's he paranoid about?" Jim inquired.

"Well, he's a bit of an agoraphobe and only gets out maybe twice a month. He hates crowds, public transit, and touching any paper product that hasn't been microwaved for at least ten seconds."

"Why's that?"

"He thinks it kills any potential anthrax spores."

*Not so paranoid,* Jim thought, recalling that one of the anthrax victims after 9/11 died in the Valley.

Rose continued, "As women aren't allowed on the resident floors, we usually just beep our horn and meet Phil on the fire escape to give him his meds. You'll be our first nurse who won't have that problem."

Soon the behemoth SUV pulled up to the brick YMCA building, which had been converted from a defunct National Guard armory. The YMCA had a more traditional castle-like appearance than Richard's abode, but it was also much older and more decrepit. Rose gave a quick blast of her loud horn, and within seconds Phil appeared outside the fire escape door on the second floor.

"You gotta make sure to give Phil all of his meds in a small baggie and the MAR in a separate baggie. Once a new nurse made the mistake of giving him pills in a regular coin envelope, and he ruined them in the microwave."

Phil was a tall and husky African American man with tightly cropped hair and a neatly trimmed mustache. Over time, Jim would learn that Phil usually wore ironed dungarees with a clean T-shirt, or a smartly pressed button-down shirt. He always wore running sneakers, but never shoes.

"How are you today, Phil?" Rose gently asked.

"Okay, I guess, but I couldn't get out of bed until 4:30 p.m. this afternoon. Do you think they could increase my dose of Ambien?"

"I don't see why not—you're a pretty big guy. I'll have Cindy call the doctor first thing in the morning. By the way, this is Jim. He's going to be coming out on the nights that Vicky's off."

Phil glanced up at Jim with a slight smile and nod of acknowledgment, which Jim returned.

"What happened to Joanne? I liked her," Phil said.

"Her husband got a better job, so they're moving down south at the end of the month."

Phil let out a slight sigh and took the small baggies from Rose that contained his pills and the MAR. "I'll be right back, Rose."

Phil then slipped back into the building.

"Phil has to remove the MAR from the baggie with tongs before he microwaves it and signs," Rose explained.

Phil reappeared moments later, returned the MAR, and said his goodbyes to Rose and Jim.

After they descended the fire escape, Rose said, "Jim, you really should try to relax and smile more often. These people may have psychiatric problems, but they can sense if someone's not comfortable with them."

Jim was taken aback by her comment and replied sheepishly, "Not a problem."

As Rose walked around the driver's side of the car, Jim discreetly popped a chalky piece of nicotine gum into his mouth.

After they entered the SUV, Rose stated, "Next, we'll head over to see Walter and Sally Waterman in Brickton. They're brother and sister. Sally's a patient, but Walter should be also. He's truly a very filthy, unpleasant, and maladjusted human being. She's psychotic and borderline mentally challenged. Her IQ is somewhere between seventy and eighty, I believe."

Rose continued, "Sally and Walter lived in a small colonial that was their parents' homestead years ago. Walter always aspired to become, and eventually became, a retired federal bureaucrat. Sally never worked or went past the ninth grade. Her parents always took care of her before their deaths, after which Walter assumed the role of caretaker."

Walter usually wore a dark blazer, with cotton chinos or corduroys. Due to his deteriorating eyesight to the point of legal blindness, he wore dark sunglasses. He was accompanied by his tired and crippled eye dog, Thunder.

Sally always wore a nightgown, or large muumuu to allow her pendulous body parts freedom of movement. Her hair was unkempt and filthy, much like the rest of her dirt-stained body.

"Sally's obsessed with Jesus and Santa. Santa. and Jesus, those are her favorite topics. Also, she's always looking to get hot coffee. It drives Walter nuts. Sometimes I think he just keeps her around for his sadistic amusement. He genuinely puts her down."

"What do you do about that?"

"Usually, his comments are fairly benign but mean-spirited nonetheless. I try to tune him out—or if he's being particularly obnoxious, I'll tell him to knock it off."

Jim and Rose found the front door partially opened and entered a quaint vestibule. The floor revealed a beautiful marble mosaic design that was covered with numerous layers of filth and funk. The door to the house was likewise open, so they entered a larger receiving room. It was an appalling sight: broken floorboards, tattered and moldy curtains, cracked windows, trash, and other debris scattered around. The stench of cheap cigar smoke and feline urine dominated. Walter sat upright in a torn and partially eviscerated recliner while puffing a large Churchillian cigar. Thunder laid docile at the side of the chair.

"Heya Rose, how ya doing?"

"Good Walter. How've you been?"

"Can't complain."

"Where's Sally?"

"Down the hall watching a Christmas film, I guess."

Rose and Jim went down a short and dark hallway into the living room that made Wanda's abode look immaculate. Cats roamed freely on and around Sally.

"Hey, Rosie, I got hot coffee today! I'm watchin' an old movie about Santa having Christmas Angels. Howboutthat, Jesus and Santa both havin' angels! I pray to see them every day. Angels from Jesus and Santa, Jesus and Santa, Jesus and Santa…"

Sally continued extolling the merits of Jesus and Santa over the next couple of minutes until Rose gently placed the pills in Sally's hand and tried cueing her to take them.

Finally, Walter yelled, "Just take your pills, Sally—don't keep these nice nurses here all day!"

Sally glanced at the pills in her hand. She then closed it, except for her index finger, and made the sign of the cross with her fingertip traversing from forehead to sternum, then up and across to each shoulder. Afterward, she lapped up the fistful of pills from her palm with the enthusiasm of a cat cleaning itself. Rose introduced Jim briefly to Sally and then to Walter. Soon they were outside, breathing fresh air.

"How can they live like that?" Jim asked.

"It's kind of a game for Walter. Every five years or so, someone complains to the health department about their squalor. The state then inspects the home with the threat of condemnation. Walter immediately does some cosmetic repairs like painting and spackling, but then when the state backs off, the downward cycle begins again. You've gotta be very careful with Walter. It is rumored that he's abused Sally over the years."

"In what way?"

"At least physically, but Sally never admits to any abuse. So, it's virtually impossible to get anyone at the state to take it further than an investigation."

"Now we're going to see Mike over in South Ellingford," Rose went on. "He's twenty-two and lives in a modest house with his mom. He has a mild traumatic brain injury from an accident a couple of years back."

"What type of meds does he get?"

"Anti-epileptics for the mild seizures that he's developed. He's a very nice young man. If you didn't talk to him for more than a couple of minutes, you wouldn't know that there was anything wrong with him."

They then pulled into his driveway and caught sight of Mike doing some mulching around the front shrubbery. He was a big kid with wide shoulders and a friendly smile.

"Hey, Rose, how's it going?"

"Pretty good. How 'bout you?"

"Not bad. I'm trying to get this mulching done to surprise Mom before she gets home."

"Mike, this is Jim. He's a new nurse who's gonna be working evenings."

The two shook hands and exchanged a brief smile.

"How's your Uncle Joe doing?" Rose inquired.

"He's fine. I'm supposed to help him with a couple of jobs later this week and maybe go fishin' afterward."

"Jim, Mike's uncle Joe is one of the best handymen in the Valley and is teaching young Mike everything he knows."

"I'll never be as good as Uncle Joe. Besides, what I want to do is work outside as a landscaper."

"Well, by the looks of this yard, it seems like you have real potential."

Mike smiled, then said, "What's the result of my Dilantin level from last week?"

"Perfectly normal. Have you had any seizures since Christmas?"

"Nope."

"Please let Vicky or Jim know if you ever get any more, even if they're slight."

Mike nodded, then Rose went on to wrap up their visit.

"We only see Mike in the evenings to give him Dilantin. His mom works a lot and is sometimes a scatterbrain. Mike's memory isn't the best, either. After his accident, he was having fairly frequent seizures, and then it was discovered that he hadn't been compliant in taking his Dilantin. Since we took him on as a patient, he's only had a few seizures."

"What kind of accident did he have?" Jim asked.

"He fell from a ladder while working outside cleaning gutters and hit his head on a metal post. That's one reason his mom's not crazy about the thought of his going into landscaping."

Jim stared at the successive blocks of dirty steel mills as they headed into Ellingford. It was a city of about 150,000 residents and was the hub of the Valley's steel industry. Although it was a blue-collar municipality, it had much more diversity and opportunity than the smaller surrounding Valley towns. It also had more dangerous locations for its psychiatric patients.

"For nurses' safety, I won't let any new psych nurses work in Ellingford," Rose said. The thought of working in Ellingford didn't bother Jim too much, however, as he was accustomed from his Army life to be prepared for dangerous situations.

Soon they passed through Ellingford and were traversing through safer neighborhoods in East Ellingford.

"Our last stop will be St. Monica's, about ten or fifteen minutes from here. It's a minimally supervised living apartment with three patients: Rob Reilly, Nick Fane, and Lucinda Rosado. They also have twenty-four-hour unlicensed staff to report any problems and to give any standby meds. Unfortunately, it's a current trend with the state. There's such a nursing shortage, they're now allowing non-licensed personnel to give out certain meds. I think it's a huge lawsuit just waiting to happen."

Rose continued, "Lucinda lives alone in the third-floor apartment, which is unusually spacious for one person. I'm sure that her family's political connections arranged for that. Rob and

Nick share the second-floor apartment, although they never really talk to each other."

"What's wrong with them?"

"Well, Rob is a schizophrenic who has a split personality issue. He is also a cross-dresser, so don't act surprised or judgmental when you see him wearing female attire. Nick is a paranoid schizophrenic with extreme antisocial personality disorder, and Lucinda is mildly schizophrenic with anger, depression, and anxiety issues. Unfortunately, all three have issues with substance abuse."

"What type of stuff?"

"Rob occasionally drinks to excess, which is usually when his alter-ego, Shane, will surface. Nick is no longer using anything, but he is a recovering alcoholic who previously had problems with cocaine. He's replaced his addictions with hyper- religious zealotry—predicting the end of the world on a regular basis. Lucinda sometimes drinks socially, which unfortunately has led to her using marijuana and ecstasy on occasion."

"What type of political connections does her family have?"

"We're not quite certain, but suffice it to say that her father is very powerful in Washington regarding issues of national security. If anyone should be more paranoid, it should be her, not Nick."

Rose's monstrous SUV pulled up parallel to a large brick apartment building that was covered with sinuous ivy and topped off with red clay tiles on the roof. They dismounted and entered the lower level, where they were met by June, a middle- aged caretaker who was working that evening.

"Hi, Rose, how are you today?"

"Fine. This is Jim. He'll be working evenings when Vicky is off."

"Nice to meet you, Jim," she said with a smile, which Jim returned.

"Are the troops ready for us?" Rose inquired.

"They're lining up in the kitchen as we speak."

June led the way to a brightly lit kitchen with sparse furnishings and a dingy linoleum floor.

Rob appeared in front of them wearing a loose-fitting summer dress with unassuming flats and a thin layer of rouge on his face. He also had thin mascara surrounding his eyes. After a brief introduction and exchange of pills and paper, Rob disappeared out the back door.

A provocative female, who appeared to be in her early to mid-twenties, suddenly appeared in Jim's visual field. She had tight denim cutoffs and a snug white tank top that flattered her firm bosom. Her taut arms and legs were well-defined, but certainly not bulky. Her face was accented by prominent, high cheekbones and a sloping nose that broadened slightly at the base. She had full, well-rounded lips that overlooked her strong yet mildly dimpled chin. Her hazel and brownish eyes were iridescent, but nonetheless piercing. Surrounding her face was the wildest tangled mane of dyed, dirty-blond hair that he had ever seen.

"Hi, Lucy. How are you?"

"Good, Rose. Who's your boyfriend?" she said playfully, pointing to Jim.

"This is Jim. He'll be working evenings."

"Pleased to meet you," she said, extending her hand and flashing a flirtatious smile.

"Likewise," Jim responded, shaking her hand firmly.

After signing the MAR and taking her pills, she exited through the living room.

Something about Lucinda immediately reminded Jim of his first love, Maria. Jim and Maria had been high school sweethearts in a small and dusty town near the Wahatoya Peaks of Huerfano County, in southern Colorado. Even though they were teenagers, Jim felt an ease and comfort when being with her that he had never experienced with any other woman. She was a simple Mexican beauty who was as good-natured, honest, and family-oriented as Jim, and she often joked that she wanted to start a large family together. They had planned on getting married right after high school, but her tragic death in their senior year ended that. Jim was also the person who discovered her naked and brutalized body in the dumpster next to the restaurant where she had worked. He'd been dogged by recurrent episodes of sadness ever since. After her death, everything in town reminded Jim of Maria. Once graduating high school, Jim quickly joined the Army.

The next patient, Nick, appeared in front of the table. He was wearing his typical garb: tattered blue jeans, a T-shirt, and a red, white, and blue bandana that reined in his long and dirty gray hair. His unkempt hair was equal in length to his long and filthy beard.

Upon seeing Jim, he shouted, "Have you accepted Christ as your Lord and Savior, son?"

Jim was surprised and unsure how to answer; then Rose intervened: "Nick, you don't even know Jim yet—why don't you speak to him before asking such questions?"

"Time is short! The boy should know Christ before it's too late!"

Changing the subject with a sigh of exasperation, Rose said, "Jim, this is Nick; Nick, Jim."

The two shook hands. Nick then took his pills and signed the paper. "Pleasure meeting you, Jim. We'll talk on this later."

After Jim and Rose returned to the SUV, she said, "Don't be fooled by ol' Nick. He'll seem very nice and interested in you at first, but then he'll react very poorly to any perceived slight."

"Has anyone else had any problems with him?"

"We had a nurse a couple of years back yell at him when he accused her of dressing like a slut. Nick got so mad, he stripped naked and ran down Jackson Avenue screaming that the whores of the apocalypse were invading East Ellingford. You should also know that he's obsessively punctual about getting his pills because he usually goes to AA meetings at 7:45 p.m. every evening."

Following a pleasant and quiet ride back to the office in Ashton, Rose said, "We'll see you tomorrow at 2:00 p.m. for the staff meeting."

"See you then."

Soon Jim arrived at his second-floor apartment in South Ashton. He went into the spacious upstairs foyer and began his typical end-of-the-day activities, which he performed in no particular order. Jim organized the mail with the most frivolous on top and the more interesting ones toward the bottom; pulled out a bottle of small-batch bourbon from a nearby liquor cabinet; checked his email; and had a final cigarette for the day. All of these items (except the email) had been neatly arranged on top of his smaller steamer trunk, which Jim had done before leaving for work. He used the trunk as a coffee table and had it stationed in front of a futon sofa that doubled as a guest bed. Occasionally, Jim fell asleep on this futon after a busy day and bourbon. More often than not he preferred to fall asleep in his bed, sometimes while watching TV.

While pouring a small amount of Woodford Reserve over randomly placed ice cubes in his glass, Jim checked his email. There was only one message, and it was from his younger sister Jenny. She was an earthy and compassionate forest ranger, who was simultaneously focused and ambitious (much like their older sister and father). For three consecutive years, she had been a finalist for Ranger of the Year, once placing second. The message was a raunchy joke, which made Jim laugh out loud and almost spill his drink. It also brought back touching memories of how Jenny took care of him with constant attention, good humor, and unbridled sympathy after Maria's death. Jenny was a good-hearted hippie chick. If she hugged a tree, it would undoubtedly hug her back. In appearance, people often accused her of looking like Sacagawea.

Jim turned his attention to the mail, which was mostly junk. Same old flyers from credit card companies and other nursing agencies promising better hours, higher pay, more satisfaction. The national nursing shortage ensured that there was always a steady stream of prospective employers soliciting his services. He knew that as long as being a registered nurse was public information to be gleaned from the health department, the avalanche of solicitous junk mail would be never-ending. As Jim couldn't do agency work at hospitals and nursing homes due to his bad hip, visiting psych patients seemed to be the least strenuous and most lucrative job opportunity at the moment.

He quickly smoked one cigarette, and then unexpectedly lit a second one. Jim didn't like to chain-smoke and usually avoided having more than one at a time. He took great pains to avoid becoming a hardcore smoker and never smoked more than ten in a pack before throwing them out. Also, he shunned smoking first thing in the morning. He would even occasionally try to quit by chewing nicotine gum.

Tonight, he was still feeling a bit uneasy about Rose's remark concerning his stultified bedside manner. He began wondering if this job would be a repeat of his last. He seriously considered it and thought maybe there was something genuinely wrong with him. *How come I can sizzle during a job interview but end up disappointing bosses with the steak?* he thought. *Was I being disingenuous during interviews? Overpromising? Obsequious?*

Gradually his thoughts devolved into painful remarks he received during different jobs. *"You're not as experienced as I thought you were...I thought you could stand on your own two feet for a whole shift...I thought that you had a better understanding of the workers' comp field..."* And now: *"I thought you would be more confident and less stiff around my patients."*

Soon his gaze fixed upon the dimly lit crucifix that was hanging on the far side of his room. Although Jim didn't think of himself as particularly religious, he truly liked that crucifix because his Aunt Ruthie had given it to him just before she died. Staring up at it, Jim wondered how Jesus would do in today's workforce. Would he succeed or would he hear those awful words: *"Sorry Jesus, we just don't think you're a good fit for this company."*

# CHAPTER TWO

The staff meeting convened at the agency's Ashton clinical office, which occupied a nondescript storefront in a small strip plaza. The office's only unusual characteristics were its lack of a sign out front and that it was concealed by tinted windows.

Rose introduced Jim to Carol, Cindy, Vicky, and Stella at the start of the meeting. Carol and Cindy were slightly frumpy but very pleasant and competent nurses with several years' experience. Vicky, a lady about Jim's age in her late twenties, looked more like a biker babe than a nurse. She also worked the evening shift. Stella, a Cuban nurse who had emigrated to the United States as a child, was the evening supervisor from 2:00 p.m. to 10:00 p.m. She had several years of psychiatric nursing experience. Stella often dressed in flamboyant Caribbean clothes and had a penchant for speaking her mind, regardless of the consequences.

"Jim, where did you work before coming here?" Vicky asked.

"I was a nurse case manager for Acme Insurance's workers' compensation unit in Manhattan."

"Wow, pretty swanky. What the hell brings you here?"

"Just wasn't my cup of tea."

Rose, sensing Jim's apprehension about the subject, opened the meeting.

"All right, ladies and gentleman, let's get started with addressing the ongoing tardiness and incompleteness of some of the MARs that I receive. You all should know and should be setting a good example for our new nurse in showing him that

MARs are due promptly every Friday. This is how we get paid. Please remember that."

Rose's audience looked somewhat bored, as they had heard that speech several times in the past.

Rose continued, "Remember also to document any visit in which you perform any patient education or detailed patient assessment—such as in a hypertensive or hyperglycemic episode—as a skilled nursing visit. That's how we get paid well."

"Damn shame Helga ruined it for the rest of us!" Vicky exclaimed, to the amusement of everyone else in the room.

Jim didn't interrupt her to ask what she meant by this remark. He found out later that Helga was a private agency nurse who had been working sixteen to eighteen hours daily doing nursing visits, and she had made over $300,000 in one year. When the politicians got word of this from the medical lobby, they couldn't tolerate the thought of any nurse making more than a doctor. Thus, they devised a two-tier reimbursement scheme to pay visiting nurses. A skilled nursing visit was paid at the prior and higher rate and involved delivery of extraordinary care; whereas, a routine visit (just to give medicine) was paid at a newer and much lower rate.

The meeting continued for another half hour or so and eventually deteriorated into a bitch session about insurance companies, doctors, difficult patients, and their families. Rose didn't seem to mind, as she seemed to share most of those same frustrations.

After the meeting ended, she said to Jim, "Starting today and up through next Wednesday, I want you to shadow Vicky for her evening shifts. Once your orientation is done, call Vicky, Stella, or me if you have any questions while on the road."

"Great. I'll give Vicky a call to set it up."

Jim's evenings with Vicky passed by quickly, and soon he was striking out on his own. He enjoyed working with Vicky more than Rose, as Vicky offered no criticism but displayed rank candor and wicked humor, which made her a favorite of both the patients and nurses. She was a feisty lady whose roughness around the edges of her personality was ameliorated by the voluptuousness of her frame. If she wasn't married with two kids, Jim most certainly would hit on her.

Jim arrived at Wanda's decrepit door at 4:00 p.m., knocked firmly, and awaited her appearance. About a half-minute had passed when it occurred to him that he'd forgotten to rap three times to alert her to the presence of a non-solicitor. He immediately knocked three distinct times, hoping to produce her at the door. After a momentary pause, the door creaked open and Wanda looked through it. She then opened it wide and invited him in.

"Feliz Cinco de Mayo!" she said in a pseudo-Spanish accent.

"Gracias," Jim replied, feeling a little awkward that he didn't know how to say "likewise" in Spanish.

As his eyes adjusted to the dark shadows of the room, Wanda's image came into focus. She was wearing a faded white sombrero and a colorful poncho. Surprisingly, Bubba was perched on her shoulder, wearing the same attire. Not wanting to get too close to the odd-looking bird, Jim followed at a few paces behind them. Luckily, she deposited the parrot back into his metal cage before they went into the kitchen.

After taking her blood glucose reading and exchanging pills and paperwork, Jim said, "How are you feeling today? Have you been hearing or seeing anything strange or unusual?"

"I have this really large boil on my butt, and it's makin' vibrations inside my body. The vibrations are causin' voices in my head."

"Can I take a quick look at it?" Jim asked reluctantly.

"Sure," she said, simultaneously standing up and dropping her pants.

Jim looked at what appeared to be a slight blemish on her left cheek, then said, "How long have you had it?"

"For about a week or so."

"Have you been running a fever at all?"

"Nope."

"Why don't you clean it with peroxide in the morning and at night and put a dab of antibiotic ointment on it after each cleaning?" Jim instructed.

"Where do I get that stuff?"

"I'll call Cindy and have her get an order for it tomorrow."

Jim then left for Sir Richard's on the other side of Ashton.

Arriving at the front door of the railcar, Jim was greeted by Sir Richard, who was wearing a red blazer, a black flowing cape, and an unusual feathery hat.

"Good afternoon, Mr. Goldmann. I'm Jim from Harmony Nursing Agency. May I come in?"

"I remember you, young man. Please come in, and you may call me Sir Richard."

Jim entered and hesitated, then asked, "Do you mind if I ask why they call you Sir Richard?"

"Years ago, I was inducted into the sacred Knights of Malta and have retained the honored regalia and indicia of my class. I only wear the uniform, however, on the most special occasions."

"What's the occasion?"

"It's my birthday!"

"Happy birthday, Sir Richard."

Jim's own birthday was a sore subject, as he had missed being Colorado's first baby of the Bicentennial year by eight seconds. So, instead of having the distinction of being Baby Bicentennial New Year, his was just another anonymous birth under the sign of Capricorn. If only his ever- accommodating mom had breathed more and pushed less (against medical advice), the honor would have been his.

Richard and Jim then traveled across the front railcar, through the darkened rotunda of one of the upside-down tanker cars, then emerged in the east wing railcar. This car had been converted into a large laboratory with numerous beakers, burners, and other various scientific equipment. The two exchanged pills and paperwork, and then Richard took his blood sugar reading.

"It's 285, young man."

"Are you feeling okay?"

"Most definitely. I shall draw up my insulin according to the sliding scale."

As Richard drew it up and nonchalantly stuck himself with the insulin needle, Jim spied a large drafting table in the corner of the room covered with numerous maps.

Richard, noticing his curiosity, said, "Would you like to see the maps, my boy?"

"Sure."

He escorted Jim over to the table and showed him several maps that depicted diagrams of a wall that was V-shaped, like the Vietnam Memorial, but it did not slope downward from its center.

"These show the proposed additions in height that I want to make to the existing wall to keep prying eyes away from my Paramatter research. The vectors and coordinates are laid out in perfect symmetry. It would take an atomic blast to bring it down."

"Is this what you're trying to get approved by the zoning board?"

"Yes, but my neighbors and this town have consistently hampered and sabotaged my research and efforts to keep it private. A couple of years ago, they even sent in state inspectors based on fraudulent allegations that my laboratory was dangerous. Big mistake. I have never maintained an unsafe lab, and they all knew that."

Soon Jim's visit with Richard was over, and Jim was off to see Phil.

Jim's visit with Phil was brief and without incident; however, Phil looked defeated and bedraggled in a weathered bathrobe that covered his faded pajamas, but he denied any depression whatsoever.

After leaving the Y, Jim lit a cigarette to help blunt his senses before going over to Sally's and Walter's. He arrived at their hovel and found the doors unlocked again, and he ventured inward with caution. Walter was bolt upright in his chair, smoking another smelly cigar.

"Heya Jim, how you doing?"

"How'd you know it was me?"

"Well, I heard the doors open, and it smelled more like Old Spice than Chanel, so I figured it was either you or a well- groomed burglar."

"Where's Sally?"

"She's in the kitchen eating cereal with coffee."

As Jim cautiously entered the kitchen, the twitching antennae of a half-crushed cockroach caught his attention. While feeling some sympathy for the creature, Jim didn't want to kill it in front of Sally for fear that it might startle or offend her. The roach was positioned adjacent to Sally's big bowl of cereal, but she was completely oblivious to anything but the food in front of her.

"Hey, Jim, got hot coffee in my cereal!" she exclaimed, with a small stream of coffee dribbling down her stubbly chin.

Jim nodded politely.

"Know what else?" Sally asked.

What's that?"

"I saw Jesus and Santa today!" she replied.

"Where?"

"Jesus is working at the convenience store—he gave me free coffee!"

"Was Santa with him?"

"No, silly, Santa's on the VCR."

"What makes you think you saw Jesus?" Jim queried.

"It said so right on his name tag: J-E-S-U-S!" she said.

"What did he look like?"

"He had long dark hair, dark skin, and a long, beautiful beard!"

"Did he tell you that he was Jesus?"

"He kept tryin' to tell me that his name was Heyseuss, but he couldn't tell me why Jesus was on his shirt. After a while, he gave me a cup of coffee, then said goodbye."

Not wanting to undermine her faith, Jim smiled and waited for Sally to consecrate her pills with the sign of the cross before taking them. After taking them and signing the MAR, Jim found himself outside smoking an unusual second cigarette to kill the lingering odors from her house.

Following a smooth ride to Mike's, Jim rang the doorbell. A strawberry-blonde and Rubenesque woman appeared and introduced herself as Betty, Mike's mom.

"Mike's not here right now. He went to his TBI (Traumatic Brain Injury) support group."

"When will he be back?"

"Probably in a couple of hours, but Vicky usually just leaves his pills with me, and Mike signs off on them later."

He gave her the pills in a small manilla envelope, then left for St. Monica's Apartments in East Ellingford.

Once at St. Monica's, Jim went through the open door and found June sitting on a sofa and watching TV.

"Hey, Jim, how are you?"

"Pretty good, and yourself?"

"Not bad. Let me go round them up. They usually don't get down here for Vicky until 7:20 p.m."

"Thanks," Jim said as June got up and made her way to the back door.

Jim then went to the kitchen table and started unpacking his meds and paperwork. Soon, Nick, Rob, and Lucinda entered the rear of the kitchen.

Nick immediately stepped forward while Lucinda helped Rob primp his hair and makeup in the corner of the kitchen.

"How are you feeling today, Nick?" Jim asked.

"Blessed and delivered. Do you know Christ, my son?"

"Sure. Hey, are you having any thoughts of hurting yourself or others?"

Nick appeared visibly insulted by Jim's query, then said, "There is no need to hurt if you believe in Christ—and if you knew him, you would know that as well!"

"I don't mean any offense by the question, but Rose expects me to ask such things."

"Well, if you were a true believer, then you would educate Rose about not insulting Christians by asking such offensive questions!"

He took his envelope of pills, then stormed out of the kitchen without signing the MAR. Jim promptly wrote "refused to sign" in the appropriate box of the MAR.

Lucinda then appeared before him. She was wearing a tight leather dress that was cut dangerously close to her bottom along with fishnet stockings and bright red pumps. Jim tried diverting his glance from the hint of her cleavage that glistened with body sparkle.

"Hey, cutie, how are you?" Lucinda said playfully.

"Not bad. How you doing?"

"Okay. Rob and me are gonna take the bus down to the Philthy Dawg."

"What's that?"

"A strip joint down the road. It used to be a firehouse, but when the town built a newer station, a local bar owner bought it and decided to put the pole to better use," she said, while simultaneously pantomiming the gesture of a stripper descending a pole.

Lucinda laughed loudly as Jim turned red.

"Anyway, I'm going to show Rob the ropes down there—he hasn't had a date in months."

"How do you know the ropes?" Jim asked, immediately realizing the potential insult of this question.

"Why, Jimmy—you're not implying that I would take off my clothes for money, are you?!" she replied, feigning angry indignation.

"No, no—it's just that—"

"Aw, I'm just messin' with you. I actually bartend there. There's no amount of money that strangers could pay me to take a peek at these bad boys!" she exclaimed, while pridefully clutching her breasts from the bottom. After taking her pills and signing the papers, she said, "Robbie, I'll meet you outside. See ya later, Jimmy."

"See ya."

Next, Rob stepped up wearing a bright floral shirt, heavy eye makeup, and tight jeans.

"Hey Rob, how ya doin' today."

"Not bad. Just hopin' that Lucinda will keep me outta trouble."

"Good luck."

After the pills and paperwork were done, Rob pranced out the door to catch up with Lucinda.

It being a Friday night, Jim decided to pop in at a local Irish pub called Sully's. It was within walking distance from his apartment, so he didn't have to worry about driving under the influence. Jim was pleased to see that Taco was tending bar. Taco was an older gentleman of Native American or Mexican ancestry. Jim wasn't quite sure why they called him Taco. He heard that it was because he loved making tacos, loved eating them, or had killed a man named Taco when he was younger. Jim doubted that Taco was a killer, as he had the best bar-side manner. Taco's advice was usually very insightful, and after a few drinks, he could be downright prophetic. Taco also made the best chili Jim had ever tasted. Sully's was famous for it—straight from the pot or on top of hot dogs.

# CHAPTER THREE

The days following Jim's orientation unraveled like the spring blossoms in the Valley. His daily assignment changed slightly after Rose noticed the times of his visits on the MARs. She instructed him to start at least at 5:00 p.m. instead of 4:00 p.m. to give the diabetic medications closer to suppertime. So, instead of working from about 4:00 p.m. to 8:00 p.m., he was now working from about 5:00 p.m. to 9:00 p.m. Jim and the other staff nurses weren't paid by the visit but by the hour. However, on any given shift, they would usually work four or five hours and be on call for another three or four. Thus, they would get paid for eight hours per shift when they usually only worked four or five. Jim thought that this was a good deal, as working only twelve to sixteen hours per week while getting generously paid for twenty-four to thirty-two hours would give him plenty of free time to find another job in corporate healthcare.

He was somewhat jealous that his older sister, Michele, had a serious boyfriend whose corporate career as an industrial psychologist was taking off. Jim viewed that suitor, Dr. Stanton Josef, as nothing more than a glorified marketer trying to capitalize on Michele's emerging success. She was widely regarded as one of the best new furniture makers in the greater Pueblo region. Dr. Josef had a nauseating tendency to be a brownnoser to those above his status and condescending to those beneath him.

As Jim's current job progressed, he started developing a comfort level with his patients and definitely dressed more casually. A beautiful spring Thursday was in progress when Jim began his shift wearing faded shorts, a navy-blue T-shirt, canvas, high-top sneakers, and a Cleveland Indians ball cap. Although Jim had grown up in southern Colorado, his father had been an avid Indians fan, having been raised in Shaker Heights. Jim wasn't that much into baseball, but wearing the cap made him feel closer to his dad. Shortly after Michele's birth, Jim's uncle had found Jim's dad a modest but steady job with a manure company as a sales representative south of Pueblo. Mr. Greene was a smart and gregarious yet humble man. He often joked that he would rather earn an honest living selling bullshit rather than backstab his way up some corporate ladder in Ohio. Nevertheless, his company did recognize and reward Greene's talent, which enabled him to retire in relative comfort after thirty years of dedicated service. Jim admired his dad and hoped to find the right niche in life as his father had.

Jim's visit with Wanda promised to be fairly uneventful, as her boil had healed without any problems. He was grateful because he did not enjoy the evening assessment and antibiotic treatment, although Wanda seemed to. Wanda, however, had developed other issues.

"Hey, Jim, I've got great news!" Wanda shouted.

"Oh, yeah? What is it?"

"I discovered my voices were comin' from the icebox, so I defrosted it. Now I'm not hearin' 'em anymore!"

"Are you seeing anything unusual?"

"Nope, I think I'm free and clear of this thing at last."

By this thing, of course, she meant schizophrenia. Jim didn't want to burst her bubble, so he just nodded politely, recorded her blood glucose meter reading, and ended their visit after the pills and paperwork were completed. He then proceeded to Sir Richard's.

Jim sensed apprehension once he entered Sir Richard's. "Is everything okay?"

"Not today, my good man. I've heard that the secrets of Paramatter shall be unveiled to me by the end of the year!"

"Who did you hear that from?"

"I don't know—it just came to me," Richard replied.

"Have you been seeing any unusual things?"

"No, but you fail to understand the importance of this message. Time is short. I must complete the extension of the wall to prevent my neighbors from prying into the secrets of Paramatter," he said, walking purposefully toward the rotunda en route to the lab.

*"Time is short." Man, he's starting to sound like Nick,* Jim thought.

Once in the lab, Richard retrieved a small uncapped canister of blood glucose meter strips that had been resting near one of the bright lamps overlooking what appeared to be some sort of research field, no doubt related to the Paramatter. Richard began testing his sugar as Jim retrieved the medicine from his book bag.

"The Zoning Board works at a snail's pace," Richard continued. "It may take weeks, nay, months before I have a decision. And if I lose, it will likely take more months to appeal it to the next level. I just don't have that kind of time!"

"Well, won't these shades keep prying eyes away?" Jim said, pointing to the shades above each window in the railcar's lab.

"Yes, that may keep some eyes from watching, but not infrared eyes. Infrared binoculars can see through these walls and shades. The addition to the height of the brick wall will include lining the entire back of the wall with a lead shield."

Just then the blood glucose meter beeped, indicating that the reading was complete. It read 348.

Taking notice of the number, Jim asked, "Are you feeling okay?"

"No, I told you that I must complete that wall before the secrets of Paramatter are revealed!"

"No—are you feeling thirsty? Having blurred vision? Having to pee a lot?"

"Nothing like that. Just anxious to complete my work on the only worthwhile scientific pursuit remaining. Many scientists believe that there are five types of matter. But where does any matter come from? It has to come from something. If the light just came forth from the darkness, what is darkness made of?"

Jim nodded with interest as Richard continued, "Paramatter is the primordial substance from which all else comes. Just as white light contains all the colors of the spectrum within it, Paramatter contains all the potentialities of matter within itself."

Unsure what to say, Jim turned the subject back to his work. "Well, Sir Richard, make sure that you don't get so engrossed with your research that you let your sugar skyrocket out of control. You should probably check it again at bedtime. Let me give you my cell number if you have any questions or problems. It's 203-555-0977."

Richard accepted Jim's number and promised to do what he asked.

Within minutes Jim was at the side of the Y honking for Phil. After a few moments, Phil appeared on the fire escape on the side of the building, wearing well-creased jeans and a crisp black T-shirt.

"Hey, Phil, how are you today?"

"Pretty good, son. I got up earlier than yesterday."

"What time?"

"About 2:30 p.m. this afternoon."

"How's that increased dose of Ambien working for you?"

"Not bad, but I would probably sleep better if I didn't watch so much TV at night."

Jim smiled empathetically.

"Why don't you come on in?" Phil suggested.

After entering Phil's room, Jim was impressed by its spartan appearance. It contained a neatly made twin bed, two wooden chairs, a large footlocker on which a small TV sat, a bureau with a microwave oven on top, and a clean but tattered state police Stetson hanging on a hook behind the door.

After carefully retrieving the MAR with tongs and placing the paper in the microwave, Phil removed the pills from the other bag (except for the Ambien, which he left for bedtime) and swallowed them. When the microwave beeped, he removed the paper, signed it, and gave it to Jim, who was distracted by a story on a cable news show about another suicide bombing in Iraq.

Noticing Jim's distraction by the segment, Phil said, "Barbarians."

Jim nodded, then asked, "Are you having any thoughts of hurting yourself?"

"I've already been hurt enough, thank you very much," Phil wryly answered.

As the cable news story ended, so did their visit.

Jim then headed over to see Sally, who was in her typical Jesus, Santa, and coffee-focused frame of mind. He couldn't get out of there quickly enough and again indulged in an uncharacteristic second cigarette afterward to fumigate any lingering aroma of Sally's residence.

As Jim approached Mike's house, he found him in the garage tinkering with a lawnmower.

"Hey, Mike, howya doing today?"

"Not bad. How 'bout you?"

"Pretty good. Have any seizures or other problems?"

"Nah. Just a problem living here. My mom's a real pain in the ass. She doesn't hardly let me do anything, other than work with Uncle Joe. Sometimes she treats me like I'm brain dead, not brain injured."

"Does your TBI support group help much?"

"It's okay, but most of the people there are older. They don't understand what it's like to be an adult but to be treated like a child. I tell you; I really need to get the hell outta here, sooner than later."

"Well, if you decide to move at some point, please let us know."

Mike nodded, and after the pills and paperwork were swapped, Jim was on his way to St. Monica's. Once there, Jim found Nick in the kitchen. Maureen, another caretaker, was working instead of June. She told Jim that she would phone the other patients from the staff office near the pantry. Soon they began entering the kitchen.

"Good evening, Mr. Fane," Jim said, hoping not to provoke Nick.

"So, how long have you known Christ, my son?"

*Damn! He's starting with that stuff again!* Jim thought with increasing frustration, then answered, "Pretty much my whole life."

"No, no, no—when did you accept him into your heart as Lord and Savior?"

Jim remained silent.

"If you can't recall when you were saved, then you truly don't know Christ!" Nick exclaimed.

"I believe it was when I was in the Army. It was a long time ago—ten years, I believe it was then."

"Well, if Christ came into your heart, you'd remember it as though it were yesterday."

"Well, it was about ten years ago, but it seems like yesterday," Jim replied.

Nick nodded skeptically, then said, "I have to go to my AA meeting, but we'll talk more on this later." He then exited the front door to walk to his meeting.

"Do you know where Rob and Lucinda are?" Jim asked Maureen.

"Nah, they didn't pick up the phone. Why don't you go upstairs?"

Jim was annoyed by her answer, as June was more helpful and would've gone to their apartments to see if they were there. Jim's knocking was unanswered at the second-floor door of Rob and Nick's apartment, so he went upstairs to Lucinda's. After turning the corner at the top of the staircase, Jim found her reclining on a wicker lounger and wearing a bright orange tankini. Lucinda's body glistened with coconut-scented oil, and her abdomen displayed an intriguing tattoo: a dark tribal spider that surrounded her inverted belly button.

"Hey—howya doing today?" Jim asked, with a hint of embarrassment in his voice.

"Just fine. Whatcha lookin' at?" she replied, noticing that he had focused on her tattoo.

"Just never saw one quite like that."

"Wanna know what it stands for?"

"Sure."

"It's a black widow. They kill their partners after they mate."

"So, you're a mankiller?" Jim replied, with a bit more confidence in his voice.

"Nah, but I don't want guys to think I'm an easy score," she said jokingly.

Jim laughed, then said, "Don't you think it's a little too early in the season to be tanning?"

"Never too early to tan. Besides, it's almost Memorial Day. Anyhow, I should probably wrap it up 'cause the sun's about down," she replied, simultaneously standing and putting a towel around her waist. "Why don't you come in?"

"Sure."

Jim followed her into the spacious apartment and noticed another tattoo. It was a pitchfork on her lower back. "What's the pitchfork on your back for? Are you a devil?"

"Nah, it's something that I saw on the Discovery Channel. It's supposed to symbolize psychology. I figured since my folks already think that I'm fuckin' nuts, why not get a tramp stamp to prove it? Do you like it as much as the black widow?" she asked, her eyes beaming flirtatiously.

*Jimmy, keep your mind out of the paravertebral gutter. This chick will make you lose your license,* he thought, but then he answered sheepishly, "Oh, it's nice."

"Just nice?"

"Yeah, nice. You know—I like, I like them both about the same. Say, um, why do your parents think you're nuts?"

"Well, it's a long story—but the bottom line is that it was tough growin' up in the shadow of a doctor and dead baby."

"How's that?"

"Well, when my parents finally had a boy—after my older sister and me—they were thrilled—you know, havin' someone to carry on the family name and all the machismo bullshit that goes with it. But then at four months, he died of SIDS. My folks never really recovered. My dad resigned from Congress and returned to his prior work at the NSA. He just couldn't stand the publicity of public life anymore—you know, kissin' babies and kissin' ass. After Vincente died, Dad just wanted to be anonymous."

"What about the doctor? Did he commit malpractice?"

"No, the doctor I'm talkin' about is my older sister, Vanessa. They spoiled the shit out of her 'cause she was brilliant from day one. IQ of 153. She got a full scholarship to Yale Med and now works at Mount Sinai. So, I was always the black sheep."

"Sorry to hear that."

"Hey, I'm used to it."

After their visit was over, Jim stopped back at Rob's door to find that he still was missing in action. So, Jim wrote "not available" on Rob's MAR, then headed home. Once there, Jim began routinely going through the motions of his evening routine. Soon he found himself on the couch sipping cold bourbon and trying not to think about Lucinda.

*Damn, what a gorgeous-looking girl,* he thought. The image of her dark body, resplendent with sweet oil in the afternoon sun, kept creeping into his bourbon-soaked consciousness. He was both enticed and disturbed about his bourgeoning feelings for Lucinda. Suddenly, he found himself on his cell phone searching for "Latina belly button tattoos." After clicking on the images tab from the toolbar on top of the screen, he scrolled down. Most of the pics were of athletic young women exhibiting well-chiseled abs and intricate artwork surrounding their navels. The more Jim scrolled down, the fewer clothes the women were wearing.

Jim put the phone down and slowly pushed it as far away from himself on the couch as possible. As he was recovering from this stretching endeavor, his eyes fell upon Jesus' abs from the crucifix. They seemed to be a perfect six-pack, and he appeared to have zero percent body fat. Jim wondered if that was the way he really looked and, if so, how did he get such well-defined abs by just walking around the desert?

Jim closed his eyes while reclining on the couch. The cadence of Lucinda's sultry voice captivated his fleeting thoughts until he was asleep.

# CHAPTER FOUR

*Another beautiful spring afternoon,* Jim thought as he knocked methodically three times on Wanda's door.

She answered, looking more disheveled than usual. Her hair appeared even more unruly than ever. "Come in, Jim," she said gruffly.

"Are you okay?"

"Nope. This fuckin' bitch at the corner store just ripped me off!"

"What happened?"

"I give her twenty bucks for a pack of smokes, and she only gives me $4.50 back. I say, 'Where's the rest of my change?' Then she says, 'You only gave me a ten.' When I keep arguin' for the rest of my change, she threatens to call a cop. That fuckin' bitch! I could fuckin' kill her!" Just then, Bubba starting nervously crooning an old Patsy Cline song.

Jim paused to think, then said coaxingly, "You mean that you were so mad, you *wished* she were dead?"

"No—I wanted to reach over the counter and plunge a fuckin' knife into her chest!"

"Do you still have a bow and arrows?"

"Nope, I gave them up. If I had one, I'd shoot that fuckin' bitch right between her beady eyes!"

"Do you have any guns or knives?"

"Just some dull kitchen knives," she replied with a hint of irritation. "Why do you ask?"

Sensing she felt insulted, Jim replied, "Wanda, you know I like you, right?"

Realizing that Jim indeed liked her, she softened and said, "Sure, I do."

"Well, I don't want to get you in trouble or anything, but what you just told me about the clerk, I gotta tell someone else, at least Rose—or I'll get in trouble."

Wanda nodded quietly, with a look of recognition that there might be something wrong with her behavior.

Jim continued, "I'm not gonna call the cops unless Rose insists. I'm just gonna go back to my car and call her from my cell phone, then I'll be right back."

Jim went to his sedan and quickly dialed Rose's number. "Hey Rose, I got a problem. Wanda just threatened to kill a store clerk. What should I do?"

"Does she have a plan or the means of carrying it out?"

"Not really. She said that she just has some dull kitchen knives."

"Why does she want to kill this clerk?"

"She said the clerk ripped her off over change from cigarettes."

"Well, cigarettes are like a food group to her. Go ahead and call the Valley Crisis Center and report what happened to a counselor. Also, call her later to see how she's doing."

Jim finished up with Wanda's blood glucose meter reading and pills and then did as Rose instructed. He found himself about twenty minutes behind schedule by the time he reached Richard's. Richard again appeared stressed about the upcoming Paramatter revelation and his perceived inability to keep it from his neighbors' eyes. Again, his sugar was high.

"My sugar is 401," Richard said matter-of-factly, glancing at the blood glucose meter that was on the edge of the brightly lit, sterile field of Paramatter materials.

"Are you feeling okay?"

"Just feeling under the gun about the Paramatter."

"Do you mind if I make a call from here?"

"Certainly not."

Jim decided to call Stella instead of Rose, as Rose had sounded like she was heading out during his last phone call.

"Stella, how you doing?"

"Fine, baby, how 'bout you?"

"Not bad. I'm sorry to bother you, but Richard's sugar is high again. It's 401. He's not symptomatic, though."

"Well, they just raised his clozapine, so that might have something to do with it. Tell him to check it later, then call back and see what it is. If it's over 450, or if he becomes symptomatic, call him an ambulance," Stella instructed.

"Okay, thanks."

Jim followed her advice, then arrived at Phil's about a half hour behind schedule. Phil was taciturn but didn't seem overtly depressed. In fact, he denied being depressed at all and just quietly consumed his pills following the microwave processing of the MAR.

Given the brevity of his visit with Phil, Jim found himself almost back on schedule when he arrived at Sally's and Walter's. As usual, he entered the unlocked house and found Walter sitting in his decrepit chair holding a plain white manuscript, which had a logo on the cover. Walter feverishly moved his fingers across a page dotted with Braille. When Jim took a second look at the logo, he realized that it was a Playboy bunny.

*There's someone who truly gets Playboy for the articles,* Jim thought. "Hey, Walter, howya doing today?"

"Not bad. How 'bout you?"

"Okay. Where's Sally?"

"In the living room listening to a Christmas album."

As Jim headed down toward the living room, he glanced at the MAR and noticed that Sally was scheduled for her haloperidol shot this evening. *So much for catching up,* he thought.

"Hi, Sal. How are you today?"

"Good. Just listening to Christmas Carols and drinkin' my hot coffee."

"Jesus still giving you coffee?"

"Yep, and he even gave me a day-ol' donut today."

"Why don't you take your pills while I draw up your haloperidol shot?"

"Only one CC, right? Santa told me I only get one CC. Any more knocks me out."

"Just take the distemper shot, you freakin' beast!" Walter bellowed from the other room.

"You the—you're the beast, you're the devil! Santa says I only get one CC!" Sally shouted angrily.

"Hey, Walter, you're really not helping me out over here," Jim interjected.

"Sorry, Jim, I just get tired of hearing her same ol' BS every time she has to get her shot."

"Sally, just calm down. I'll only give you what you're ordered—nothing more, nothing less," Jim said reassuringly.

Of course, Jim didn't tell Sally that she was ordered two CCs, which she apparently needed. While Sally methodically blessed the pills, Jim drew up two CCs from a glass vial. He then tapped the excess air to the top of the syringe. Jim expelled the air by pressing gently upon the plunger. Once completed, he positioned a small biohazard container nearby and opened the top of it.

"All done," Sally said nervously.

"Just look out the window—I'll be done in a minute."

Jim then put the end of the plunger (which was attached to the syringe and needle) between his lips for a moment, like a dangling cigarette, freeing his hands to clean her shoulder with alcohol. Afterward, he rapidly plunged the needle into her elephantine arm and pulled back on the plunger to ensure that he hadn't hit an artery. Then Jim firmly pressed the plunger, expelling the medication into her deep tissue. He quickly cleaned up, had the MAR signed, and was soon outside having another cigarette to blunt the olfactory insult that he had just endured.

Arriving at Mike's, Jim was still behind schedule and found Mike's mother outside trimming a rosebush

"Good evening Betty. Is Mike around?" Jim asked.

"Nope, he's staying at my brother Joe's tonight. I'll give you the address."

She neatly wrote the address on the back of Mike's MAR. Jim was relieved to see that it was in East Ellingford, so he could go there last and not be further behind schedule for arriving at St. Monica's.

Since he was running later than usual, June had the patients waiting in the kitchen for him. Lucinda was first in line.

"Hey, Jim! Howya doin', sexy?"

"Just fine. How you doing?" Jim asked nervously.

"Not bad. Wanna see a picture of the new tattoo I'm thinkin' of gettin'?" she asked while reaching into her pocket.

"Hurry up, Whore of Babylon! I have an AA meeting to go to!" Nick angrily interjected.

"Why don't you suck my left tit, you hypocritical bastard?" Lucinda yelled, while simultaneously grabbing her left breast and pointing it in his direction.

"Whore! Whore! Whore!" Nick screamed as he ran out of the kitchen.

Noticeably upset, Lucinda readjusted her shirt and then said, "Sorry about that, Jimmy. That idiot really pisses me off."

"No problem; I understand."

Flustered by what had happened, Lucinda quickly took her pills. She then signed the paper and exited out the back door.

Rob, wearing a pink halter, next approached Jim. Their visit was brief and uneventful.

Jim then reluctantly went up the back stairs to find Nick.

Once Nick answered the door, he exclaimed, "Whore of Babylon! That's all she is! Her throat is an open grave! Her words are as smooth as silver but are as bitter as bile once swallowed! No one who goes down her path ever returns to the path of life!"

Jim felt hot with anger at Nick's tirade and tried immediately to change the subject. "Mr. Fane, I have your pills. Would you please take them?"

Nick greedily consumed the pills, then continued, "That whore! That prostitute! She made me miss my meeting!"

"Why don't you pray for her?" Jim said with a hint of sarcasm.

"There is no higher power that can save that slut!"

*Great, this guy's an authority not only on knowing Christ but also on who can be saved or damned,* Jim thought.

After composing himself, Jim tersely stated, "Please sign right here," pointing to the appropriate block on the MAR.

Once he had it signed, Jim quickly said goodbye and retreated to his sedan for a relaxing cigarette on the ride home.

At home, Jim engaged in his usual routine of mail reviewing, bourbon sipping, cigarette smoking, and general relaxation. After sifting through a small pile of junk mail, he spied a personal letter from the Rushmore Health Management Corporation, to whom he had sent a resume in response to a want-ad. It read: "Dear Mr. Greene, thank you for your interest in Rushmore Health Management. Unfortunately, we have no position suitable for your qualifications at this time..." *What the hell does that mean? Am I overqualified or underqualified? Screw those ambiguous weasels!* Jim thought as he finished off his cigarette.

After extinguishing his smoke, Jim booted up the PC to check his email. He had two new messages. The first one was from the patronizing Dr. Josef on the subject of getting ready for the "high-powered corporate interview." It was an opportunistic attempt to curry Jim's favor, as Dr. Josef knew of Jim's situation and was obviously trying to exploit it as a means of further ingratiating himself to Michele. This was all the more evident by the fact that he had copied Michele on the email. Jim immediately deleted the message without opening it. He was incredibly frustrated that his usually savvy and intelligent older sister could fall for such a jerk.

Unfortunately, Michele had been struggling with self-image issues most of her adult life. She was virtually flat-chested and had unusually thick ankles, as well as abnormally elongated front teeth. Jenny's resemblance to Sacagawea probably taxed Michele's self-esteem to a degree, although she never admitted that to anyone. What Michele lacked in glamorous looks, however, she made up for with her impeccable work ethic and generosity of spirit. When someone who called himself a doctor took an interest in her, everyone else in Jim's family seemed to understand how she could fall for him.

The second message was from the online dating service through which he had met Holly. Briefly, Jim perused the message after opening it. It contained special offers and a calendar of upcoming events for local singles. Jim likewise deleted this message, as he thought it more prudent to get a good job before getting a good girlfriend.

# CHAPTER FIVE

About a week later, while Jim was getting ready for work, he listened to his voice mails from his agency cell phone. There was one message. It was from Rose asking that he have Mike sign off on his MAR from Thursday of the previous week. *Damn! I forgot to give Mike his pills after leaving St. Monica's last week,* Jim thought. He pondered about it some more, then realized that Rose thought that Mike forgot to sign his MAR, not that he didn't get his medicine. Jim was unsure whether or not Mike would cover for him and sign the MAR nonetheless.

After a few more minutes of agonizing, Jim decided that he would tell Rose. The only criticism that she'd leveled at him since orientation was the brevity of some of his narrative nursing notes.

Jim nervously dialed the phone and was surprised when Rose answered on the first ring. "Hey Rose, how are you?"

"Okay. What's up?"

"Well, I got your message about Mike signing the MAR, and the problem is that I forgot to visit him that night because he was at his Uncle's in East Ellingford, and I just forgot to go there after St. Monica's."

After a brief pause, Rose said, "We'll have to fill out an incident report and notify his doctor. Also, we'll have to develop some sort of remedial plan to ensure that it won't happen again."

"Thanks," Jim replied. Then they hung up.

Shortly afterward Jim was starting his shift, and he found Wanda in better spirits.

"Hey, Wanda, how are you today?"

"Not bad. Yourself?"

"Okay," Jim said. "Any more thoughts about hurting that clerk?"

"Nope. I figure if she wants to rip me off, then fuck her. I'll go to the mini-mart down the road in Brickton. They have the cheapest cigarettes in the county. Besides, they have a real cute Spanish guy working the counter."

"What's his name?"

"Heysuess, or Jesus—something like that."

*No doubt Sally's savior,* Jim thought.

After finishing their visit, Jim made his way to Richard's.

Once in Richard's laboratory, Jim was concerned by Sir Richard's blood glucose meter reading of 545.

"Sir Richard, are you feeling well?" Jim asked.

"Just aggravated by the demands of this Paramatter research. It doesn't seem to be going anywhere, but I am told the secrets shall be revealed to me by the end of the year. It just doesn't seem to add up yet."

"Well, unfortunately, your sugar is very high, and you should probably go to the emergency room now. Would you like me to call an ambulance for you?"

"An ambulance? Heavens, no. What would people think of someone of my stature being wheeled into the hospital like a commoner?" Richard replied. "Would you be able to drive me there, my boy?"

"Well, how would you get back?"

"There is a member of my fraternity at the hospital. He would certainly arrange for suitable transportation back to my abode."

"I'm pretty sure driving sick patients to the hospital is probably against the rules. You know, because of insurance regulations and things like that," Jim responded.

"I'm not truly that sick, and you have it on my royal honor that it shall forever remain a secret between you and me."

Jim, not wanting to impair his rapport with Richard, finally acquiesced. "All right, but you have to call me later and tell me if they are keeping you overnight or sending you home."

Although Jim was a bit nervous about breaking the rules, he wasn't overly concerned, as County Hospital was on the way to Phil's. Within twenty minutes Richard was deposited at the hospital without any complications, and Jim found himself on the Y fire escape, waiting for Phil to appear in response to his horn.

"Hey, Phil. How are you today?" Jim asked after Phil opened the fire escape door.

"Not bad. Got up about 3:00 p.m. Why don't we head inside, Jimbo?"

Once inside, Phil initiated his usual microwave ritual with the MAR.

"So, how long were you with the state police if you don't mind me asking?" Jim said, pointing to the Stetson hanging on the door.

"About seven or eight years. It was the best job I ever had."

"Rose tells me you used to work at the Trade Center before that?"

"Yes, sir," Phil replied.

"I used to work a few blocks from there with a large company, Acme Insurance."

"Oh, yeah? What did you do for them?"

"I was a workers' compensation nurse manager. I'd work with injured employees and their lawyers to see that their claims were properly handled."

"Sounds pretty swanky. Why'd you leave?" Phil queried.

"Well, they thought that they, the insurance company, were paying out too much money on the cases I was working on— that I was being too fair to the injured workers."

"Is there any such thing as being too fair?"

"So, after about six months, I was told that the department was downsizing by two people," Jim said.

"Who was the other person?"

"This nice fifty-eight-year-old nurse, who wasn't producing quite as much as her younger colleagues."

"Damn insurance companies."

"How long did you work at the Trade Center for?" Jim inquired, subtly trying to change the subject.

"A couple of years. If I had known what was going to happen on 9/11, I would've been working there that day."

"Are you having any thought of hurting yourself?" Jim gently asked.

"No, I'm resigned to my current fate," Phil replied bluntly.

Soon their visit ended, and Jim was nervously inhaling a cigarette on the way to Sally's and Walter's home. Once there, he found Walter in his usual chair and Sally glued to the TV watching another Christmas video.

"Hi, Jimmy. How ya doin'?"

"Good, Sally, and you?"

"I'm good. Jesus gave me free coffee and a cigarette today!"

Jim was surprised, as he hadn't known that Sally was a smoker.

She continued, "Walter don't let me smoke. Says it's too expensive, but Jesus saved me with my favorite cigarette. It's menthol. I love Jesus. I love my cigarettes. I love Santa! And you know what, Jimmy?"

"What's that, Sal?"

"They love me too! They told me so!"

Jim nodded, and soon, their visit had concluded. Soon he was outside again. He quickly smoked one of his own cigarettes, as he always despised the smell of menthols.

Approaching Mike's, Jim was a bit apprehensive about the missed visit from last week. Mike either never noticed or didn't care because he hadn't brought it up previously during the current workweek. Regardless, Jim knew and felt guilty. He also felt guilty that he hadn't apologized yet to Mike. Jim envisioned the worst-case scenario: Mike would go into a prolonged seizure and die from missing one dose. It wasn't a particularly plausible scenario, but it haunted Jim nonetheless. Jim's prior military experience had morphed him into a worst-case scenario kind of guy. As Jim pulled into Mike's driveway, he found Mike laying on the front lawn and thought that the worst-case scenario was coming true.

Running quickly across the wide lawn, Jim shouted, "Mike, are you okay?"

"Sure. Just got tired mowing the lawn, so I figured I'd take a little break."

"I thought you had passed out or something."

"Nah, just enjoying the sunshine," Mike replied, lifting his head and shoulders off the grass.

"Hey, sorry about not catching up with you last Thursday at your uncle's."

"No biggie. We actually went to the movies, so you probably wouldn't've found me anyhow," he replied. "Say, when's my next Dilantin level due?"

Checking his notes, Jim replied, "About two more weeks. Have you been having any seizures?"

"Nope. I was just curious when the lab work is due."

Following a few more instructions from Jim on the importance of maintaining a therapeutic Dilantin level, their visit ended with the necessary exchanges.

After a couple of songs on his car radio, Jim soon arrived at St. Monica's and set up shop in his usual spot in the kitchen.

Rob appeared wearing a faded denim shirt and dungarees.

"How are you, Rob?"

"It's Shane. I'm fine, me fella."

Jim recalled that Shane was Rob's Irish alter-ego.

"Are you feeling okay today?" Jim asked.

"Like I said, just fine, lad. Lookin' forward to gettin' on me boat 'tis evenin' and watchin' the stars."

"Well, if you have any unusual thoughts or feelings, please let June or someone know."

After Rob took the pills and signed the MAR, he said, "No problem, lad. We'll see you later."

Jim was amused about exactly who "we" were.

Suddenly, Nick was in front of him with a condescending smirk on his face. "Where do you worship Christ, my son?"

"Well, being a nurse and all, I don't always get a chance to go to church."

"Nonsense. There's always time to worship Christ. If you are a true believer, then you must worship among them."

"Well, I go to St. Francis Xavier down near Ashton—when I'm not too busy working."

"St. Francis? A Catholic church? No, no, no! You can't be a follower of Christ and a Catholic too!"

Jim sensed himself hot with anger. He had encountered some less than opened-minded Christians before when he was in the Army, but at least those guys had the faith to jump out of airplanes with him.

Jim then took a deep breath and replied, "Mr. Fane, you believe what you believe, and I believe what I believe. Why don't we just leave it at that?"

Nick shook his head disdainfully, took his pills, and signed the MAR in silence. He then stormed out.

Jim went to June's small office near the kitchen. "Where's Lucinda tonight, June?"

"She's working. Why don't you leave me her pills, and I'll see that she gets them?"

"Does she ever drink while working?"

"Never. She has too much self-respect to drink or do drugs at her workplace. It's only when she visits her friend, Rita, that Lucinda seems to get into trouble."

"Okay," Jim said, handing Lucinda's pill envelope to June.

On the ride home, the pain in his left hip became more noticeable and acute. Sprinting to save the lounging Mike was the first running Jim had done in years. Now he was paying for it. Once home, Jim put a large ice pack on his left hip area and had a couple of extra bourbons. Shortly afterward, he checked the inbox on his computer. The message that he had been fearing for some time now projected ominously from his screen. It was from Michele, and the subject line simply stated: "WE'RE ENGAGED!" Jim reluctantly read the attached message, which gave scant details on the logistics of the wedding but rather exuded general proclamations of mutual love. After rereading the message three times, Jim thought it best to log off without replying under the influence. He then succumbed to a restless night's sleep.

# CHAPTER SIX

As the remaining days of June passed, the rudimentary elements of Michele's wedding plans began to take shape. Also, by the start of the long holiday weekend, Jim was comfortably acclimated to his not-so-new job.

It was drizzly on the Fourth of July; thus, Jim donned a green rain slicker and his old, tattered ball cap. Once with Wanda in her apartment, Jim noticed that she again seemed somewhat excited.

"Wanda, what's goin' on?"

"Great news, Jimmy! I finally figured out how to get rid of the voices!"

"I thought defrosting the icebox took care of that?" Jim asked.

"Nah. The box was bare for less than a day before the voices came back. But today I found an old Christmas wreath in the closet. As soon I threw it out, the voices stopped. Man, what a relief."

Jim nodded, showing his support for her newfound happiness, but he also felt saddened by the recurring torment that she was suffering. Soon their visit was over, and he was on the way to see Phil, as Richard had gone out of state to visit some relatives for the holiday. Naturally, they had made suitable arrangements for Sir Richard to travel, including securing his pills in advance.

Once Jim was at the fire escape of the YMCA, Phil met him, and then the two went inside to conduct their business. Phil was watching TV, which was broadcasting some patriotic documentary in commemoration of Independence Day.

"Amazing how some people still think that America is a democracy," Phil remarked cynically.

"What do you mean?" Jim asked.

"I tell you, boy, America's not much more democratic than the English aristocracy that we broke away from."

"How so?" Jim asked.

"Well, how representative is our government—of the people, for the people, and by the people—when so many friggin' members of Congress are millionaires?"

"It makes you wonder if they truly feel the pinch—or empathize with us voters—when things like gas and interest rates soar," Jim mused.

"Exactly! What's even worse is that the special interest groups, not the people, keep these bozos in power by funding their multimillion-dollar campaigns. If they withdrew their support from any given campaign, it would collapse like a house of cards. It's a real boondoggle how these folks get elected."

"Maybe there should be caps on the amount spent on campaigns, or simply have the government pay an equal amount to each candidate, like what's done in some other countries," Jim suggested.

"That's not a bad idea, but term limits would eventually help solve the problem," Phil suggested.

"How so?"

"Well Jimmy, if you limit the amount of time that these jokers can serve, then you'll destroy the elitist gerontocracy and end the reigns of politicos like Strom Thurmond and Robert Byrd— guys who treat elected office like a lifetime appointment."

Jim chuckled, then added, "Happy Birthday, America!"

Phil laughed also, but then spoke more softly. "Don't get me wrong; I love this country. I just hate what's happened to it."

Jim nodded, then shortly afterward they finished up their business. Even though Jim was a nurse, he enjoyed following politics and current events. Since 9/11 Jim had taken a particular interest in Middle Eastern affairs and the war on terror. Rarely a day went by when Jim didn't know what color the national threat level was.

Within minutes Jim was at Sally's and found her and Walter on the front porch barbequing.

"Hey, guys, howya doing?"

"Good," Walter replied, taking a stubby cigar out of his mouth. "Would ya like a dog or a burger?"

Not wanting to offend them but also not wanting to consume anything that came from their house, he opted for a little white lie: "No, thanks, I just ate."

"Hey Jimmy, Jesus gave me a free devil dog today!" Sally exclaimed.

*Jesus doling out devil dogs. How odd,* Jim thought with amusement.

"He's probably being nice to you because he's looking to get laid," Walter said.

"He's not tryin' to—he's my—the lord and savior! He's not tryin' to get laid!"

Jim quickly interjected, "Don't worry about that, Sally. Just don't let him touch you. You know he's divine, and it just wouldn't be right for him to go around touchin' mortals."

She nodded at Jim's response and seemed less agitated, while Walter smiled knowingly at Jim's shrewd move. Jim then hurriedly finished up and left for his visit to St. Monica's, as Mike had received his meds earlier from Cindy.

After an unusually brief trip to St. Monica's due to the holiday, Jim was greeted by Maureen, who was sitting on the couch watching television. Rob was in the kitchen, so Jim began with him.

Rob was unusually quiet but offered no complaints. He wore a plain summer dress and had a thin layer of foundation on his face. After Rob was done, Jim found himself alone in the kitchen for a moment. He then went to the threshold of the living room to talk to Maureen.

"Hey, Maureen, do you know where Nick and Lucinda are?"

"Nick got his envelope earlier from Cindy. He went to an AA picnic tonight. And Lucinda's working the closing shift at the PD."

"PD?"

"Yeah. You know, the Dawg," she replied.

"What time is she due back?"

"I dunno."

Jim nodded and then said goodbye. As many of his patients were out for the holiday, Jim was running ahead of schedule. Knowing from June that Lucinda never drank or did drugs on the job, Jim figured he'd venture out to the Philthy Dawg to discreetly give her the medication there. He was disappointed that June hadn't been working because he would have trusted her to wait up for Lucinda to give her the medication.

Once at the Dawg, Jim took a seat at the corner of the bar, which afforded him a complete view of the bar and the rest of the place. A burly bartender approached and asked what he wanted to drink.

"I'm not here to—is Lucinda working?"

"Who's asking?" the man gruffly inquired.

"Oh, I'm a friend—I guess I'll have a seltzer. Is she due back soon?"

"She's on break. Shouldn't be gone too long," he tersely replied.

"Thanks."

After a couple of minutes, Jim was approached by a scantily clad and scrawny stripper who had just finished a routine on stage. The pungent aroma of cheap perfume preceded her.

"Hey, buddy, howya doing?" she inquired.

"Not bad, and yourself?"

"Good. What's your name, big boy?"

"Jack," he deceitfully replied.

"Like the ripper?"

Jim chuckled, then replied, "Yeah, and what's yours?"

"Venus."

"Like the flytrap?"

Now she laughed, then replied, "Yeah, something like that."

After a brief pause, she continued, "Say, you seem like a guy who could use a lap dance. What do you say?"

"Well, thanks, but I'm really here to see—I'm just waitin' for a friend."

"A friend," she said sarcastically. "Sure, a friend. Hey, well, it was nice talkin' to you, anyway."

Suddenly, and much to Jim's relief, Lucinda appeared behind the bar. Her hair was dyed a deep auburn, and she was wearing a short white belly shirt with navy blue spandex shorts. She was the most attractive female in the place.

"I like your outfit. Very patriotic," Jim said.

"How nice of you to notice. What the heck brings you here?"

"Maureen's working, so I figured that I'd come down to give you—"

"Why don't you just give me what you owe, then I'll mark the IOU as paid in full," Lucinda replied.

Jim nodded and smiled while sliding her the coin envelope containing her meds and a piece of paper. She nonchalantly tucked the envelope beneath her bra strap, then signed and returned the MAR.

Right after the transaction was completed, she said, "Hey, sorry about yelling at Nick in front of you last week. I didn't mean to put you in a bad spot."

"No problem," Jim replied.

"You know, Nick used to be a regular in here."

"Really?"

"Yeah, his AA meetings are held at the Knights of Columbus Hall across the street. He used to come in faithfully to preach to the strippers."

"No kidding!" Jim remarked.

"Yep. He saddled up to the stage, and whenever a stripper bent over to whisper in his ear, he'd respond with warnings about the end of the world. Most of the strippers didn't care and were more than glad to take his singles, but some were offended by his remarks. So, one night this stripper, Jumpin' Jasmine, decided to expose Nick for the fraud that he is. She was a spicy Dominican. They used to call her JJ for short."

"What did she do?"

"Well, JJ was probably the most aggressive performer and lap dancer that ever worked at the Dawg. So, after one especially erotic routine on stage, she decided to offer Nick a free lap dance."

"He took it?" Jim asked.

"Not only did he take it—the more he'd rant and rave about the apocalypse, the harder she'd thrash and thrust upon him. Man, she kept coming at Nick like a crazed bronco to a cornered rodeo clown!"

"What did he do about it?"

"Soon as the dance ended, Nick bolted to the men's room. Charlie the bouncer saw it and rushed in after him, thinking maybe he was sick."

"Was he?" Jim questioned.

"Not physically. But soon as Charlie burst in, he caught ol' Nick committing an act of self-service with his unleaded pump— if you know what I mean," Lucinda said while making the appropriate corresponding hand gesture.

"What did Charlie do?" Jim asked, laughing.

"Threw his ass out. But once management heard what happened, they banned Nick from ever returnin'. He tried comin' back a few times but never got in. After a while, he got the hint."

Once Jim finished his seltzer, he said goodbye to Lucinda and was soon on the way home, but not before taking a short detour to Sully's for a couple of chili dogs and a cold beer.

At his apartment, Jim decided to skip the bourbon as he did not want to mix drinks. He perfunctorily checked his email. Most of it was spam or crap forwards, completely devoid of any interest or substance.

Suddenly, Jim found Lucinda's tucking the coin envelope under her bra strap replaying in his mind. *Damn, anytime a smoking hot babe plays with her bra strap or hair, it's a huge turn-on,* Jim mused. He kind of felt bad that he was still having mildly erotic thoughts about her. He wasn't sure if he felt guilty because they were now friends or because she was still his patient. His thoughts somewhat segued onto Maria. *They're both beautiful women, but totally different. Maria was as smooth as a pearl, but Lucinda is cut like a diamond,* Jim pondered while struggling to sleep.

# CHAPTER SEVEN

An unusually hot July day was underway when Jim arrived at Wanda's. She was in a good mood, and her sugar and voices were well controlled. Soon he was traveling to the YMCA. Jim had gotten a voice mail from Cindy informing him that Richard's sugar was 610 and that he had been admitted to County Hospital for observation.

At Phil's, Jim blasted the horn, and an angry man appeared from a third-floor window. The man shouted, "Can you not beep your horn when you come here! I've gotta work nights, and you're wakin' me up!"

Jim was embarrassed and proceeded cautiously up the iron fire escape. Within seconds Phil appeared, seemingly oblivious to the recent exchange. Phil was wearing a pair of neatly pressed khaki shorts and a fresh white T-shirt.

"Hey, Phil, how are you?"

"Fine. How 'bout you?"

"Good. You stayin' cool today?" Jim asked.

"Yeah, I went shopping at the supermarket down the street. It's so damn hot, I purposely stayed in the frozen food section for a couple of extra minutes," Phil replied.

"Don't you have an air conditioner?"

"Yeah, but it's low wattage and old. I got it at a yard sale last year. It's not that great, but it's the only thing I can afford."

They both went into Phil's warm room to finish their visit, and shortly afterward Jim was back in his air-conditioned car, heading over to see Sally. Once Jim arrived, he found Walter on the porch. He was perusing what appeared to be a brochure to a tropical resort.

"Hey, Walter, whatcha reading?"

"A brochure about a condo complex in Florida from my old IRS partner, Mitch. Soon as we get enough money saved up, we're gonna get one together. Shouldn't be too much longer."

"Sounds nice. Where's Sally, inside?" Jim queried.

"Nope. She's probably off visiting her mini-mart messiah."

"Please tell her I'll stop by later."

"You bet."

Jim was annoyed that he'd have to make a second trip to Sally's, but at least he was ahead of schedule.

Arriving at Mike's, Jim saw him sprawled out in a hammock beneath some shady trees.

"Hey, Mike, you comfortable?"

"Yeah, this hammock is a lot less itchy than just layin' in the grass. Besides, no one will take me for dead and give me CPR by mistake for being in here."

"Sorry, I didn't mean to worry when I ran across the grass."

"Ah, don't worry about it. I'm just messin' with you," Mike quipped.

"How you feeling today?"

"Kinda bummed out. I cut my hand on a jagged nail working with Uncle Joe last week. Had to get five stitches across my palm. My mom completely freaked out, and now it feels like I'm under house arrest 'cause she won't let me work at all."

"She'll let you go back once the stitches are out?" Jim asked.

"She better."

Within minutes their visit was over, and Jim pulled up to St. Monica's (still slightly ahead of schedule) and found Nick in the kitchen.

"Do you have my pills?" Nick inquired.

"Sure."

"Are you still going to that popish church near Ashton to worship Christ?"

*Damn! He's at it again!* Jim thought. "I haven't been there in a while. Just too busy lately."

"That's good. You should not worship any cone-headed old man wearing a white robe!"

"If the Church is that bad, how come AA holds their meetings at her Knights of Columbus Hall?"

"What? How do you know that I go to meetings there? Have you been spying on me? Are you a secret agent from Rome?!"

"As agency nurses, we know the location of all nearby AA meetings, and the Knights' hall is the closest one from here." *Another white lie to the rescue,* Jim thought. "Look—I don't mean to upset you, but I'm just tired of hearing you insult my church."

"Well, you must know Christ before it's too late!"

Jim sighed again but refused to answer. He then handed Nick his meds, who took them without protest. After the MAR was signed, Nick exited out the back.

"Hey, June, where's Rob?"

"He's out back on the boat. You know Lucinda went away for a couple of days with Rita, right?"

"Yeah, thanks."

Jim went out into the backyard, where he found an old and weathered boat, more than twenty feet in length, sunk into the ground.

"Hey, Rob, how ya doing today?"

"It's Shane; Rob's too much of a pansy to commandeer such a magnificent vessel."

"How are you feeling today, Shane?" Jim asked.

"Just fine. And yourself, me boyo?"

"Not bad. Nice boat you got here."

"Aye, lad! And once I fix her up, I'm gonna take her back to the home of me ancestors, in Ireland."

"Oh yeah, what part of Ireland are they from?"

"Ellingford."

Jim fought back his laughter, as he was certain that there was no such corresponding town on the Emerald Isle. They talked for a couple more minutes, then Jim ended their visit with the usual exchanges.

Jim was happy that Sally was back at her home when he arrived, and their visit was brief and without any troubles.

Once in from work, Jim commenced his usual routine and began with sipping Knob Creek while opening his inbox, as he had not gotten any regular mail for the day. Other than a couple of impersonal spam messages, there was only one email. It was from Jenny, who was sharing some preliminary ideas about wedding patterns and dresses. After perusing it quickly, Jim decided to check out some news online and also the status of the national threat level (which he usually did first thing in the morning).

Once he finished that, he logged onto his old internet dating site to see if there were any hot new pics. With an increased sense of frustration, Jim viewed page after page of a seemingly endless array of tired-looking middle-aged women. Many of them candidly proclaimed themselves to be a "hard-working single mom, looking for a fun relationship with a kind, caring, and fully employed man." For about fifteen minutes Jim searched, and then he toggled back to his inbox for a final glance. Much to his surprise, he discovered a new email from Paramount Mutual Insurance Company.

Reportedly, they were the Cadillac of new healthcare insurers in the New York marketplace. They were contacting Jim to arrange for an interview in response to Jim's recent application to them. Jim promptly replied to the email with dates and times of his availability to meet. After logging off, Jim poured a second glass of bourbon, then went to bed to look for a mindless sitcom on TV.

# CHAPTER EIGHT

Jim got up fairly early the next day, as he had several errands to run. He began by stopping in at Gus' Diner to get a newspaper and a large cup of coffee, light, no sugar. Although he was hungry enough for breakfast, he figured he'd wait until after he returned from the gym. After leisurely reading the paper over the next half hour or so, Jim then headed out for the gym.

The gym was fairly empty most mid-mornings, which Jim preferred. Only a few middle-aged homemakers were working out, and there was no waiting for any of the machines that he wanted. It always disappointed him that he couldn't do squats anymore. He used to be able to squat 360 pounds before his parachuting accident. Now he generally didn't do any weight- bearing exercises for his lower extremities, except for gently warming up and down on an elliptical machine. Over the next forty-five minutes, Jim completed a circuit routine for his upper extremities. He was pleased that he could still bench press about 300 pounds. Unfortunately, the cute trainer who worked the counter was out at the time; otherwise, he would have spent at least a few minutes flirting with her.

After leaving the gym, Jim stopped back at Gus' to grab a sandwich to go. Once home, he ate, then reviewed his resume to make some minor changes to its layout. He decided to change the color of the paper from gray to ivory, which he thought was more of a power color. He also decided to pick a slightly thicker bond. *I've got that interview coming up, gotta get ready,* Jim thought as he left for the print shop.

He dropped off the resume with the printer, then went to a big and tall store to check out some new suits. It had only been months since Jim had stopped wearing suits daily; however, he noticed that when he tried his on recently, all of the pants were snug. Jim always despised shopping for clothes, as they never had anything cool in his size, or if they did, it was prohibitively expensive. *Man, I wish I was still dating Holly. She always could find me clothes that fit,* Jim thought. Soon he left the store without having purchased anything.

He returned home and decided to start doing some of his narrative nursing notes, as they would be due at Rose's office in the next couple of days. He reviewed his handwritten notes from the previous week and realized that he wanted to follow up with what was going on with Richard. Picking up the phone, he dialed Stella's number and got her answering machine. Instead of leaving a message, he decided to call Vicky.

"Hey, Vicky, how you doing?"

"Not bad. What's up Jim?"

"Just wanted to follow up on what's going on with Richard."

"Yeah, it's the strangest thing. Once he got to the hospital, his sugar dropped from 600 to about 390. The ER staff noticed the same thing happened the last time he went in on your shift," Vicky replied.

"So, what did they do?"

"They watched him for a while. He wasn't symptomatic, so they sent him home. Rose is thinking that maybe it's a mechanical malfunction, so she's having someone from the blood glucose meter company come to check it out."

"You know—if you have time—I also wanted to talk to you about Nick," Jim said.

"Sure, what's going on with him?"

"He's driving me bananas. He's always berating me with religious questions and insulting what I believe."

"Yeah, he can be a real Bible-thumping pain in the ass. You should tell him what I told him," Vicky said.

"What's that?"

"That you belong to the Church of the Avenger, about sixty miles from here."

Jim starting laughing, picking up on Vicky's sarcastic tone of voice, which clearly implied that no such church existed.

"Aren't you afraid that Nick will try to attend with you sometime?" Jim inquired.

"Nah. Sixty miles is too long for Nick to bum a ride there, but he does love the picture of the church that I've painted for him. I told him that it has a tall white steeple overlooking a strong white building, both of which are surrounded by a sturdy white fence. If he knew that I was Wiccan, he'd have me burned at the stake."

After Jim stopped laughing, he said, "Thanks a lot, Vicky. I appreciate that."

"No problem. If you ever have any questions on the road, please call me."

After their conversation ended, Jim completed his narrative notes and prepared an early dinner of steak and beans. Once dinner was done, he checked his emails: a few bad jokes from his folks and a couple from his friend, Chris, in Iraq. Chris sent pics from one of Saddam's palaces that he had stayed in for a few days during a medical conference. It was plush and looked absolutely extravagant. He was happy for Chris but also a little envious. Jim missed being an Army medic and would've liked to have become an Army nurse, had his hip permitted.

After checking his regular mail, Jim then enjoyed a leisurely glass of bourbon while watching an old episode of *M\*A\*S\*H*.

# CHAPTER NINE

Soon another hot July day was underway, and Jim was heading out for his first visit.

He found Wanda dripping with sweat in her cramped apartment, malodorous from the summer heat. Bubba cooed quietly in the corner of the main room.

"Hey, Jimmy, howya doin' today?"

"Not bad—how 'bout you?"

"Pretty good since I threw my fan out yesterday," she replied.

"Why'd you throw the fan out?"

"The vibrations were causing voices to bounce off all the walls. It was starting to get on Bubba's nerves."

"The fan was causing your voice and Bubba's to echo in here?" Jim asked.

"No, not our voices—I don't know whose—but it was really starting to piss off Bubba."

"When was the last time that you had your clozapine level checked?"

"I dunno."

"Are you feeling okay other than the voices?" he questioned.

"Yep. No problems."

Jim made a quick note to himself to follow up on the clozapine issue as Wanda checked her sugar, took her pills, and signed the MAR.

Minutes later he was greeted at the railroad castle by Sir Richard wearing his white lab jacket.

"Hello, Sir Richard. How are you?"

"Just fine, my good man. How are you?"

"Good. Why don't you take your sugar while I get your pills?"

"The nice lady from the blood glucose meter company was out today and gave me a new machine and test strips," Richard said.

"Terrific. How have you been feeling?"

"Splendid! I got some great news today. I won the variance for my wall. Now I can contact a master mason and have it heightened and fortified with the lead backing."

"Good for you," Jim replied.

Just then the blood glucose meter beeped, and Richard said, "Two-oh-five. Not bad, wouldn't you say?"

"Not bad at all," Jim answered.

They soon finished their visit, and Jim made his way to Phil's. Once inside the Y, Jim went to Phil's room and found a documentary about WWII playing on TV.

"WWII, now that was a war, boy," Phil said.

"Yep, war seems portrayed as simpler back then," Jim responded.

"Yes, sir. At least you knew who your enemies were."

"Yeah, and you were able to win their hearts and minds after beating them," Jim opined.

"But how the heck do you win the hearts and minds of defeated jihadists—like the Taliban—who, after legitimately losing on the battlefield, keep thinking that it's perfectly acceptable to strap on a bomb and continue their fight in a crowded market of civilians?" Phil queried.

"That just strikes me as being a sore loser, militarily speaking."

"Sore losers or not, if we continue to underestimate them, as the Romans did the barbarians, we will surely go out the same way the Romans did."

"I suppose the real battle should be for the hearts and minds of the angry young people who aren't yet terrorists but who make up the jihadists' recruiting pool. We should target them and show them that they have better options than blowing themselves up," Jim suggested.

"Man, that's easier said than done. Especially when you got Arabic news networks spewing anti-American propaganda 24/7."

Jim nodded, then their visit ended after exchanging the pills and paperwork.

Following a brief ride, Jim arrived at Sally's and found her on the couch surrounded by several mangy cats who roamed around her.

"Hey, Sally, how are you?"

"Good, Jimmy. How are you?"

"Good. Did Jesus give you a muffin today with your coffee?" Jim inquired, pointing to the large half-eaten muffin in her right hand.

"Yep, Jesus is the best! Jesus and Santa! Santa gives away presents! He's the best, too! If Santa gives me a nice present, I'd bring it right over to Jesus and give it to him!"

Jim smiled, then they finished their visit in the typical fashion.

Jim's visit with Mike was uneventful. Mike's hand was healing nicely, without any symptoms of infection or dehiscence.

Shortly after arriving at St. Monica's, Jim set up shop in the kitchen while June greeted him from the nearby office. Nick was the first to approach Jim from the table.

"Do you read the Bible about Christ, my son?"

"Usually, when I go to church," Jim replied.

"Just like you Catholics, paying attention to Jesus and his word only while in church," Nick said with a sigh. "What's your favorite passage?"

"Probably the one about not judging, lest you be judged," Jim replied with a hint of sarcasm.

Nick seemed nonplussed and continued, "Mine is Paul's sixth letter to the Ephesians, the one about putting on the full armor of the Lord to advance against and smite the heathen enemy—to go forth wearing the breastplate of righteousness and belt of pride, armed with the sword of vengeance, the dagger of retribution, and the battle-ax of spite."

"Well, if you *must* smite and spite the heathen enemy, you really should have at least those weapons at your disposal," Jim said with even more sarcasm.

"Amen! Amen! 'Vengeance is mine,' sayeth the Lord!"

Nick took the pills, signed the MAR, and left the kitchen whistling "Onward, Christian Soldiers."

"Hey, June, where are Lucinda and Rob tonight?" Jim asked.

"Rob took a bus to Ellingford to see a bridal show. Why don't you just leave me his meds?"

"Sure. What about Lucinda?"

"Oh, she told me to send you up."

"Okay. Thanks."

Jim went out the back door and up the flights of stairs to Lucinda's apartment. Once arriving at her back door, he found only her screen door shut. He gently rapped on the flimsy door.

"Hey, Jimmy! Come on in, bud!"

"Hey, Lucinda. How are you?"

"Great. Check out my new tattoo."

Jim peered at her flexed left arm, where the base of her deltoid merged into purposefully bulging triceps and biceps musculature. He saw two bands of interwoven thorns that circumnavigated her arm; however, he was a bit more distracted by her darkened cleavage.

"Cool. Very tribal," Jim said.

"Look closer, and you'll see some tiny drops of blood painted beneath some of the thorns."

Jim took a second look and indeed saw what she'd described. Then, he replied, "Wow, I've never seen a tattoo armband that involves fake blood."

"Yeah. My best friend Rita got the same thing, except hers is in on the right arm. I guess that makes us blood sisters or something like that."

"Hey, how was your trip to see her?" he asked.

"It was excellent! After we got these tattoos, we went to a slammin' all-night rave where we met some interestin' people. But most of the guys were pervs who kept trying to look down our shirts. Rita's great, though, and really knows how to handle men."

"How'd you guys meet?" Jim inquired.

"She used to be a stripper at the Dawg. Best fake boobs I've ever seen—her surgeon did a bang-up job. Rita made enough money to put herself through school for massage therapy and had enough left over to buy a new convertible. She now works for an exclusive spa just outside of Ellingford," Lucinda said. She then put the pills in her mouth and swallowed them.

"Hey, do you have a pen? I seem to have lost mine," Jim said.

Lucinda stuffed both hands into her snug denim cutoffs and quickly retrieved a short, stubby pencil. "This is all I got. It's from the bar."

"No problem," Jim said while handing her the MAR. As she signed, he continued, "You work 'til closing?"

"Nah, I usually don't work late evenings unless I'm covering for someone. Since I'm their youngest and smallest bartender, they're nice enough to let me work mostly the day shifts and happy hours. It's more of a white-collar crowd. Better tippers."

Jim smiled, and then the two said goodbye, and Jim headed back to his apartment.

Once Jim got home, he laid out his dress clothes for his interview with Paramount Insurance Company, as it was first thing in the morning.

# CHAPTER TEN

Jim felt cautiously optimistic following his interview with Paramount Insurance Company, and he promptly fired off a thank-you letter to Mr. Gordon, the executive who had interviewed him.

At the beginning of the following workweek, Jim discovered that they had increased Wanda's clozapine dose by fifty milligrams per day—twenty-five in the morning and twenty-five at night. His visit with her was brief. Her sugar was slightly elevated, and her auditory hallucinations were unchanged.

Arriving at Richard's, Jim found Sir Richard in an unusually good mood.

"Hello, Sir Richard, how are you today?"

"Just splendid, young man! And yourself?"

"Fine. What's going on?" Jim asked.

"I've just received three quotes from different contractors in the past week, and it looks like I'll be able to afford the addition to my wall. They can start next week," Richard said while checking his sugar. It was 305.

"Are you feeling okay? Your sugar's a little high."

"Oh, I'm fine. Just excited to resume my Paramatter research with absolute secrecy," he said just before taking his pills.

Once they reached the lab, a foul stench emanated from some large pots that were cooking on large hot plates. Richard asked him to inspect the pot of a Paramatter prototype brewing in the corner. It stunk like rotten eggs and mustard. The concoction appeared somewhat like pasta e fagioli but had none of its olfactory appeal.

"Richard, I'm sorry. It doesn't look like much of anything to me," Jim said reluctantly.

"Nothing at all, my boy?"

As a courtesy, Jim took a second look, then said, "Sorry, nothing."

Richard nodded slightly, showing his appreciation for Jim's opinion. Then he said, "Well, my muses seem to be eluding me today."

Jim nodded and then slid him the MAR, which he promptly signed and returned. Within seconds Jim was on his way to the YMCA.

Once at the Y, instead of honking, Jim climbed up the fire escape and gently knocked on the door, as Phil's room was near the exit. He knocked repeatedly, but there was no response. Finally, a younger man answered the door and let him into the corridor. Jim knocked on Phil's door, and after almost a minute Phil appeared, unshaven and disheveled.

"Hey, Phil, are you okay?"

"Late night. I was up watching a documentary."

"What about?"

"9/11 hijackers—the magnificent nineteen," he replied with a tone of disgust.

An awkward pause followed as Phil began his usual ritual with the meds, microwave, and MAR. After he completed it, Jim noticed that Phil hadn't made eye contact with him once during the visit.

"Say, Phil, are you having any thoughts about hurting yourself?" Jim gently inquired.

"No, sir," Phil replied with a quiet, strained tone of voice.

"If you feel that you need to talk to someone, please call me," Jim said as he patted Phil on the shoulder.

Phil nodded, then Jim left to go see Sally.

After arriving at Sally's, he entered the unlocked house and made his way to the living room, where he found her on the couch, drinking a coffee and eating a large muffin.

"Hey, Sally, how are you?"

"Good! Jesus gave me another muffin today!" she replied.

"Good for you."

"Jesus loves me! He gives me muffins!"

"Have you been hearing any voices or seeing anything unusual?" Jim asked.

She shook her head no, and suddenly a large chunk of muffin became dislodged and bounced off her knee onto the floor. Immediately, a spry kitten pounced upon it like a hungry lioness on a stray wildebeest in the Serengeti. As this episode was right near Jim's feet, he instinctively jumped back. After regaining his composure, he quickly finished their visit and was soon in his car smoking his usual post-visit cigarette.

At Mike's house, Jim found Mike again lounging in the hammock under the shade of a tree.

"Hey, Mike. How's it goin'?"

"Not bad. Just waiting for Uncle Joe to pick me up to help him move some supplies for a job that he's starting tomorrow."

"How's the hand?"

"Pretty much healed. How's yours?" Mike replied sarcastically.

"Just fine, thank you. What kinda supplies are you moving?"

"Some lumber to build a deck across town. Mom's pissin' me off, though, 'cause she won't let me work with Uncle Joe unless I wear these thick gloves that she bought me," he said, holding up a pair of gloves beside him in the hammock.

"I'm sure she's just trying to look out for you," Jim said.

"That's what bugs me. She's always trying to protect me from everything. Besides, I hate these gloves. They make my hands itchy and sweaty."

Soon their visit was over, and Jim was on the way to St. Monica's. Once inside, Jim found June at the table, reading the newspaper.

"Hi, Jim. How are you?"

"Fine, and you?" he replied.

"Not bad. Lucinda went out dancing with Rita and some other friends, and I believe that Rob went to the Dawg. Why don't you leave me their meds, and I'll go get Nick for you?"

"Thanks."

She and Nick almost bumped into each other at the back door while she was leaving to get him. Nick immediately sat down at the table.

"Good evening, Nick. How are you?"

"Blessed, and yourself?"

"Pretty good," Jim answered.

"Have you explored the word of Christ?"

"Yeah—it's like I told you before. I read it when I go to church."

"Not good enough, young man! You must read the word of Christ daily to be saved!"

Jim paused, then said, "Well, I got this Gideon Bible from the Army once—and I do look at it now and again."

"Have you ever heard of the Reverend William Roberts?"

"Nope. Never heard of him."

"He's the minister of the First Church of the Lord and Savior. And for just $149.99 you can get a brand-new King James Bible complete with gilded pages, biblical maps, and an exhaustive concordance from our church store."

"No, thank you—I'm okay with my Army Bible," Jim replied.

"If you want, for only $49.95 you can get a collection of sermons by the Right Reverend Roberts on CD," Nick proposed.

*Like it wasn't bad enough that he keeps mocking my beliefs. Now this huckster wants me to spend money on his,* Jim thought with exasperation. "I'm just fine with my church and Bible, but thank you anyway."

"You must read the Bible daily! You must be saved! The Reverend William Roberts can take you there!" Nick exclaimed as he signed the MAR after taking his pills.

After Nick had finished up, June joined Jim at the table.

"Sorry about Nick bothering you. I couldn't help overhearing him."

"Thanks, but it's not your fault."

"I know, but you're a good guy and don't deserve to be treated like that," she said with genuine sympathy in her voice.

"Is he like that with everyone?"

"Basically, but I think most folks don't even engage him in his religious rantings after a while," she replied.

"Well, I don't even want to talk to him about religion, but it seems that's his only topic of conversation."

She nodded understandingly. They bantered for a few more minutes, then Jim headed home.

At his apartment, Jim began with his usual routine, and as he sorted the mail, he spied a letter from Paramount. After going through other pieces of junk mail and tossing them on the floor to be later discarded, he took a deep drag from his cigarette and opened the Paramount Mutual letter. It read, "Dear Mr. Greene: We are pleased to invite you to our corporate headquarters on Park Avenue for a second interview with our risk management group..." *Holy shit! I got a shot at being back in the city again!* he thought with a renewed sense of excitement.

Jim then poured himself a healthy tumbler of Knob Creek to try and coax himself into a good night's sleep.

# CHAPTER ELEVEN

Arriving at Wanda's, Jim found her unusually nervous, with her left hand twitching from extrapyramidal tremors, likely caused by the increase in her meds.

"Wanda, are you okay?"

"Nope. I've been hearin' voices from that trophy up there," she said, pointing to a cylindrical-shaped object about a foot tall with a small chrome-plated archer on top. It was located on her TV credenza.

"Are the voices saying anything to you?"

"Yeah, they're tellin' me that I'm bad and nasty. Every time that I change the TV channel, I keep hearing things like 'no good dirty whore!'"

"Are you sure they're not coming from the TV?"

"Nope. I can't imagine any TV show saying something like, 'We're gonna shoot flamin' arrows at your vaginary zone 'til you bleed to death, you filthy little cunt!' They're gonna shoot flamin' arrows! They're gonna shoot flamin' arrows 'til I bleed to death! I'm so ashamed by what they're saying, but I don't want to throw it out—it was the one that my mom was most proud of." Wanda started to sob heavily.

"How long has your hand been twitching?"

"I dunno."

"Are you having any thoughts of hurting yourself?" Jim gently inquired.

"No—I just, I just want these goddamn voices to stop. It's killing me!"

"What does your psychiatrist say about your voices?"

"Oh, he never really talks to me much. There's no money in it for him. Usually, we just chat for a minute or two every few months. Then, he renews my prescriptions."

"Well, if you ever feel like hurting yourself, please call me, Vicky, or someone else and let us know. In the meantime, I'll call the doctor about your hand."

She nodded, then they went on to wrap up their visit. Before heading over to Richard's, Jim made a note to himself to follow up with Vicky or Stella about Wanda.

Soon Jim was at Sir Richard's, where he found him in a distraught mood, as evidenced by the look on his face.

"Sir Richard, what's bothering you today?"

"Bad news, my boy! Take a look," Richard said, handing Jim what appeared to be a small stack of legal papers.

"What's this?" Jim queried.

"Some sort of application for a temporary restraining order pending a zoning appeal!"

"So, what can you do about it?"

"Well, that's just it—now I have to either spend money on a lawyer to fight this or save the money for the wall addition and fight this myself."

"Well, you did win it yourself at the last hearing, didn't you?" Jim said.

"Yes, but these papers come from a law office, and my neighbors didn't have lawyers at that last hearing. Since they lost, they are determined to crush my research by now retaining some unscrupulous lawyers! Do you know of any inexpensive but honest attorneys?"

"Nah, I generally try to avoid lawyers," Jim replied.

"Well, this again demonstrates my neighbors' willingness to continue their surveillance of my research. It must now go underground!"

"What do you mean?"

"If I don't have the protection of my lead-enforced wall, then I must work during the middle of the night to minimize their chances of discovering my project."

Just then the blood glucose meter beeped, reading 385.

"Sir Richard, are you feeling okay, physically?"

"Just defeated. This setback will surely put me several weeks, if not months, behind schedule."

"Well, if you start feeling really thirsty or urinating a lot, please call us immediately."

Richard nodded, then the meds and MAR were exchanged in a routine way. Within seconds Jim was on his way to the YMCA.

Once at Phil's, they went into his room, where there was a documentary playing about the history of flight.

"Hey, Phil, how are you?"

"Pretty good. I woke up at 2:15 this afternoon," he said with a hint of pride.

"Good for you. Whatcha watching, something on the Wright Brothers?"

"A program on the history of flight from Kitty Hawk to the Space Shuttle."

"Do you like flying?" Jim asked, suddenly realizing the potential insult of his question given how Phil's wife had died.

"I used to love it, but I got no use for it anymore."

"Sorry, I didn't mean to bring it up."

"Don't worry about it," Phil replied. "It amazes me at the capacity of folks to use good technology to kill and maim each other. I wonder if the Wright Brothers ever thought that their dream of flight would someday result in the nightmare of fully fueled planes crashing into buildings."

"If inventors thought like that, then nothing would probably ever get accomplished."

"It doesn't matter. The jihadist hillbillies would find some other way to use current technology to get our goat," Phil flatly responded.

*Such as low-tech box cutters,* Jim thought. *Too bad those jihadist hillbillies won't just turn on each other like the Hatfields and McCoys.*

Soon their visit was over, and Jim headed to Sally's. As it was Friday night, the visit was a bit longer due to Sally's receipt of her regular haloperidol shot. He arrived at Mike's slightly behind schedule and found Betty at home instead of Mike.

"Hello, Betty. How are you?"

"Just fine. I let my brother take Mike out for dinner and a movie tonight. If you want, you can leave me his medicine."

Jim obliged and had Betty sign Mike's name on the MAR.

After a brief ride, Jim found himself inside the kitchen of St. Monica's and was approached by Maureen, who said, "Did you hear about what happened to Rob?"

"No, what's up?"

"He got the shit kicked out of him last night by some gay- bashers. He's at Valley Memorial Hospital in Ellingford."

"Man, that sucks! How'd it happen?"

"When he went to the Dawg last night, some other guys got pissed off that the strippers were flirtin' with him and askin' him about makeup tips. After he left the bar, they started following him back here. Then they pummeled him. When he was found by the police, he barely had a pulse. One of those assholes stabbed him and left him for dead," she explained.

"How's he doing now?"

"I got an update from Cindy, who said that he's out of ICU and is expected to make a full recovery."

"Thanks for letting me know."

Nick soon appeared, wearing a bright white T-shirt that read, "In case of Rapture, this shirt will be unoccupied."

"Evening, Nick. Got your pills ready for you," Jim said, hoping to keep their visit focused and brief.

"Amen! Amen! Have you heard that the Lord has exacted his vengeance upon that fa**** sinner Robert Reilly?"

"That wasn't the vengeance of the Lord. That was the work of some jealous and hateful scumbags!"

"Vengeance of the Lord, nonetheless!" Nick shot back. "Haven't you ever read that the Lord will often use sinners to exhibit his power and glory? Indeed, the Lord repeatedly hardened the heart of sinful Pharaoh in order to unleash a multitude of plagues on Egypt. In doing so, he used a sinner to facilitate an awesome display of his retribution and vengeance!"

Undaunted, Jim replied, "And haven't you read that story of the Good Samaritan who took in a total stranger, beaten by the roadside, and cared for him as a brother?"

"How dare you lecture me on the Word! You who've been steeped in sin and popery since birth! I smite you mightily in the name of Jesus Christ, my Lord and Avenger! You shall burn for an eternity in the everlasting lake of sulfur!"

After having said this, Nick turned away from Jim and headed toward the back door.

"Mr. Fane, do you want your medicine or not?" Jim shouted at him.

"I smite you, Nurse James! 'Vengeance is mine,' sayeth the Lord!"

After Nick left the room, Jim signed "refused" in the appropriate space on Nick's MAR.

Maureen re-entered the kitchen and sat across from Jim. "What a fuckin' idiot! I'm so sick of hearin' him babble on about being saved and what the righteous Reverend Billy Bob can do for our souls," she said.

Jim nodded in agreement, then asked, "Where's Lucinda?"

"She's upstairs."

"Great. I'll see you later," Jim said, then headed up to Lucinda's.

Once at Lucinda's he found her visibly distraught, with mascara running down her face from prolonged crying. Her normally electrifying eyes were glazed over and reddened.

"What's wrong, Lucinda?"

"Rob's almost dead, and it's all my fault!"

"How can that be your fault?"

"If I never brought him to the Dawg, he wouldn't be lying in the hospital right now!"

"You can't blame yourself for that. It's not your fault some asshole bigots attacked him."

"I know. I just can't help thinkin' that if I never showed him the place, he wouldn't have gotten hurt."

"Well, I'm sure Rob won't hold it against you."

"You know the funny thing is, he's not even gay. He just loves all things feminine, like blouses and makeup. He even once told me that if I wasn't such a muscular tomboy, he'd totally eat me up."

After a couple more minutes, their visit ended. Jim left confident that even in her guilt, she wouldn't do something stupid.

Once back in his car, he checked his agency cell phone and discovered that indeed Cindy had left him a message regarding what had happened to Rob. Jim decided to stop in at Valley Memorial Hospital to see him before going home. He checked in at the hospital and learned from Rob's nurse there that Rob's stab wound had ripped through his spleen and nicked his stomach. She said that if it had been a few inches higher, it would have punctured his lung and killed him. Jim quietly entered Rob's room and found him sleeping while connected to a couple of IV lines and pulse oximetry. His face was badly swollen and severely bruised. The sight made Jim even madder about what had happened and at Nick's heartless, self- righteous remarks.

Once home Jim engaged in his usual routine but was still disturbed about what had happened to Rob. Nonetheless, Jim managed to fall into an unsettled sleep after his evening routine.

# CHAPTER TWELVE

Jim's Saturday shift began with a large hot cup of coffee, as he had not gotten a restful night's sleep. Arriving at Wanda's door, he rapped on it three times and was greeted by her. She looked a little less haggard than the previous day but was still having fine tremors in her left hand.

"Hey, Wanda, how ya doin'?"

"Just sad since I threw out the trophy yesterday. My mom must hate me now."

After an awkward silence, Jim asked, "Are you having any thoughts of hurting yourself?"

Wanda shook her head defeatedly.

"Are you still hearing any voices?"

"Not since I threw that little bitch into the garbage."

"Well, it sounds to me like you took aim at a problem and hit the mark," Jim said, at once feeling unprofessional for this outright deception. "Don't you think that your mom would be proud of you for that?"

"Maybe you have something there," she replied, her expression lightening up a bit.

"Hey, I tried calling the clinic to get you something for your tremors—"

"What tremors?" she interrupted.

"In your left hand, from the clozapine," Jim said politely.

She nodded in acknowledgment.

"Anyway, the doctor covering last night wouldn't increase your Cogentin. They usually won't prescribe anything during the weekend unless it's an emergency. So, if your hand starts shaking more violently, or if the tremors spread, please give me a call. If you feel like you're about to have a full-blown seizure, just call 911."

She again nodded with a look of comprehension, then they soon ended their visit.

Once at Richard's, Jim observed that Sir Richard looked unusually disheveled and unkempt.

Richard explained that he had been up all night doing his research. "Will you please take a look at this, my good man?" Richard inquired, pointing to a pot of bubbling solution that reeked like a combination of garlic and dirty socks.

"What am I looking at?" Jim queried.

"A Paramatter prototype, I hope."

Jim was unsure how to answer, as he could not believe that the blueprint for all matter could smell so foul.

"What do you think?" Richard asked.

"Well—I dunno—I'm no scientist or anything," Jim replied sheepishly.

"That's exactly why I want your opinion!"

Jim reluctantly stepped closer to the solution and saw that it looked like a churning conglomeration of slimy vegetation interspersed with chunks of a cheese-like substance. "It looks interesting."

"But does it mean anything to you?" Richard asked with the enthusiasm of a psychoanalyst presenting inkblots.

"Honestly, no. Is it supposed to?"

Richard looked disappointed, then said, "I was hoping that someone else would see what I saw so I might confirm my working hypothesis."

"What is your working hypothesis, Sir Richard?"

"That the orderliness of Paramatter and eventually matter itself did arise from biochemical chaos," Richard sheepishly replied. "I suppose that perhaps I've been too preoccupied with legal matters lately to do justice to my Paramatter research."

Richard confessed that he had spent a good deal of the morning, as well as most of yesterday, researching local law firms online. His sugar was elevated at 387. Jim gave him the usual cautionary instructions, and then they ended their visit.

Soon afterward, Jim and Phil found themselves again in front of the TV during Jim's visit. A special was playing on the Travel Channel.

"Hi, Phil. How are you today?"

"Just fine, thanks."

"Whatcha watchin'?"

"A special on summer homes in the Adirondacks," Phil replied.

"Ever been up there?"

"Yes sir, my family settled in that area after moving from Georgia. My brother still has a cabin up there, not too far from Sagamore Hill. Debbie and I went up there for a couple of weeks when we were first married. I used to tease her about probably being the only high-powered female executive in New York who could reel in largemouth bass. It was the happiest time of our lives."

Jim hesitated, then reluctantly asked, "Are you having any thoughts of hurting yourself?"

"Nah. The memory of Debbie is the only thing that gets me out of bed at all. Even in death, she is still my main reason to live," he said matter-of-factly.

Shortly after their visit, Jim was en route to see Sally. Arriving at Sally's, he was surprised to find the house locked and nobody answering the door. He decided to move on and found Mike in his mom's garden doing some watering. Their visit was brief, and then Jim headed over to St. Monica's.

Upon entering St. Monica's, Jim was glad to see June working. She greeted him warmly and said, "Nick went out. Why don't you leave me his envelope?"

"Where'd he go?" Jim inquired.

"He went to an AA dinner. Rob and Lucinda are in their apartments. They told me to send you up."

Taking the envelope out of his bag and handing it to June, Jim said, "Thanks, I'll see you later."

Jim was nervous as he knocked on the door to Rob and Nick's apartment, not quite knowing what to expect. Rob answered. He was wearing a chiffon blouse and had an uneven layer of foundation on that poorly masked the terrible bruising on his face.

"Hey, Rob. How are you feeling?" Jim gently inquired.

"I've had better days."

"Do you mind if I look at your belly?"

"Nah, go ahead," Rob replied, lifting his shirt.

Jim noticed a large swath of hair that had been shaved off over Rob's left upper quadrant area from the surgery and several stitches in a horizontal line in the middle of the hairless patch. He took out his stethoscope and listened to Rob's abdomen over several locations to ascertain the return of normal and active bowel sounds. Jim was relieved that the repeated movement of the stethoscope seemed to elicit no pain. Jim glanced up from Rob's wound and spied a pewter crucifix through his sheer blouse.

"Nice crucifix," Jim said.

Rob, pulling it out from his blouse, remarked, "I got this from my mom when I was a teenager after my pop really beat the shit of me once." His voice trembled before he paused a moment. "She told me that everyone has their own cross to bear, but that some crosses are heavier than others."

Jim nodded sympathetically before continuing his physical assessment of Rob. "Are you having any pain anywhere?" Jim queried.

"Just where the stitches are."

"How's your appetite been since leaving the hospital?"

"It's coming back."

"Have you moved your bowels since the surgery?"

"Just once in the hospital."

"Was it difficult?"

"Nah, about average."

"Well, please let us know immediately if you get constipated. We don't want those stitches, or the internal ones, poppin' out or anything while you're strainin' on the toilet."

"You bet," Rob replied.

"Have you been walking around much since coming home?"

"No more than usual."

"Just make sure that you don't loaf around on the couch all day—that'll make your lungs lazy and maybe even give you pneumonia. Just make sure you get around enough."

Rob nodded, then asked quietly, "Why can't people just accept me for who I am?"

"Those bastards at the Dawg were just jealous 'cause the strippers were payin' more attention to you."

Rob smiled, then replied, "Yeah, I noticed that one of those guys looked totally pissed when a girl wrote her number on my single and stuffed it down my tube top. You know, I almost called a cab before I left, but when I was leavin' they seemed preoccupied with another girl on stage."

"Other than your old man, have you ever been attacked like this before?"

"I got the crap kicked outta me when I was in the Valley Mental Institute."

"Do you talk about any of this with your doctor or counselor?" Jim calmly inquired.

"Nah, I'd rather just leave the past in the past." Gently putting his hand on Rob's shoulder, Jim replied, "Well, if you ever want to talk or need a ride, just let me know and I'll take care of it."

Rob nodded again, and the two finished up their visit with the typical exchanges. Soon Jim was at Lucinda's door and entered when she told him to do so. He found her on the couch wearing a baggy gray sweatshirt and boxer shorts. Her hair was completely unkempt, and she wore no makeup but still looked pretty.

"You okay, Lucinda?"

"I'm really bummed out."

"What's botherin' you? Are you still upset about Rob?"

"No, I talked to Rob; we're cool. What I mean is the dark spirits of summer have returned."

"How's that?"

"It was about this time of year that my brother died. It always haunts me, literally. Some years I even feel this dark presence following me around."

"Are you seeing or hearing anything unusual?"

"There was a dark shadow standing on my back porch this morning. The more I focused on it, the more awful it appeared. Then, it quickly bled through the screen door and rushed at me."

"Did you pray?" Jim asked, feeling a little awkward about his question.

"Not really. I just closed my eyes and quickly turned around 'til I felt it was gone."

"Are you having any thoughts of hurting yourself?"

"Nah, I just want peace for me and my baby bro."

"Have you ever gone to a counselor?"

"Nope. I don't do counselors anymore. They're all a bunch of fuckin' quacks."

"Well, if you ever change your mind, please let us know, and we can find you a good one."

"I won't, but thanks, anyway."

"Well, if you do ever feel like hurting yourself, please call me."

She smiled, then replied, "I know that I can always count on you, Jimmy."

The visit ended shortly afterward, and then Jim made his way back to Sally's. Once there, he found the front door unlocked and entered. Walter was in his usual chair, and Thunder lay motionlessly by his side.

"Hey, Jimmy, my boy! How's it goin'?" Walter inquired.

"Oh, just fine, and you?"

"Terrifically. Thanks for asking," he replied with a hint of condescension.

"Where were you guys earlier?"

"We went out to dinner at Gus' Greek diner up in South Ellingford."

"Sounds like a fun Saturday night out."

"Gus is great. His food is dirt cheap, and he has the most beautiful daughters who work there."

*How does he know? Did he feel them up?* Jim pondered, then asked, "Where's Sally?"

"Down the hall listening to Christmas Carols or somethin'."

"Thanks."

Jim made his way to the dimly lit living room and found Sally next to an old and slightly dilapidated record player.

"Hey, Sally, how are you?"

"Nervous."

"Oh, yeah? What's the matter?" Jim quietly asked.

"I don't know what to get Jesus for Christmas."

Jim paused, then said, "Sally, Christmas is more than five months away."

"I know. But I don't know what to get Jesus for his birthday."

"How about a heart full of love and kindness and goodwill toward your fellow man?"

Sally seemed flummoxed, then replied, "Nah, I was thinking of something more like a sweater or scarf. I used to crochet all the time when I was a girl."

Jim smiled, then said, "Well, he'll need that to be warm should he decide to pop in and visit Santa at the North Pole."

"Hey, you're right!"

She went on to engage in her usual blessing of the pills before consuming them, and then they ended their visit.

After a short and smooth ride from Sally's, Jim arrived back at his apartment. Once Jim was there, he mindlessly went through his usual end-of-day activities and soon fell asleep on the couch in his foyer.

# CHAPTER THIRTEEN

Jim didn't get up until the middle of the morning on Sunday, but he still managed to get to church on time. It was the first time that he had gone in a couple of weeks. He felt that his life was in a bit of a slump, and he was desperately looking for some sort of inspiration. Also, he was increasingly nervous about his interview in the city the next day and figured it couldn't hurt to pray.

He was excited to learn that Father Paul was saying the Mass. Father Paul was the most bohemian Jesuit that Jim had ever encountered. Jim liked him because he wasn't afraid to do daring things like raise his voice or use props and exhibits to get his message out. Once he even brought in a Guatemalan folk dancer to make a point about the importance of nonverbal communication. He had concluded that particular sermon by paraphrasing a quote attributed to St. Francis: "Preach the Gospel at all times, and sometimes even use words." Jim didn't get too much out of this service, however, as he was far too distracted with thoughts about returning to work in the city.

After church, Jim bought a newspaper and a large coffee and then plopped himself on the couch to watch one of the many political news programs that aired on Sunday. Soon his coffee was gone, the paper was read, and it was time to go to work.

At Wanda's, Jim found her fairly quiet and somewhat nervous.

"Hey, Wanda, how ya doin' today?"

"Not good, not good at all. The fruit flies from the kitchen brought the voices back with them," she said anxiously as her palsied left hand gestured toward the dining area.

"What have they been saying to you?" Jim queried.

"They sounded Germanic and kept telling me, 'Don't eat the vatermelon; you're not vorthy!'"

"Do you have any watermelon or fruit around the house?"

"I threw it all out after these voices started, but the flies keep coming at me with their taunts," she said with tears in her eyes.

Bubba then began quietly singing an old Roy Orbison song from the other room.

"Are you having any thoughts of hurting yourself?" Jim gently inquired.

"No, I just want these goddamn voices to stop. I want my old life back. I want to be able to pick up a bow and arrow again," she sobbed while looking down at her tremulous left hand.

"Are you still hearing voices from the trophy?"

"Nah—just from those fuckin' flies."

"Do you want to go down to the hospital to talk with a doctor?"

"Nah, they don't give a shit about people like me any more than my regular shrink does."

"Well, if you change your mind or start having feelings about hurting yourself, please give me a call."

Wanda nodded through her heavy sobs as Jim tried to encourage her at the end of their visit.

Soon, Jim found himself inside of Sir Richard's castle.

"How are you feeling today, my royal friend?" Jim queried.

"Frazzled, my good man. I've been up all night conducting my research."

"Are you hearing or seeing anything unusual?"

"My muses tell me that I must redouble my efforts to discover the Paramatter before it's too late. They also said that if my heart is not pure, then the secrets of Paramatter shall never be revealed to me. I must discover the Paramatter—God does not play dice with the universe!"

"Well, I certainly don't want to keep you from your work too long, so why don't you check your sugar?"

Richard nodded, then went on to do so. After several seconds, the blood glucose meter beeped and read 510.

Jim looked concerned as he glanced down at the number. "Say, Sir Richard, are you feeling okay?"

"Just demoralized," he replied.

"Well, your sugar's very high again. What do you say about me driving you to the hospital?" Jim tactfully proposed.

Sir Richard gave a slight nod of acquiescence, then said, "Can you give me a minute to pack a few things, should they want to keep me overnight?"

"Certainly."

Within minutes Jim had dropped Richard off at the hospital.

Jim then drove to Phil's at the YMCA. Jim found the door on the fire escape cracked, so he made his way to Phil's door. He gently knocked a few times, and then after a long pause, Phil appeared. He looked disheveled and half-awake. His usually neat room likewise was disarrayed.

"Hey, Phil. How ya doin' today?"

"Tired. Another late night in front of the TV."

"Is the Ambien not working for you anymore?"

"Shoot, I forgot to take it."

"Well, tonight just take the one in the baggie that you forgot last night."

Phil nodded, then began his usual ritual with the MAR and microwave. After Phil took his pills and signed the paper, Jim departed.

Jim found Sally in more of an upbeat mood than usual.

"Hey, Sally. What's goin' on?"

"Nuttin'. Just relaxing and watchin' a Christmas movie," she said while deeply exhaling a drag from an obnoxious menthol cigarette.

"Jesus give you another smoke?"

"Yep. He loves me very much, and I'm gonna get him something good for Christmas!"

"Well, I got some good news for you," Jim said while reaching into his book bag.

"What is it?"

"My neighbor was having a tag sale and had some yarn and needles that weren't sold, so she gave them to me," Jim said while handing Sally two large balls of yarn, one green and one red, along with a blunt crocheting needle.

*Another little white lie won't hurt,* Jim thought, knowing full well that he had purposely bought the stuff for her. He didn't want to make her feel awkward by taking a gift.

"You must be an angel or an Apostle or something! That's it! You must be Jesus' Apostle James!"

Feeling embarrassed about his impromptu canonization, Jim replied, "No, I'm not an Apostle. I was just in the right place at the right time."

Sally was ecstatic and started to laugh and clap her hands together like a little girl.

Now Jim was feeling even more embarrassed and hoped that Walter wasn't eavesdropping. "Hey, Sal, why don't you take your pills? I'm running a little bit behind today," he gently prodded.

She nodded, then engaged in her cruciform calisthenics before taking the pills and signing the MAR. Unexpectedly, after signing she embraced Jim in a big bear hug. He was physically repulsed but glad to see her so happy. Soon he was outside, smoking one of his cigarettes.

Once at Mike's, Jim likewise found him in a cheerful mood.

"Hey, Jimmy boy, whuz up?"

"Not much. Why you so happy?"

"Met a girl at lunch with Uncle Joe at Gus' Diner. Man, she's a slammin' hottie!"

"Hey, that's great. Did you get her number?"

"Yep. She wrote it for me on the check that she handed to Uncle Joe, but she was really obvious about what she was doin'. Even ol' Uncle Joe picked up on it."

"What's her name?" Jim inquired.

"Penelope."

"Good for you."

After a few more minutes of chatter, they finished up their visit.

Jim arrived at St. Monica's a short time later and found Maureen lounging on the couch.

"Hey, Maureen, how are you?" Jim inquired.

"Not bad, and you?"

"Terrific. Where's the gang?"

"Nick and Lucinda are upstairs, and Rob is out back on the boat."

"Thanks," Jim replied as he turned to make his way to the back door.

Arriving at Nick's door, Jim knocked gently in the hope that maybe Nick wouldn't hear him. *No such luck,* Jim thought as Nick approached the door.

"Hello, Mr. Fane. May I come in?"

Nick nodded and walked away from the door as Jim opened it.

"Say, Nick, I just want to apologize for raising my voice to you last visit. It wasn't very professional of me," Jim said sheepishly.

Nick neither acknowledged nor showed any signs of accepting Jim's apology. Rather, he changed the subject by saying, "Be careful, boy! You're on the edge of slidin' down into the slimy pit!"

"What exactly do you mean?" Jim asked tersely.

"You can't condone Reilly's homosexual behavior. It's as bad as the ancient Israelites who co-mingled and intermarried with the worshipers of Baal. Eventually, those sinful heathens brought Israel down to its destruction!"

Jim fought the anger welling up inside him, not wanting to give Nick the satisfaction of getting the better of him. Jim also didn't want to reveal Rob's true sexual identity, as that would be a betrayal of Lucinda's trust. After thinking for a few moments, Jim inquired, "Well, what can be done about it? They're pretty much everywhere."

"Oh, I know it! It seems like when I was a kid you couldn't even talk about such things in public, but nowadays you can't even watch TV without encountering at least one of their homosexual shows. We must resist! We must eradicate them!

We must put on the full armor of the Lord and smite them mightily in his power!"

Not surprised by Nick's answer but also not wanting to respond angrily to it, Jim calmly replied, "Seeing how I am one not without sin, I really don't feel comfortable throwin' stones at Rob or anyone else."

"Well, you must repent! You must change your ways! Look at King David. He grieved the Lord by sleepin' with Bathsheba, but he changed his ways and put on the full armor of the Lord! You must do the same! You must put on the full armor of the Lord!"

"Well, I'm no King David—and I just can't bring myself to condemn someone else for their sexuality."

"Time is short! You must repent! You must put on the full armor of the Lord!"

Jim gave a vague nod, then nonchalantly slid the pills and MAR across Nick's kitchen table where they were sitting. Nick seemed slightly confused but took the pills and signed the paper nonetheless.

Soon Jim was at Lucinda's door, and she answered his knocking wearing nothing but a hot pink bath towel and copious beads of hot water.

"Oh, gosh—I'm sorry," he said. "Do you want me to come back in a few minutes?"

"Don't be silly. I just got outta the shower and will be dressed in a minute," she replied. "Sit down, relax."

Jim sat on her deep and comfortable sofa with his back facing away from the entrances to her bathroom and bedroom. He was watching some mindless video on TV when Lucinda returned wearing jean cutoffs and an old concert T-shirt. She purposefully plopped down beside him on the deep pillows.

"How you doin' today?" Jim asked.

"Not bad," she said softly.

"Hearing or seeing anything unusual?"

"I heard the faint sound of a baby crying early this morning at the same time that a shadow passed in front of the sun. It darkened my bedroom."

"Anything else?" Jim gently inquired.

"Nah, just still feeling blue about Vincente."

"Are you sure you don't want to talk to a professional psychologist?"

"Why would I want to talk to some crackpot shrink when you're listening to me just fine?"

Jim smiled, then replied, "Well, they have many more years of schooling than me and could probably give you better insights into your situation than I ever could."

"Bullshit! Besides, they would never take me seriously, with my tattoos and all—not the way you do."

Jim laughed out loud, then said, "I won't bug you about it anymore, but if you do change your mind, please let me know."

She nodded, and soon Jim was on his way to see Rob.

Jim found him sitting on a flimsy aluminum chair on the deck of the old boat. The strong scent of whiskey surrounded him.

"Hey, Rob. How are you?"

"Rob's not here. I'm Shane."

Jim paused, then inquired, "How are you doing, Shane?"

"Not very good, me lad. I've got this horrible pain over me stomach."

"Do you mind if I take a look at your abdomen?"

Shane nodded, then lifted his white shirt to allow Jim to inspect him. Shane's suture line looked red and angry, with a small amount of green, purulent drainage oozing from one end. His belly felt like it was on fire, and palpation near the sutures elicited immediate and excruciating pain.

"Do you mind if I check your vital signs?"

*Why the hell doesn't Rose give us thermometers, not even the semi-accurate strip kind; what kind of nursing are we practicing?* Jim thought with frustration as he checked Shane's other vital signs. As Jim suspected, Shane's pulse and respirations were somewhat elevated.

"How much have you had to drink?"

"What the hell does that have to do with anything?" Shane angrily retorted.

"I'm not implying anything. I'm just wondering if you can stand and walk."

No sooner had the words left Jim's mouth when Shane rose from the chair and wobbled unsteadily toward Jim.

"Hey—let's wait a minute here. Why don't you just sit down?" Jim nervously remarked.

"Not a bad idea, lad! I'm feeling a bit woozy," Shane said as he reached for the folding chair behind him.

Suddenly, the chair gave way and buckled, and Shane's body twisted. He hit the deck with a loud crash. Jim rushed over and noticed a small laceration over one of the badly bruised areas of Shane's face. It immediately began to bleed profusely. Jim quickly reached into his bag for gloves and gauze.

He adroitly put the gauze pad over the affected area, then asked, "Are you okay?"

"Yeah. What the hell happened?"

"You fell. I'm gonna call an ambulance."

Shane nodded, then put his head on the deck. Jim pulled out his agency cell phone and attempted to dial, without any luck. *Great, no thermometers and cheap phones! Anything to save a buck!* Jim thought. Instinctively, he pulled out his own cell phone, which was barely able to muster a signal. He quickly dialed 911, then elevated Shane's knees to relieve any intra- abdominal pressure. He continued to monitor him while the paramedics were en route.

About a half hour later Shane was safely in the ambulance, and Jim headed home. Although it was late and Jim was exhausted, he felt compelled to shine his shoes for his interview the next day. He did so while intermittently sipping bourbon. He probably could have gotten away with just buffing them, as they weren't in bad shape, but Jim never underestimated the value of a good shine. After a few more minutes, his shoe polishing was completed, and he quickly turned in for the night.

# CHAPTER FOURTEEN

Jim slept in that Tuesday, tired from his interview in the city. Sleep had not come as easily to him on Monday night, as he'd still been wired from his trip.

When he got up, he decided to skip the gym and headed straight to the office, as he did not have any of his patients' meds ready for the week.

Arriving at the tinted-windowed office, Jim found it quiet and empty. Today he appreciated the silence in his fatigue. Jim always viewed preparing medications as just as important as an artilleryman's duty of plotting coordinates, as he knew poor preparation could be fatal. He set up his usual empty three drinking cups and pulled the first drawer full of medications open. One cup was for five o'clock meds, one for seven's, and one for nine's. Jim always felt like he was playing a perverted and inverted version of the shell game whenever he starting popping pills into the cups. Not all patients received medications at those times, so often it was a fairly simple game. He always double-checked the cups, however, to ensure that the right pills (usually recognizable to him by their shape and color) ended up in the right cups. Today he decided to triple check them, as he had been very distracted by the Paramount Mutual interview and kept replaying it in his mind. Jim began to wonder if he had done as well as he'd initially thought. He then put the pills into the coin envelopes.

On the way to Wanda's, he realized that she'd just started receiving an increased dose of Cogentin for her tremors. He hoped it would work for her. After Jim's triple knocking was completed, Wanda led him into her dingy kitchen.

"How are you feeling today?" Jim inquired.

"Tired. I've been up all night scrapin' paint," she replied.

Looking around the kitchen, Jim noticed that the walls had indeed been stripped in several places of any loose paint chips.

Suspecting that her reason for stripping was not good, he asked, "Why'd you do that for?"

"The loose chips were tauntin' me. They kept saying that I was a no-good dirty girl and that I would never amount to anything."

"Are you having any thoughts of hurting yourself?"

"Nope. I just want these goddamn voices to stop!" she replied angrily.

Jim was surprised that despite the increase in clozapine, her blood sugar was pretty well-controlled. He also noticed that unlike Wanda's prior excited epiphanies about discovering the source of her voices, she no longer displayed the same confidence or enthusiasm.

Soon Jim was on the way to Sir Richard's. Once there, Jim found him in an unusually spirited mood.

"Good afternoon, my good man! How are we doing today?" Richard inquired while opening the door.

"Just fine, and you, Sir Richard?"

"Superb! I just retained a seasoned property litigator and should have enough money left over to finish the addition to my wall."

"Wow, that's great! When's the zoning appeal scheduled for?" Jim asked.

"Next month, but I can have some preliminary preparations done to the wall in the meantime."

"What did they do for your sugar when you were at the hospital the other day?"

"Well, they checked it again and it was only 345. They suggested that the blood glucose meter people replace my meter again. I told Cindy yesterday, and Rose is making the necessary arrangements."

Richard then checked his sugar, which was 360. Since he denied having any hyperglycemic symptoms, Jim just gave him the usual cautionary instructions before he left for the YMCA.

Once at Phil's, they sat down to a documentary program about the Minuteman Project.

"So, Jimmy, what do you think of these Minuteman guys out west?" Phil inquired.

"I'm not sure. I don't know much about them."

"Their concept's similar to the original Minutemen, except these guys guard the Mexican border."

"Seems like they might give some competition to our National Guard," Jim jokingly responded.

"Well, seeing how many Guard and Reserve units are deployed overseas, it's not a surprise that someone else would try to fill the void."

"How many Minutemen are there?" Jim asked.

"I'm not exactly sure, but their presence is more symbolic than anything else."

"How effective could a bunch of civilians be in securing such a large, unfenced border? And what about our larger border to the north with Canada?"

Phil, looking thoughtful, replied, "The only way I think a Minuteman-type project would work is if everybody assumed the mentality of the original Minutemen."

"How's that?" Jim queried.

"Well, if all able-bodied citizens assumed that the enemy was imminent—at all times—and were sufficiently prepared to react."

"I think the original Minutemen had it easier, as all of their imminent enemies wore bright red uniforms," Jim replied.

"Yeah, no kidding. I mean, even professional law enforcement wasn't able to effectively ferret out any of the magnificent nineteen," Phil responded. "You know who I feel sorry for? That poor Maryland trooper who had one of the hijackers pulled over for speeding just hours before their attack. Besides racial profiling, how the hell would he have known what that driver was really up to?"

Jim nodded, and then Phil turned his attention to the pills and MAR.

Within minutes Jim was at Sally's, watching her drink coffee and crochet a bright red swatch destined to become Jesus' sweater. Their visit was fairly brief, and Jim was making pretty good time as he arrived at Mike's.

Once in Mike's driveway, he was greeted by Betty, who was outside watering some flowers.

"Hey, Jim. How are you?"

"Good, and you?"

"Can't complain."

"Mike around?"

"No, he's on his way to go out with that little Greek trollop from Gus' Diner."

Surprised by her answer, he said, "How do you know her?"

"I've seen that little tramp wait tables for a couple of years now. She's always wearing clothes two sizes too small, especially with that enormous chest of hers. I mean—come on—what's Gus really trying to sell?"

"Well, can you please make sure Mike gets this?" Jim said, extending a coin envelope with his right hand.

"No problem. I told him that he had to be home by ten," she replied.

"Thanks, I appreciate it."

Jim then headed over to St. Monica's and was encouraged to see that June was working.

Rob approached Jim and now had what appeared to be at least a few stitches on his left cheek.

"Hey, Rob, how ya feelin'?"

"Not too bad. Rosie's got a medical nurse coming out to give me an IV in the morning and late afternoon," he said.

"Do you mind if I take a look at your abdomen?" Jim asked.

"Not at all," Rob responded while lifting up the loose-fitting blouse he was wearing.

The wound was no longer red, angry, or oozing. It looked completely healed.

"Where are they giving you the IV medicine?" Jim inquired.

"Right here in my arm," Rob replied, pointing to the IV site on his forearm.

They then exchanged the usual pills and paperwork, and Nick appeared wearing a colorful red T-shirt that read, "Put on the Full Armor of the LORD!"

"Hey, Mr. Fane. How are you today?" Jim asked.

"Have you put on the full armor of the Lord yet?" he quipped.

*Not again!* Jim thought. He again searched for an appropriate answer to fend Nick off without alienating him from taking his medication.

Jim replied, "You know, I used to be in the service, and I just don't like the thought of putting on armor anymore."

"No, no, no—I'm not talking about real armor, boy! I'm talking about putting on the armor of the Lord! It's a spiritual battle! You must repent and put on the armor of the Lord to go forth and mightily smite the heathen enemy!"

"Just the same, I'd rather help my fellow man than smite him."

"You cannot tolerate the heathen enemy. You must convert yourself and them, or you will both be destroyed!"

"With all due respect—I don't mean to offend you or anything—but I'd rather do what Christ said and love my neighbor as myself," Jim replied.

"Well, Christ also said that He came to bring not peace but a sword!" Nick retorted.

"Again, Mr. Fane—I mean no disrespect—but Christ also taught that 'those who live by the sword will also die by the sword,' so I'd rather just live in peace and leave the smiting to someone else," Jim replied softly.

"Boy, time is short! You'd better change your ways before it's too late!" Nick shouted.

Jim shrugged and nodded slightly while extending the coin envelope to Nick. Nick took the pills with one of the cups of water that had been put out on the table for the patients, then signed the MAR.

"Time is short! You must repent and put on the armor of the Lord before it's too late!" Nick again exhorted. He then left out the back door.

"Hey, June, where's Lucinda tonight?" Jim inquired.

"She told me to send you upstairs," she replied.

"Thanks."

Once at Lucinda's door, Jim knocked on the screen door that appeared unlocked and cracked open slightly.

"Hey, Jimmy, is that you?" she asked.

"Yep."

"Come on in, bud."

Entering the room, he discovered her on the far side of the kitchen sitting on a chair. She was hunched over with her legs spread and one elbow resting on her inner thigh as she lifted a dumbbell.

"Hey, Lucinda, pumpin' iron?"

"Yeah. Whatcha doin', checkin' out my crotch?" she replied.

"No, I was just checking out your form. I wasn't—"

"Shut up! I'm just screwin' with you!" she retorted playfully.

She then put the dumbbell down and leaned back in the chair while crossing her arms and legs. Her body glistened with sweat, which even dripped down her forehead. Likewise, her yellow tank top was also soaked with sweat stains.

Jim felt that he was being somewhat intrusive seeing her in such a state. "Say, want me to stop back in a few minutes?" he tactfully inquired.

"What? Do I smell or something?" she said jokingly while raising one arm and inhaling deeply from her armpit.

Jim burst out laughing, then replied, "Well, if you're okay with your odor, then how can I complain?"

"Got my drugs, buddy?"

"Yep. Right here," he said, extending a small coin envelope, MAR, and pen.

She ripped the envelope open and took the pills with a bottle of water that she had at her feet. Then she signed the MAR and returned it to Jim. "Wanna see the rest of my gym, Jimmy?"

"Sure, why not?"

"My pops set me up with such a large pad that I didn't need the second bedroom, so I converted it into a gym."

The two then walked through the gym door, and he viewed a large Nautilus-type apparatus in the middle, which was covered with what looked like numerous pieces of wet laundry. Various dumbbells and barbells laid scattered on the floor.

"Hey, I like what you've done with your Nautilus equipment," Jim said wryly.

"Thanks. It took me a while to get it like that."

"Which do you like better, free weights or Nautilus?" Jim asked.

"Free weights. It forces you to achieve better balance and form."

Jim nodded and then said, "Yeah, but you can't lift heavy free weights without a spotter."

"Not a problem for me. I'm lookin' to get ripped, not massive. I can see by your cannons that you go more for the higher weights with low reps," she said while suddenly grasping his formidable right arm.

Jim laughed, then asked, "Where did you get the Nautilus equipment? It looks pretty sophisticated underneath all those clothes."

"I dunno. Daddy dearest got it for me after Vanessa graduated from medical school."

"Wow. That's a pretty good deal. She graduates, and you get a gift!"

"Well, she got a Mercedes for her graduation present. After he overheard me complainin' to my mom, he decided to throw me a bone," she said, pointing to the Nautilus machine.

Not quite knowing how to respond, he said, "Does he know that you use it as a clothes hanger?"

"Yeah, that's the best part. Whenever he asks me if I like using it, I tell him that my clothes are drying nicely on it."

"Well, at least you have the privacy of your own gym and laundromat, all in one room," Jim quipped.

"I know. I hate going to gyms and laundromats. They're just meat markets," she replied. "What I really want is a heavy punching bag. I could use Nick downstairs, but that would probably get me arrested."

Jim laughed, then they said their goodbyes, and he started home. Once back at his apartment, Jim sat down at his computer and banged out a thank you letter to the executives at Paramount Mutual. He also printed off another copy of his resume, as he had another interview coming up with an insurance company in Ellingford the following week.

Jim then poured a glass of bourbon and leisurely went through his end-of-the-day routine. Soon enough, the bourbon tumbler was empty and his mail was read, and Jim settled into his bed as a beautiful array of stars lit up his bedroom. Jim felt glad that although his apartment was older, the landlord had installed a skylight as a present for the former tenant, who happened to be the landlord's sister. Within minutes of gazing up at the starry sky, Jim slipped into sleep.

# CHAPTER FIFTEEN

The rest of that week flew by, and it was already early Friday afternoon when Jim realized he hadn't done his nursing notes due from the previous workweek. He quickly sat down and scribbled them out. Throughout his life, he had consistently been criticized for his deplorable penmanship. It was the only class that he had ever received a D in during his academic career. Now he viewed it as an asset, as the more difficult his penmanship was to read, the harder it would be to critique the contents of the writing. He presumed that employers and any potential medical malpractice attorneys would just gloss over his notes and spend more time and attention on others that they actually could read. After finishing his notes, he double-checked his book bag to ensure that he had all the right meds and supplies ready to go. Soon he was off to the local coffee shop, and then on to Wanda's.

His repeated knocks were answered by Wanda, who looked even more tired and haggard than usual. She denied any increase in hallucinations and claimed that her voices had seemed to level off since she completed the removal of all the loose paint chips in her apartment. She also denied the consumption of those paint chips. Soon Jim was on the way to Sir Richard's.

"Good afternoon, Sir Richard. How are you today?" Jim asked as Richard opened his door to greet him.

"Splendid, my good man! The blood glucose meter lady finally deduced what was causing my falsely elevated sugar readings."

"Oh, yeah, what was it?"

"Well, she took a reading using my strips and my meter and saw that my blood sugar was elevated. Then she took a reading from my meter but using her strips and realized that the number was much lower. After examining my quarters, she determined that my strips had been altered by their exposure to the bright lights next to my research field," Richard said enthusiastically.

"Wow. That's great. Hopefully, that will end your trips to the ER."

"More importantly, I now have one less thing to distract me from the Paramatter research. My good fellow, I must tell you the turn that my research took this morning. I had a vision of a miniature universe swirling inside of my shrubs this morning. It contained the most wonderful arrangement of stars, asteroids, and other such bodies that were blinking and exploding with brilliant light. And all the while these majestic objects were humming quietly, as if you could hear the notes of their centrifugal symphony!"

"Are you seeing or hearing anything else out of the ordinary?"

"No, my dear James, but certainly this revelation must lead to the ultimate discovery of Paramatter!"

Jim and Richard then finished their visit after a few more minutes of conversation.

Once at the Y, Jim found Phil half-awake and disheveled. He denied any suicidal ideations and simply claimed that he hadn't slept well. After further questioning, Jim found out that it was Phil's wedding anniversary.

After completing the transaction with the pills and paper, Jim asked, "Do you talk to a psychiatrist or counselor at all?"

"Every couple of months for a few minutes, when I need to get my pills renewed. She always seems in a bit of a hurry and distracted. Her waiting room is always overflowing," Phil replied.

"Do you feel like you're getting anything out of it?"

"Just pills."

"Do you want me to see if I can ask Rose to get you a different doctor?" Jim inquired.

"It wouldn't do you any good. I only have coverage to go to that clinic, and I hear that the other doctor there is just as rushed," he replied. "Thanks, anyway."

Soon, Jim was off to Sally's and Walter's. At their house, Jim entered through the perpetually unlocked doors and made his way past Walter, who was puffing a foul cigar. Thunder, his lame eye dog, lay quietly next to him. Jim then found Sally glued to the TV, with a cup of coffee in one hand and the partially made sweater next to her.

"Hey, Sally. How's it goin'?"

"Good! Got my coffee from Jesus today!" she shouted gleefully.

"Hey, how's the sweater comin' along?"

"Pretty good. I'm almost done," she said, holding up a lopsided piece of fabric that consisted of a large red swatch with one uneven green sleeve protruding from it.

"That's great. You ready for your pills and shot?"

"I'll take the pills, but Santa says I don't have to take my shots no more."

*Damn! That's a tough excuse to beat,* Jim thought. "Sally, you know I like you, right?"

"You bet, Jimmy!"

"And you like me, right?"

"Besides Santa and Jesus, you're my favorite!"

"Well, if you don't let me give you this shot, my boss will get mad at me. I might even lose my job," Jim said, instantly feeling remorse for this little white lie.

She looked distressed, then nervously replied, "Okay, but just one CC."

"Only what the doctor ordered," Jim responded, feeling guilty for another misrepresentation about what he was going to give her.

When the injection and pills were finished, Sally signed the MAR, and then Jim was on the road to Mike's.

Pulling into Mike's driveway and walking up the sidewalk, Jim discovered Mike with the young Greek girl on the front porch swing.

"Hey, Mike. Who's your friend?" Jim asked, feeling suddenly awkward about his use of the word "friend," as he was not sure if the girl had already attained girlfriend status.

"This is Penelope. Penelope, this is my friend Jim," Mike replied somewhat nervously.

"Pleased to meet you," she said, extending her delicate hand.

Jim shook it gently while not trying to laugh at her squeaky voice. Penelope was garbed in tight spandex shorts and a bright red tube top. The top's elasticity was challenged by her gargantuan breasts. *Shit, I don't wanna embarrass Mike in front of this girl by giving him his meds right here,* Jim thought.

"Hey, Mike, I got that piece of equipment that your Uncle Joe's been waiting for," he said. "Why don't we go inside real quick, and I'll show you how to teach Uncle Joe how to use it?"

Mike smiled, then replied, "Great. He's been waiting for that high-torque ratchet set for a while. Excuse us for a minute, Penelope."

Then Mike and Jim disappeared for a couple of minutes to complete their transaction.

After taking his pills, Mike said, "Thanks a million, Jim! I really appreciate your discretion in not giving me my pills in front of Penelope."

"No problem," Jim replied.

Once back on the porch, Jim extended his hand and said, "It was a pleasure meeting you, Penelope."

"Likewise," she replied, her voice sounding as though she had just inhaled a balloon full of helium.

*Man, ginormous boobs and a squeaky voice. I wonder how well this girl would do at a corporate job interview*, Jim mused.

On his way to St. Monica's, he found himself quickly sucking down a new cigarette to settle his nerves.

Once there, Jim found no patients had come to the kitchen. "Where's the gang?" he asked Maureen, who was sitting on the couch, watching TV.

"I dunno."

Annoyed by her answer, he left by the back door and headed up the stairs. He knocked on Nick's back door and found him inside, wearing a T-shirt that read, "First Church of the Lord and Savior, where our members are armed and ready for the Lord!"

*Here we go again,* Jim thought. "Hey, Nick. How you doin' today?"

"Blessed and delivered!"

"Ready for your pills?"

"Have you repented and been baptized?"

"I was baptized years ago in Colorado."

"How old were you, son?"

"I'm not sure. I was kinda young."

"An infant?" Nick asked.

"Yeah," Jim reluctantly replied.

"Baptism as an infant cannot save your soul!" Nick exclaimed.

"Well, then, exactly what type of baptism do you suggest?" Jim retorted.

Nick, not perceiving Jim's aggravation, quickly replied, "The Right Reverend, William Roberts, has a three-part program: pre- baptism preparations, baptismal events, and post-baptism reflections, available for only $299 per part."

*Nick doesn't have that kind of money. How the hell did he afford it?* Jim wondered. He then calmly inquired, "How did you pay for such an expensive process?"

"I was baptized by the Reverend Robert's predecessor for free. But if you enroll now to do all three programs, without interruption, then the Right Reverend will eliminate one payment," Nick said.

*Is this guy trying to save souls or make a buck?* Jim wondered. "Money's kinda tight with me right now, so I don't think I'll be able to do it—but thanks, anyway," he replied tactfully.

"If you act now, the Right Reverend will allow you to pay on a monthly installment program, with only nineteen percent interest."

"Well, I'll have to check my finances and get back to you. Are you ready for your pills now?" Jim inquired.

Nick nodded, then took the pills and signed the MAR.

"Say, you don't happen to know where Rob is, do you?"

"That butt pirate's on the ship out back, probably swabbing his deck!"

Jim nodded while thinking what a hypocrite Nick was. He decided to see Lucinda before Rob, as her apartment was closer.

He knocked on the door and was greeted by Lucinda, who was wearing a bright peach summer dress with tasteful shoes.

"Hey Lucinda, whatcha all dolled up for?" Jim asked.

"Going to a spa party with Rita. It's like a Tupperware party, except she's selling spa products," Lucinda replied.

"Sounds like fun."

"Why don't you come? You'll probably be the only guy there, and you might get lucky. You know, with all those women talkin' and thinkin' about exotic soaps and lotions!" she said while pretending to lather herself with an invisible bar of soap.

Jim felt himself turning red with embarrassment and replied, "I've still got patients to see, but thanks, anyway."

"Jimmy, you're so easy to embarrass! That's why it's so much fun!" she riposted playfully.

They both began to laugh, and then Jim asked, "Are you still hearing or seeing anything unusual?"

"Yeah, but it's happenin' less often. After the anniversary of Vincente's death in August, I should be good until the anniversary of his birth next summer."

"You don't hear voices or see things at any other time of year?"

"That's it. I only hear babies cryin' and see dark images during the anniversary of his brief lifespan."

Saddened by her response and unsure how to answer, Jim changed the subject to giving her the pills for the evening.

Soon their visit was over, and he was climbing onto the boat in the backyard to look for Rob or the seafaring Shane. Jim saw him near the far end of the stern, sanding down one of the ship's banisters. He was wearing a faded lavender camisole and denim culottes.

"Shane, is that you?" Jim asked.

"Who's Shane?" Rob responded.

"Oh, never mind," Jim replied. "I've got your meds for you."

Rob nodded, then took the pills with a cup of coffee resting near the banister.

"That rail you're working on is looking good," Jim said.

"Thanks. I'd love to finish this whole boat by next summer and sail over to Europe. I hear that they're much more accepting of people over there."

"I have a friend from Copenhagen. He's always been an open-minded guy," Jim replied. He then went on to assess Rob's wounds, which were healing nicely, and soon their visit was over.

Jim soon settled into his place, booted up the computer, and deleted most of the new messages that were predominately junk. There was one, however, from Jake and his wife announcing the birth of their triplets and indicating that a suitable hard copy announcement would be sent soon.

The final message in his inbox was from his old dating service. It had a calendar of events for the rest of the summer and also invited Jim to check out the profiles of their newest members. Jim gave in to curiosity and clicked on the link. Soon he was scrolling through several pictures and bios, none of which caught his attention. Toward the end, however, he did see one that looked intriguing. Her name was Marsha, and she had an elegant photograph posted that had been taken from a side view. It looked as though she was posing for a Canadian quarter. Marsha's profile indicated that she was in her twenties and a municipal employee. The remainder of her profile, including what she was looking for in a man, was equally vague. Although interested, Jim decided to go to sleep rather than reply, as her profile had just been posted, and he did not want to appear desperate.

# CHAPTER SIXTEEN

The weekend passed by quickly, and soon another workweek was bearing down on Jim. As it had been an unusually cold and damp weekend, Jim's hip had ached the whole time. Thus, he didn't end up doing much of anything, other than loafing around and watching TV.

Checking his agency voice mail, Jim was embarrassed by one from Rose, who was looking for his weekly notes and MARs. He had forgotten to drop them off on Friday, which wasn't like him. Even before he'd joined the military, he had put a premium on punctuality. It was something that his father had instilled in him. He went to the Ashton office and dropped them off, as well as prepared his medicine envelopes for the week.

At Wanda's, Jim was surprised to see her answer the door with a painter's cap on and paint stains on her face and hands.

"Hey, Wanda. How you doin' today?"

"Good. I'm painting things up in here. That should put an end to the voices."

"Where'd you get the paint supplies from?"

"Vicky was telling me last week how they just painted their house and had some left over. She was nice enough to give me some."

"So, you're gonna paint this whole place?"

"Nah, I'm no Michelangelo. I'm just gonna touch up the areas that peeled."

Jim was pleased that she had regained some of her spunk and optimism and hoped that it wouldn't be short-lived. They finished up their visit in the typical fashion, and then Jim soon arrived at Richard's.

His visit with Sir Richard was fairly brief and unremarkable. He was vigorously at work on the Paramatter project and enthusiastic about his upcoming zoning appeal. Since solving his blood glucose meter malfunctioning, his sugar readings were running only slightly above normal.

Soon afterward, Jim found himself back in his car and on the way to Phil's.

At Phil's, Jim sat down to a documentary about reality TV shows.

"Say, Jim, what's your favorite reality show?"

"I dunno. I haven't given it much thought. I used to like *Survivor* but kinda lost interest after a couple of seasons. I do like the concept, though, of people trying to rough it in the wild. What's your favorite?"

"Probably *The Apprentice*," he replied.

"I never really watched a full episode," Jim remarked.

"Man, having someone at the end of each show being told that they did a lousy job and are getting fired—now, that's reality."

*My reality, unfortunately. At least the Donald has the guts to fire rather than to call it downsizing,* Jim thought. "It does seem a bit contrived, though. I mean, it's all about the personalities rather than the abilities."

"How's that?" Phil asked.

"You get all these highly qualified people to join teams for a limited purpose and for a limited amount of time. Any one of those candidates who fail might excel with other coworkers in other settings."

"Well, I suppose that's the unreality about reality TV. Anyhow, the Donald's a blast to watch. Man, I tell you what, when you got that kinda juice, you don't need to pull punches with anyone."

"I just don't know, though, how much longer any of these reality TV shows are gonna last. The market for them seems a bit oversaturated."

"Yeah, it's gettin' to the point where everyone will have their own reality show for fifteen minutes," Phil replied.

Jim laughed, then said, "With my luck, they'll probably cancel them just before shooting mine."

The two talked for a few more minutes. Phil denied any harmful ideations, and then they methodically exchanged the pills and paperwork. Soon, Jim was on his way to see Sally and Walter.

Once there, he made his way through their unlocked abode to find Walter and Sally in their usual locations: chair and couch.

"Hey, Jimmy! Look!" Sally exclaimed, holding up a lopsided sweater that already showed signs of feline abuse.

"Very nice. I think Jesus will enjoy it very much, especially when he goes to visit Santa."

"Come on, who you kidding? Unless Jesus was resurrected as a child of Thalidomide, that sweater's a joke!" Walter bellowed from the other room.

*This guy not only reads* Playboy *in Braille but also critiques knitwear,* Jim mused.

"You're a joke! Jesus loves me and will love my sweater too!" Sally retorted.

"You just don't get it. You have just as much chance of meeting Jesus as you do Santa Claus! Neither exists, except in that frickin' crazy melon of yours!" Walter responded.

"You—you—you don't get it! Jesus and Santa do exist! And they love me more than they love you!" she said in even a louder tone of voice.

"I don't need fairy-tale characters to love me. I've got my cigars and Thunder!"

At this point, Sally started to cry and wail uncontrollably. Jim reached into his bag and handed her a tissue. After a couple of minutes, her sobbing subsided, and she took her pills and signed the MAR.

"I think your sweater is just fine, Sally. Jesus will like it very, very much," Jim said softly.

Soon Jim was in his car and smoking another cigarette, aggravated by the exchange that he had just witnessed.

Arriving at Mike's, Jim found that Mike wasn't home, but Betty was.

"Hey, Betty, how are you?"

"Okay. How are you?"

"Not bad. Mike around?"

"No, he's out with that Greek tart again! She really should get a boob reduction or wear bigger shirts. I mean, if her tops were any smaller, there'd be nothing left to Mike's imagination!"

"Can you give Mike his pills when he gets in?" Jim inquired.

"No problem. He should be in at nine forty-five tonight because I changed his curfew. He didn't get home until eleven last time he went out with whoreopolous, and I told him that for every hour he comes home late, I'm going to deduct fifteen minutes off his curfew."

Jim finished the visit and found himself making good time en route to St. Monica's.

There, Jim discovered June on the couch reading.

"Hey, how are you?" he asked.

"Just fine, and you?"

"Okay," Jim replied. "Anyone in the kitchen?"

"Nah, Lucinda and Nick are upstairs. Rob went to the rec center. Why don't you leave me his pills?"

"Thanks, I'll see you later," Jim responded, handing her the envelope.

Once at Nick's door, Jim rapped lightly. He hoped that maybe Nick was napping and wouldn't answer.

The door swung wide open. *Shit, he's awake,* Jim thought. "Evening, Mr. Fane. May I come in?"

Nick nodded and opened the screen door. The two then sat at a small and grimy table in the poorly lit kitchen.

"Boy, do you believe in prophecies from the Spirit?" Nick tersely inquired.

*Damned if I do, and damned if I don't,* Jim mused. "What exactly do you mean?"

"Prophecies from the Spirit! Divine revelation! Visions from above!"

"Well, is that the same thing as destiny?" Jim asked.

"No, I'm not talking about the predestination of Christ's elect. I'm talking about visions from the Spirit."

"Sure, I guess so."

"Well, I've seen a vision of a broken man, thin and shuddering in a dark corner," Nick replied.

Although he was pleased that Nick wasn't attacking his faith, Jim was perplexed by Nick's statement. *Is this guy having schizophrenic hallucinations, or is he legitimately seeing images from hell?* Jim wondered. "Did you see this man in your apartment?"

"No! I'm not seeing things! Do you think I'm fuckin' crazy like the other nut jobs that you visit?! This was a prophecy from the Spirit!"

*Honestly, yes, I do think that you're fucking crazy!* Jim thought. "Look, I don't mean to offend you. I just have to ask certain questions when patients tell me that they're seeing or hearing things," Jim calmly replied.

"Well, if you were truly a follower of Christ, you'd recognize prophecies from the Spirit!" Nick retorted.

"If you took any offense, I'm sorry," Jim said. "Would you please take your medication?"

Nick, still looking angry, obliged nonetheless. Jim didn't ask any further questions and was glad that Nick didn't say anything after taking his pills, instead simply signing off and letting him go.

Jim was relieved to get out of there and looked forward to talking with Lucinda.

Entering her porch, he found her sprawled on her wicker lounger wearing an indigo bikini. Her tanning lotion smelled like lilacs, which was Jim's mother's favorite flower. Lucinda didn't seem to notice Jim, as her eyes were shut and she was breathing semi-deeply. She looked angelic, and Jim just stood there for a few moments, admiring the beauty of her toned and vivacious body. He then softly whispered, "Hey, Lucinda, are you sleeping?"

"Not anymore, thanks to you," she softly whispered back.

"Gosh, I'm sorry. I should've left your pills with June," he replied.

"That's okay. I've gotta get up and get ready anyhow."

"What for?"

"Rita and some of her friends want to go out to a new dance club in Ellingford."

"Do you want me to get you some water from the kitchen?" Jim asked.

"Nah—like I said, it's time to get ready to party!" Lucinda replied as she stood up and started dancing her way to the kitchen door.

Once inside the kitchen, Jim asked, "Are you hearing or seeing anything unusual?"

"Not a lot. I only heard a baby crying once this week."

"Don't forget to go to your doctor's appointment next Tuesday at the clinic."

"What time?"

"10:30 a.m., I believe," Jim replied, glancing at his notes.

"And what if I don't?" she inquired mischievously.

"Well, then your pills won't get renewed, and I won't be able to see you anymore."

"Aw, come on! You could still see me at the Dawg!" she said jokingly.

Jim felt himself getting red with embarrassment, especially as she was so close to him with her provocatively oiled and tanned body, which was tightly wrapped up by her even darker bikini. He regained his composure, then tactfully changed the subject. "Does the doctor at the clinic ever ask you about your voices or visions?"

"Not really. A while back one of them tried to probe about it, so I told her a buncha bullshit about seeing a green-headed monster eatin' my mother out while she was on the rag. I think it had her more aroused than concerned."

Jim took the hint again that this girl truly had no use for shrinks. After a few more minutes they finished up their visit, and he left.

On the way home, Jim decided to stop in at Sully's for a quick black and tan. He was stoked to see that Taco was behind the bar. Jim took a seat and overheard that the band scheduled to play had canceled at the last minute, so there would be no live entertainment that evening.

"Hey Jimmy, what's doin'?" Taco asked.

"Not much, Taco. What's doin' with you?"

"Same ol' shit. Different day. Same toilet," he replied. "Whatcha drinkin', my friend?"

"Black and tan, please."

As Taco began pouring, he asked, "You all right? You look aggravated or somethin'."

Taco had a sixth sense about reading body language, and Jim wasn't surprised that he detected that something was bothering him.

"Just tired. Seems like there are no good available women in the Valley," Jim replied.

"How 'bout at work?" Taco inquired.

"Nah, dating women at work can be dangerous."

"How 'bout the internet?"

"Nah, I got too much self-respect for that. Besides, I've had friends who did that—and it seems like all they ever met were psychos or divorcees who were just looking to get laid," Jim replied, purposely concealing the fact that he was one of those "friends."

Taco chuckled, then said, "Well, what do you do for fun when you're not working and when you're not here?"

The question hit Jim hard. *That's it! That's the problem: I don't do much for fun when I'm not working!* Jim thought. "Other than going to the gym, I don't do much for fun. And even the gym isn't always fun—it's work. Besides, the one girl that I really loved in high school got killed. Since then, no one's taken her place."

"I know it's tough, but you can't live in the past. You've gotta find something that makes you happy *now*. A sport, hobby, job, or even a place—and lose yourself in it. Lose yourself in that happiness. Once you're happy, a good woman will find you. Happiness is the greatest aphrodisiac."

Jim finished his drink and decided to drive home instead of having another. Once upstairs, Jim fired off a quick and generic email to Marsha, expressing some (but not an excessive amount) of interest in her profile.

Soon Jim found himself in bed and noticed that the scent of Lucinda's lilac oil remained on his hands. An image of Lucinda dancing in her dark bikini flashed into his thoughts. His semi- sentient mind recoiled a bit, as he genuinely didn't want to objectify someone whom he had grown to love and respect.

He shifted his diminished focus onto thoughts and images of childhood memories of his mother singing while cutting lilac blossoms. Soon that nostalgic lullaby put him to sleep.

# CHAPTER SEVENTEEN

Upon waking up the following morning, Jim's thoughts again coalesced upon his second job interview with Paramount Mutual, like a restless tongue repeatedly probing an infected tooth. The more that he thought about it, the more anxious he felt. *Did I come across as too nervous? Too inexperienced? Did they believe that I was legitimately downsized, or did they think I was fired for being incompetent? Did they receive my thank you for the interview letter, or did it get lost in the mail? Dammit! I should've sent it certified!* Jim thought. *Maybe I should take higher doses of ginkgo, and then I wouldn't forget to send important letters certified.*

Later in the day, he arrived at Wanda's, but his mind was still trapped in an executive office in Manhattan from last week's interview. He found Wanda frazzled and unkempt.

"Howdy, Wanda. How are you today?"

"No good, Jim," she replied.

"How's that?"

"I think Bubba's sick."

"Why's that?"

"I dunno. Could you just look at him?"

Jim carefully made his way across the cluttered room, which reeked of nicotine, paint, and putrefying food. It challenged his stomach. Once arriving at the cage, he peered inside and noticed that Bubba was laying on the bottom and barely moving. Although no animal expert, Jim realized that this was not good.

"When was the last time that he was on his perch?" Jim inquired.

"It's been a day or so, I think."

"What's that strange odor?" Jim inquired as tactfully as possible.

"I'm not sure, but it's coming from the corner near Bubba. It's been getting worse over the past few days."

Jim carefully moved a few of the stacks of newspapers and periodicals near the corner and realized that the odor was getting more pungent as he did so. Finally, he uncovered what appeared to be the small carcass of a dead squirrel, which was stuck in a hole where a radiator pipe used to be. After taking a second look at the rodent and spying a thick and sinuous tail, he realized that it was no squirrel. Not wanting to alarm or insult Wanda, he politely suggested that she take Bubba on the back porch for some fresh air.

After she left the apartment with Bubba, Jim donned a set of non-sterile gloves and unraveled a plastic biohazard bag. He then removed the rat from its hole and put it inside the bag. Once the rat was in the bag, Jim cleaned up a thin layer of maggots that surrounded the hole, then covered it with some thick medical tape. He quickly left the apartment to dispose of the remains in a dumpster near the adjacent alleyway. On the way back to Wanda's porch, the image of finding Maria's bloodied corpse in a dumpster recurred to Jim. It made him angry, nauseous, and dizzy.

After regaining his composure, Jim rejoined Wanda on her porch.

"Hey, Wanda. How's Bubba doing out here?" Jim asked softly.

"Seems to be perkin' up a little bit but still doesn't look right."

"How are you feeling?"

"Nervous. I can't stand to see my Bubba like this."

"Are you hearing any voices?"

"Not since Bubba's been sick."

"Why don't you check your sugar? I'm gonna call Cindy. She has a friend who works at an animal hospital not too far from here."

Wanda began doing as Jim asked while he walked over to the far end of the porch to have some privacy while talking to Cindy.

Just as Jim hung up, the blood glucose meter beeped. It read 275. Jim glanced at it and asked, "Are you thirsty or peeing a lot?"

"No, I just want my Bubba to get well," she said in a shaky tone of voice.

"Well, I've got good news for you. Cindy's friend can come over in about a half hour to check out Bubba."

Suddenly, her face brightened, and her demeanor changed. She then unexpectedly threw her arms around Jim and hugged him firmly. "Oh, thank you! Thank you! Thank you!" she exclaimed.

After a few moments, Jim tactfully extricated himself from her hug and cautioned her to tell him immediately if the odor returned. Jim, thankful that she did not ask why, was pleased that she agreed to do so. Soon he was back in his car, deeply inhaling one of his cigarettes. Thoughts of Maria's mutilated body kept coming to Jim as he drove to Richard's. He anxiously lit a second cigarette and refocused on the road.

Inside Richard's metal castle, Jim found him thoroughly focused with a large magnifying glass, reading some blueprints that were unraveled on a large table in the lab.

"Did you crack the case yet?" Jim asked in a playful yet respectful tone of voice.

"Not yet, my good sir, but I have drawn an exact replica of the celestial bodies in my shrubs on these blueprints. I hope to discern how I can translate the drawing of those glorious objects into the right ingredients to finally yield Paramatter on the hot plates!"

"Well, don't let me hold you up, Sir Richard," Jim remarked as he slid the med envelope, pen, and MAR next to the blueprints on the table.

Soon afterward, Jim found himself back in his car and on the way to Phil's.

Once at Phil's, Jim found the fire escape door locked, and he knocked gently on it. A young man opened it without comment.

Jim knocked firmly but not overly hard on Phil's door. No answer. After a few more attempts, Jim headed out to Sally's.

Inside Sally's, he found Walter smoking his usual cigar and Sally drinking her usual coffee. Next to her on the couch, he saw a bundle of red and green fabric that had been completely molested and torn by numerous kittens. Jim decided to ignore it, based on her recent fight with Walter about the quality of her work product.

"Hi, Sally. How are you?" Jim asked.

"Got my coffee. Got my Jesus. Got my Santa."

"Great, and now I've got your pills for you."

She smiled, then engaged in her usual ritual of blessing and slurping up of the pills.

After signing the paper, she asked, "What do you really think of my sweater for Jesus?"

"Well, I think it's seen better days," Jim replied softly.

She nodded in recognition that he was right, then asked, "What can I get him? There's only about five more months to Christmas."

"You still have plenty of time. Why don't you pray about it and see what happens?"

"Great idea! I will!"

Their visit soon ended, and Jim headed out to Mike's with another cigarette in his mouth. Neither Mike, Betty, nor the Greek girl was anywhere to be found at Mike's house. After a brief and uneventful ride, Jim arrived at St. Monica's, and Nick was the first to approach him in the kitchen.

"Have you decided to get baptized and saved, my son?"

*Sure, for only $999 I too can get saved!* Jim thought. He remained silent, hoping Nick would move on to some other subject. No luck.

"I said, have you decided to get baptized and saved?" he queried with even more annoyance in his voice.

"How could I possibly *decide* to get saved?"

"By accepting Jesus in your heart as your Destroyer and Avenger!"

"No, I mean how can I decide to get 'saved'? Wouldn't that amount to my saving myself, by my making the decision to be saved?"

"No, you're not getting it! Jesus must save you, but you need to decide on being redeemed!"

"Well, if Christ said 'many are called, but few are chosen,' how do I know which one I am? How do I know if I'm one of the many called or one of the few chosen? How can I know for sure—since it's not me who's doing either the calling or the choosing?"

"Christ also said that his sheep hear his voice and will follow him but will in fact run away from a stranger, so that's how you know!"

"With all due respect sheep don't have free will. They are more like Pavlovian dogs who are conditioned to do whatever their masters train them to do," Jim replied.

"But his sheep are predestined to hear his voice and to follow him!"

"But unlike sheep, people tend to hear what they want to hear. So, why would a loving God purposely create some stubborn members of the flock who are destined to ignore him and get hurt by following the deceptive voices of strangers?" Jim riposted.

"Don't make me smite you again, Nurse James! You must decide to get saved in Christ!"

*Once smitten, twice-fried!* Jim mused. Not wanting to destroy what little rapport that he had with Nick, he decided to change the subject. "Say, are you having any more visions of that thin man in the corner?" he softly inquired.

"They're not visions! That's a prophecy from the Spirit! I'm not fuckin' hallucinating! I smite you mightily in the name of my Avenger and Commander, Jesus Christ! In the name of Christ— I smite you mightily, Nurse James!" Nick yelled and stormed out of the kitchen.

"Hey, Maureen, where are Lucinda and Rob tonight?" Jim queried.

"I dunno. Upstairs, I think," she shouted back from the couch.

"Thanks. See ya later."

"You bet."

As Jim arrived at the second floor's back porch, he heard music coming from the boat in the backyard and figured it was Rob. Rather than heading back there first, he decided to go upstairs to see Lucinda.

Once at her door, he was surprised that nobody answered. *Maybe she got called into work,* he thought. He then made his way to the boat in the backyard.

While Jim was approaching the boat, he realized that Rob was not alone on board. The other voice was unmistakable. It was Lucinda's.

"Hey, guys, how's it goin'?" he inquired.

"Not bad, Jimmy. We're trying to get this ol' girl up and running for Rob's voyage to Europe!" she exclaimed.

"Yeah, and Lucinda's gonna be my cruise director, as she's the funniest lady I know," Rob said.

Jim mounted the boat and was impressed by the sanding that they were doing on the ship's deck. "Where'd you guys get all this sanding equipment?" he asked.

"Vicky let us borrow some of her equipment—she just finished remodeling her house," Rob replied.

"How are your wounds doing?" Jim softly asked.

"Completely healed up," he replied while simultaneously lifting his shirt to reveal a well-approximated scar over his left upper quadrant. The only indications that the wound had been recent were an errant piece of steristrip that was still stuck to one end of the scar and shorter hair growing over the general area.

"Great, and your face looks good, too," Jim said, peering at the scar on Rob's face.

"Got my pills, Gilligan?" Rob jokingly inquired.

"Right here, Skipper," Jim said, handing him the pills and MAR.

After Rob finished, he picked up a sander and returned to work on one of the deck's rails. Suddenly, Lucinda appeared in front of him, wearing a faded maroon tube top that was reined in by a worn pair of denim overalls.

"Hey, Jimmy, guess what I am?" she said playfully while extending both arms out in front of her.

Jim peered down at a thin layer of sawdust that clung to the black hair on her dark, sweaty, and well-sculpted forearms. *Only this girl could make sawdust look sexy,* Jim mused, then said, "I give up. What are you?"

"A breaded chicken!" Lucinda replied. She then inserted both thumbs into her armpits and began flapping her elbows up and down wildly. "Booooooooock! Bock! Bock! Bock!" she shouted while dancing in a circle around Jim.

Jim couldn't help laughing, then said, "Hey, I think I have a pill for that!"

After the laughter died down, Jim said, "Well, I hope when you guys get this ol' gal up and runnin' that you take me for a spin in the Sound before you ship out for Europe."

"Absolutely!" Rob jubilantly replied.

Jim then finished up with Lucinda's pills and paperwork and headed back to his sedan. Once inside, he decided to call Mike to see if he was home. No answer was received, and Jim hung up, not wanting to leave a message.

Shortly thereafter he arrived at Mike's and found nobody home. He was tempted to leave the envelope in the mailbox, but he didn't have permission to do that. Reluctantly, he left and went on to see Phil at the Y. Once there, he discovered that Phil had just been out on one of his sporadic shopping sprees. Phil seemed to be in a pretty good mood, and their visit was brief and without incident.

Once back at his apartment, Jim was disappointed to find no letter from Paramount Insurance Company but intrigued to find an email from Marsha.

It was a fairly bland note that read more like a Playboy bunny profile, in terms of enumerating her likes and dislikes. Marsha also disclosed that she was an assistant librarian at a local branch of the Ellingford library system. She ended her correspondence by asking Jim for his preferences and his picture. He replied by concurring with her taste in classic rock (Beatles, Stones, Eagles, etc.), as well as with her enjoyment of outdoor activities, such as hiking and biking. Jim also indicated that he was a registered nurse who was involved with both clinical practice and corporate affairs. Rather than attaching his photo, Jim took the chance of giving a written description of himself indicating that his prior top-secret military experience precluded him from sending his picture on the net. While Jim did have a security clearance during his tenure in the military, he knew that he was stretching it a bit by describing that prior service as having been top-secret. Jim then made an even riskier move and suggested that they get together for dinner or coffee.

After shooting off his reply, Jim checked the only other non- spam message in his inbox. It was from Jenny, announcing a wedding date for their sister, Michele, on July 4, 2006. Although Jim loved the Fourth of July, he did worry a bit that it could present itself as a nice soft target to any would-be terrorists in the Southwest. He considered telling Jenny about his concern regarding the choice of this date but thought that Michele might get unnecessarily anxious. *Screw it. The show must go on,* Jim thought as he logged off and headed to bed.

# CHAPTER EIGHTEEN

The following day proved to be exceptionally hot, approaching nearly one hundred degrees. Jim started his shift by purchasing a large cup of iced coffee and a new pack of cigarettes. He dreaded the anticipated increase in odors from some of his patients' homes and smoked an unusual second consecutive cigarette before arriving at Wanda's.

He rapped on Wanda's door three times and hoped that she and Bubba were in a better state than the previous day.

"Hey, Wanda, howya doin' today?" he inquired.

"Excellent! I got my Bubba back from the hospital safe and sound!"

"What was wrong with him?"

"Just a little dehydrated. They topped him off with some fluids, and he's doing just fine now."

Jim could hear Bubba happily chirping an old Johnny Cash tune as they made their way to the kitchen. Her sugar was normal, and she denied hearing any voices other than some background chatter. Soon he was back in his car and continuing with his large cup of iced coffee as he headed toward Richard's.

Jim found Richard meticulously measuring unknown ingredients on an electronically calibrated scale.

"Good afternoon, Sir Richard. Did you find the right ingredients for the Paramatter based upon your celestial blueprints?"

Richard shrugged his shoulders somewhat defeatedly and then said, "If variety is the spice of life, then what is the spice of the origin of life?"

Unsure how to answer, Jim politely directed Richard to check his blood sugar, take his pills, and sign the MAR.

After leaving Sir Richard's castle, Jim was greeted with a blast of hot air. It felt like the unforgiving southern heat that he had encountered in his younger days at Fort Bragg. Once inside his car, the temperature read 104 on the dashboard. The ice in what was left of his coffee had completely melted. He quickly swigged down the remaining coffee, knowing that it would likely become unpotable during his next stop.

Once outside Phil's door in the Y's corridor, Jim could perceive what felt like several individual beads of sweat rolling down the length of his back. Phil did not answer after a minute or so, and Jim turned around and started heading toward the fire escape door.

Suddenly, a short and bald man asked, "You looking for Phil?"

"Who wants to know?" Jim discreetly inquired.

"Look, pal, I'm not tryin' to bust your stones. Phil's my neighbor and wanted me to tell you that he's down at the pool."

"Hey—sorry. I'm Jim; thanks for your help," he said while extending his hand.

"Rocco, no problem," the man replied while shaking Jim's hand.

Jim then headed down the fire escape and around to the front entrance of the building. Once inside he followed a sign to the pool area. He was glad that the older lady at the front desk did not question his right to be there. Once in the pool area, he spied Phil lounging in the shallow end.

"Hey, Phil. Staying cool today?"

"Got to."

"Want me to get you a cup of water for your pills?" Jim asked.

"Nah, I'm feeling pretty good today. I don't think I need them."

"I thought you told Rocco that you wanted your pills down here?"

"Nope. I just wanted him to give you a heads-up as to where I am so you wouldn't get worried."

Not wanting to insult Phil's autonomy, he said, "Well, stay cool, my friend. I'll see you later in the week."

Jim then smoked another couple of cigarettes on the way to Sally's, suspecting that her home would reek more than usual. Thankfully, she was enthralled by another Christmas video, and their visit was short. Nonetheless, he had another cigarette on the way to Mike's, just to kill any lingering scent of Sally's home in his nostrils.

At Mike's, Jim was relieved when Betty invited him indoors to conduct their business, as her home was equipped with central air conditioning.

"Hey Betty, how are you?" Jim asked.

"Pretty good, but Mike's not here."

"When's he gonna be back?"

"He shouldn't be too late. That Greek prima donna had to work tonight, so he went down to visit her at the diner."

"Can you give him his pills when he gets back?"

"Oh, I still have the envelope that you gave me last week. Can I give that to him?"

"Yep, but please make sure that he takes them," Jim responded.

After Betty signed Mike's name on the MAR, Jim was again outside in the blistering sun.

About a mile or so after leaving Mike's, Jim hit a wall of traffic that was barely moving. After about fifty minutes, the traffic jam was clear, and Jim quickly called Maureen at St. Monica's to advise the patients that he was running late.

As soon as he entered, he could see Nick angrily pacing in the kitchen.

"You lazy popish heathen! You're so late, you made me miss my meeting!" Nick exclaimed.

Jim blanked out for a bit, purposely, in order not to overreact to Nick's insult. "Didn't Maureen tell you that I got stuck in traffic and that I was gonna be really late?"

"Impossible! I know all you rich nurses have expensive GPS systems to avoid such delays!" he retorted.

"Well, I'm not one of those rich nurses."

"I've heard enough! No more excuses!"

"Look, do you want to take your pills or not, Mr. Fane?" Jim abruptly inquired.

"Heathen! I smite you mightily in the name of Jesus Christ, Destroyer and Avenger! In the name of Christ Almighty, I smite you!" Nick exclaimed as he exited the back door.

After Nick left, Jim asked Maureen, "Didn't you tell them that I'd be really late?"

"Oh, yeah. I guess I forgot."

"Where's the rest of them?"

"I think they're upstairs or at the recreation center to see a movie," she replied with her gaze still fixed on the TV in front of her.

Without saying another word, Jim exited the back of the kitchen and headed upstairs. Nobody answered when he knocked on Nick and Rob's door, so he headed up to Lucinda. Arriving at her door, he saw a note posted on the screen that read, "Jimmy or Vicky, come on in." He then went into her apartment and called her name.

"Hey, Jimbo. I'm in the bathroom. Come on in."

Jim reluctantly entered the bathroom to find a few candles glowing and Lucinda slouching in the tub. He quickly glanced at her and realized that only a thin layer of bubbles and an opaque soapy film separated him from her naked body.

"Whoa!" he said, surprised. "Do you want me to come back later? I have to go to the recreation center, anyway."

"Are you afraid of me or something? I won't bite."

"I'm sorry. I'm just having a bad shift. I don't want to invade your privacy or anything—really. I can come back later."

"Don't worry. There's still some bubbles here to protect my privacy. And if they fail, you're trained as a nurse to look at titties—aren't you?" she asked playfully.

"And you forget that I've been to the Dawg before."

They both chuckled nervously, and then she said, "It's just too damn hot to do anything other than lie in a cool tub."

"Do you want to take your pills now or when you get out?"

"I'll take them here. Just get me a cup of water, please," she replied.

He did and delicately placed it on the edge of the tub, next to her pills in the small envelope that he had just opened.

She carefully lifted her left arm out of the water to take her pills.

"Are you hearing or seeing anything unusual today?" Jim asked softly.

"Yeah. I heard the shadow of a baby starting to cry around noon. It was slow at first, but then it got louder and steadier. And the hotter it got, the louder the baby cried. It pretty much piped down since I jumped in the tub a couple of hours ago."

"Seeing anything?"

"Yeah. That green, rug-munching monster was chasing me around the apartment but disappeared when I jumped into the tub. Guess he's afraid of water."

Jim was unsure how to answer until she started laughing hysterically. He began laughing also, then turned red with embarrassment, realizing that her sexual hallucination was completely fabricated.

Soon he was on the way to the recreation center. Once there, he discreetly pulled Rob away from the film to give him his meds.

By the time he was heading home, it was much later than usual, and he was still aggravated at what had transpired during his shift. Seeing how he had the next day off, he decided to stop in at Sully's for a cold beer.

Sully's was pretty empty, as the pub wasn't air-conditioned and also because it was a weeknight. By this time, though, with the sundown, the temperature had dropped into the eighties. Jim was happy to see that Taco was tending bar. He knew that Taco always had a sympathetic ear and insightful advice.

"Hey Jimmy. Whatcha havin' tonight?"

"Black and tan, please."

"What's botherin' you, amigo?" Taco asked, seeing the apprehension in Jim's posture and demeanor.

"Tough shift," Jim replied.

"Wanna talk about it?"

"Are you sure you wanna hear about it?"

"That's what they pay me the big money for," he replied while cracking a smile.

"Okay. First, I get stuck in this horrific traffic jam during the middle of my shift. That put me about an hour behind schedule. Then, this lazy bitch forgets to tell one of my meanest patients that I was running late. So, when I finally get there, he completely tears into me for being late and refuses to take his medicine."

"You're a visiting nurse, right?"

"Yeah," Jim replied.

"So, did you explain to this guy why you were late?"

"I tried, but he didn't want to hear it. He's one of those people who's always telling you that he's saved and always questioning the salvation of others."

"How does that make you feel?"

"Do you really want to talk about religion on the job?" Jim asked.

"Hey, if it's not religion, it would probably be sex, money, or politics. So, you can, if you like," Taco replied.

"Well, quite honestly, it pisses me off. Who the hell is he to put down what anyone else believes?"

"Maybe the guy's just trying to look out for you?"

"Nah, he talks about salvation in a real mean-spirited, holier- than-thou way."

"Do you believe what you believe?" Taco asked.

"Sure. Why do you ask?"

"Then why let this guy bother you?"

Jim was struck by this remark and had to think about it for a minute. He then replied, "Maybe part of me worries that he's right—that I'm not one of the chosen ones."

"So, you're really worried about your salvation, then?"

"Sure. I mean, eternity is an awfully long time."

"Well, what makes you worried about your salvation?"

"How can I know what my ultimate fate is? I mean, I try to go to church just about every Sunday, and I try to be good to others, but how do I know that I won't fall off the beam at some point before the judgment day?"

"What do you mean, 'fall off the beam'?"

"You know, like a gymnast in training. These athletes train for years and years, but only one misstep during an Olympic performance can obliterate all their years of hard work," Jim replied.

"Kinda like fallin' into the sea after walkin' on water?"

"Yeah, like that."

"Hmm, God as an Olympic judge? That's a new one to me. It would seem a bit unfair to judge a lifetime's worth of effort by just one task or event," Taco said rhetorically.

"But what if that task or event was somebody's last one? And what if they failed miserably at it? And what if their failure ended up causing tremendous pain and suffering to others? How could God just give them a free pass?"

"Maybe that's why some believe in purgatory," Taco replied.

"But what if there is no purgatory? Then all those poor saps who fall off the beam in their last performance plunge straight into hell, forever and ever?"

"Interesting dilemma," Taco remarked.

"You know what else bothers me? How could God create someone who he knew was predestined for eternal damnation? Like a Judas or a Hitler. That just seems flat-out cruel."

Taco nodded reflectively, then said, "Yeah, but was it God who forced them to pull the trigger on their evil ideas?"

"That's just it. How could God purposefully create something in someone that God doesn't have himself?"

"What do you mean?"

"Free will. How can God create free will in someone to commit the most heinous actions, when God himself doesn't have the free will to commit acts of evil?"

Taco nodded again thoughtfully, then replied, "Maybe we can't perceive the free will of God in the same way that God does."

Jim likewise nodded, then put the cash for his drink on the bar and said good night to Taco.

Soon, he was back in his apartment and engaged in his usual routine. *Damn! Still no letter from Paramount!* Jim thought as he shuffled through his mail. He was tormented with the thought of whether or not he should call Paramount to inquire but then decided to put it off. Upon checking his emails, he found one from Marsha, which he eagerly opened. Without questioning Jim's prior top-secret endeavors, she accepted his invitation to dinner and even suggested that they go to the Ellingford House, which was an elegant colonial restaurant south of Ellingford and north of Ashton. Jim quickly accepted and even suggested some dates and times.

# CHAPTER NINETEEN

Much to his aggravation, Jim had to wake up early the next morning to get ready for a job interview in Ellingford. He vigorously polished his shoes while a pot of fresh coffee brewed. Jim was uncertain as to which suit he should wear. He opted for a light tan one, as the other two were darker in color and more likely to retain heat. The forecast called for more heat and humidity, but not as much as the previous day.

He hoped that he would be back by noon, as he truly wasn't all that interested in the particular company with which he was interviewing. It was more of a minor-league type of company. Soon his shoes and coffee were done, and he sat down for a quick breakfast of peanut butter toasted English muffins.

By about 9:15 a.m. he was on the way to his interview and making good time, as most of the morning rush hour traffic had dissipated. Luckily, it wasn't too hot yet. It was perhaps in the mid-seventies, and the air conditioning in his sedan kept him cool.

The interview was about a half hour, and Jim tried his best to be focused; however, he was distracted at the thought of not getting the Paramount Mutual job. The present interview dealt with adjusting low-speed car accident claims. Soon the interview was over, and he was still agonizing as to whether or not he should call the VP with whom he'd interviewed at Paramount about the status of their job opening.

On the way back to his apartment, Jim spied a car dealership and decided to stop in and do some window shopping, as he knew that his car was getting older and inevitably would have to be replaced.

He was only on the lot for a couple of minutes before he was accosted by an aggressive salesman. After a few minutes of banter, Jim was persuaded into taking a test drive of the least expensive, no-frills, new pickup on the lot. It exuded a new car smell, which Jim always liked. They drove for about twenty minutes, including a brief jaunt off-road. Other than providing his address to the salesman, Jim did not give any inclination that he was interested in following up.

On his way back from the dealership, Jim's thoughts drifted back to southern Colorado and the first vehicle that he had had as a teenager, which was a secondhand pickup from his uncle. His memories of the open roads and open sky were exhilarating. He truly wanted another pickup; however, such a vehicle didn't fit the corporate image that he projected for himself. And if he got another job in the city, he wouldn't need a vehicle, anyway. *Man, I gotta find out about that Paramount Mutual job,* he decided as he pulled up to his apartment.

After changing out of his clothes, Jim nervously dialed the phone to the VP's office.

"Hello, this is Lisa from Paramount Mutual. How may I direct your call?"

"Um, this is Jim Greene. I met—interviewed with Mr. Gordon about a week or so ago, and he told me to call if I had any questions."

"I'll check to see if he's in. Please hold," she replied.

About half a minute passed, which seemed like hours to Jim, when abruptly a voice mail recording started to play. Jim left a brief and awkward message, thanking Mr. Gordon again for the interview and inquiring about the status of the opening. After hanging up, he agonized about the voice mail that he had just left. He hoped it didn't sound too desperate.

Jim decided to distract himself by having some lunch, then checking his emails. He had one from his old friend Jake, whose wife had recently delivered triplets. Jim was excited to hear from him and that Jake was proposing an overnight fishing trip for some time during the summer. Jim instantly replied and indicated his enthusiasm for such a trip. Thoughts of going on a hot date with Marsha and a fishing trip with Jake minimized thoughts of Paramount Insurance Company.

The next day, Jim wasn't feeling particularly motivated to do anything before work. So, he just lounged around for several hours and then grabbed a late lunch at the diner before heading out to the office in Ashton.

At Wanda's, Jim found that her apartment wasn't nearly as hot as it'd been the other day. The day's temperature was a solid twenty degrees lower than the last shift he'd worked.

As Jim and Wanda headed toward the kitchen, Bubba unexpectedly blurted out, "I'd shoot that fuckin' bitch between her beady eyes!"

Jim was uncertain what to make of this. He thought for a moment, then asked, "Have you been going back to that store where that clerk was giving you a hard time?"

"Nah. Bubba just has a keen recollection for foul language."

"How are you feeling today?"

"Not too good. I've got this toothache," she said, pulling her lip back from the corner of her mouth with her left index finger, which revealed a yellowed incisor tooth. The tooth was embedded in a red, swollen, and purulent piece of gum tissue.

"How long have you had this?" Jim asked.

"I dunno. A couple of days, maybe."

"When was the last time you saw a dentist?"

"When I was in Texas."

"If we made an appointment for you, would you go?"

"I really don't like dentists," she replied. "But this hurts like hell, so I guess I'd go if you got me one."

"Anything else bothering you?" Jim asked as Wanda finished up with her blood glucose meter reading.

"Yeah, every time food or my tongue hits that tooth, it causes me to hear awful voices."

"What do the voices say to you?"

"They say, 'You're a fuckin' filthy bitch! You don't deserve teeth! We'll yank them out of your stupid skull one by one!'"

"Are you having any thoughts of hurting yourself?"

"No. I just want the pain and voices to stop. Why won't they just leave me alone?"

Jim put his hand on her shoulder, then said, "We'll get you in to see a dentist as soon as possible. If the pain or voices start gettin' worse, or if you start runnin' a fever, you got to let us know, okay?"

She nodded quietly, then they finished up their visit.

While driving to Richard's, Jim called Rose. As she didn't answer, he left her a voice mail about Wanda's tooth.

Soon Jim found Sir Richard completely engrossed by his research. He gently asked, "Are you feeling okay?"

"Not to worry, my good man. I believe that I'm finally on the right track! And once I win the zoning appeal, then I can truly accelerate the pace of my research!"

Richard's sugar was only slightly elevated, and soon they were done.

Once at the Y, Jim found Phil watching a documentary about the outing of Joseph Wilson's wife.

"What do you think about what happened to her?" Jim inquired.

"I think it's terrible. I mean—in my parents' generation, everyone respected the idea that loose lips sink ships, even journalists. It seems like nowadays with all the twenty-four-hour news networks and the intense competition among journalists, nothing is sacred—not even the safety of an intelligence officer."

"Regardless of who leaked the information, the fact that the journalist didn't have the discretion to safeguard an officer's identity is astounding," Jim replied.

"Yep, I guess the maxim that discretion is the better part of valor went out of vogue with the notion that loose lips sink ships," Phil said. "The doggone truth is that most journalists wouldn't sacrifice an inside scoop for the safety of a public servant."

After a momentary pause, Jim asked, "Are you ready to take your pills?"

"Nah, I'm feeling pretty good today. Thanks, anyhow."

"You sure?"

"Yep."

Not wanting to destroy his rapport with Phil by trying to cajole him into taking his medicine, Jim wished him a good night. Soon he was on the way to Sally's but was still bothered by Phil's refusal to accept his medicine.

Once inside Sally's living room, Jim found her on the couch drinking coffee and watching another Christmas video. Walter was conspicuously absent.

"Hey, Sally, how are you?" Jim asked.

"Okey-dokey," she replied.

"Where's Walter today?"

"He went down to the pub to meet some friends."

"Are you seeing or hearing anything unusual?"

"Jesus told me what he wanted for Christmas!"

"Oh, yeah? What is it?"

"He wants a new throne!"

"Did he tell you this at the convenience store?" Jim asked, trying to determine if it was a genuine hallucination or if the mini- mart messiah was starting to tease her.

"Nope. He told me during a Christmas movie."

"How are you going to make it?"

"I dunno, but the Lord will provide!"

"Well, before you start using any power tools or sharp instruments, please let me or somebody else know," Jim replied.

Sally nodded innocently, then the two wrapped up their visit in the typical fashion.

Entering Mike's driveway, Jim found Mike's car inside the opened garage. At the front door, Mike soon appeared, wearing neatly pressed pants and a button-down shirt.

"Hey, Mike. How's it goin'?"

"Not bad. You?"

"Pretty good. Whatcha all dressed up for?" Jim asked.

"Penelope invited me to go with her and her family to the Valley's Greek Festival."

"You nervous?"

"A little bit. I don't think her father likes me. It always looks like he's giving me the skunk-eye," Mike replied.

"You feeling okay, otherwise?"

"Yeah, I really like this girl. I haven't dated anyone more than a couple of times since my accident. I forgot how nice it is."

"Good for you. I hope you have a great time."

"Thanks, I'll try."

Soon their visit was over, and Jim was on his way. He couldn't help thinking about his own upcoming date with Marsha.

After a brief ride to St. Monica's, Jim was pleased to see June in the living room.

"Hi, Jim. How are you?"

"Not bad, and yourself?" he asked.

"Pretty good. Rob is in the kitchen. Nick's upstairs, and Lucinda's at work."

"Would you mind giving Lucinda her pills when she gets home?"

"I was just about to ask you that."

"Thanks," Jim said while handing her Lucinda's envelope.

When he entered the kitchen, he found Rob sitting at the kitchen table.

"Hey, Rob, how you doin'?"

"Not bad. Just waiting to get back to the boat," he replied.

"Still sanding the deck?"

"Yeah, we're almost done. Then, I'm gonna paint it eggshell white," Rob replied.

"You having any problems or pain anywhere?"

"Yeah, this new lace thongboy I just got is chaffing my crotch."

"You should probably put some baby powder on later."

Rob nodded and took his pills, then signed the paper and disappeared out the back door.

Soon Jim was at Nick's door. Nick greeted him coldly, still looking resentful at Jim for his prior tardiness.

"Hey, Nick, sorry for being so terse with you last time. It wasn't your fault that I was late," Jim said.

Again, Nick neither acknowledged nor accepted Jim's apology.

"Are you having any prophecies?" Jim gently inquired.

"Yes, the traumatized man crouchin' in the corner. He's graspin' his ankles with both hands and gently rocking back and forth on his buttocks. He has darkness around his eyes and is chantin' something, over and over and over again. The end is near! You must repent and accept Christ as your Destroyer and Avenger!"

"Is that what he's chanting?"

"What?" Nick said, looking somewhat confused.

"Is he chanting, 'The end is near; you must accept Christ as your Destroyer and Avenger'?"

"No, no, no. I can't make out what he's chantin'. But when that man ends up in the corner, then the end is at hand. You must repent before it's too late."

Jim was completely unsure how to answer without running the risk of agitating Nick, so Jim just nodded politely. Nick then took his pills, and they completed their visit without any problems.

Once back home, Jim checked his inbox and found an email from Marsha confirming the time for their dinner tomorrow and specifying that she would meet him at the restaurant. After not finding any email, voice mail, or letter from Mr. Gordon at Paramount Insurance Company, Jim decided to check Paramount's website to view their job postings. Much to his disappointment, the Paramount Mutual job that he had interviewed for twice was no longer listed. Jim thought maybe it was a mistake, so he logged off and then rebooted to check it again. No change; the listing was gone. He couldn't believe it. He thought for sure he'd have at least one more conversation with Mr. Gordon to try to persuade him to take him on. Jim thought that Mr. Gordon had liked him and his qualifications. He thought he'd be back on the corporate ladder and living the high life in the city within days or maybe weeks.

After logging off, Jim had a second tumbler of bourbon and a few more cigarettes. *What the fuck do I do now?* he thought as he began nodding off on the futon.

# CHAPTER TWENTY

Jim woke up in the early afternoon the following day, completely unmotivated to do much of anything. Nonetheless, he did force himself to throw on a pair of sweats and head out to the gym, as he wanted his shoulders to look as broad as he'd described them to Marsha. At the gym, he methodically went through an upper-body workout routine that wasn't particularly challenging. Jim then took out his frustrations on a large Everlast bag that was suspended from the ceiling in the far corner of the gym. After twenty minutes of punching, Jim finished his workout and skipped the cardio machine.

On the way home, Jim stopped at a pharmacy in the Bacon Alley neighborhood of Ashton to pick up his weightlifting supplements and other supplies for the evening. Bacon Alley had previously contained slaughterhouses that colonialists had used to butcher pigs. Jim thought it a bit peculiar that this 230- year-old enclave should be revered for its history of slaughtering animals. He wondered if any of the slaughtered pigs had ever made their way to the Ellingford House, which had been used as a stagecoach stop for travelers during that era. Although he had never been there, Jim had heard good things about the restaurant and was trying to psych himself up for the dinner date enough to push out negative thoughts about Paramount.

Once back at his apartment, Jim puttered around and laid out a few different outfits on his bed. He debated on which one looked the most corporate casual—neither too stuffy nor too laid-back. After several minutes, he opted for the navy blue Dockers with a blue and white striped button-down dress shirt. Glancing at his watch, he saw it was it read 4:55 p.m. As his date was scheduled for 7:00 p.m., he thought it best to start shaving and showering.

After lathering up his face with shaving cream, Jim exited the bathroom to look for the bag from Bacon Alley Pharmacy, which contained new razor blades and aftershave. He searched his apartment for about ten to twenty minutes, with increasing anger at each passing minute. *Why would a Fortune 500 company like Paramount want to hire me when I can't even keep track of a simple bag from the pharmacy?* Finally, Jim found it near his coffeemaker, where he had left it to remind him to make a small pot before his date. Jim quickly loaded the machine with water and fresh grounds, then hit the start button.

After a thorough shave and hot shower, Jim poured himself a cup of steaming java before going to the bedroom to get dressed. Looking down at his black penny loafers, he noticed that the shine was less than stellar. He also noticed that the time was now 6:05 p.m. Rather than engage in a full shoe-shine, Jim summarily buffed them off with a soft cloth. He then dumped the remainder of the coffee in the sink and headed out.

Despite moderately heavy traffic, Jim made good time to the restaurant and found himself there about fifteen minutes early. The Ellingford House was a simple yet elegant-looking white building with tall, strong pillars lining the front porch.

Entering the restaurant, Jim was greeted by a friendly Italian- looking lady, who resembled his mother a bit. She led him to the bar area to wait for his guest. Other than a senior couple sitting at a table for two, the bar was empty. It was a fairly small room with a low colonial ceiling, decorated with a medieval motif that included a three-dimensional coat of arms with crossed swords beneath a shield and helmet of armor set above the shield. *I wonder what ol' Nick would do with this stuff,* Jim mused.

After scanning the room, Jim settled into a comfortable overstuffed chair at a table that faced the entryway to the bar.

Suddenly, a petite and perky blond waitress appeared out of nowhere and asked him if he wanted a drink while he waited. Although he wanted a bourbon to settle his nerves, he chose ice water instead so as not to appear to be a lush who drinks alone.

Before the waitress could return with his water, Marsha entered the bar. She looked to be about five-foot-two and had the physique of a ballerina. Marsha's complexion was fair, and her chestnut-colored hair was neatly pulled up into a stereotypical librarian bun. She was attired in navy blue nylons, a Black Watch tartan skirt, and a short-sleeve navy sweater that was cut low enough to be alluring but high enough to be respectable. In the area above her collar, an exquisite strand of baby pearls encircled her ivory neck. As she drew closer, he noticed that she had delicate, clear blue eyes that were accentuated by a suitable amount of mascara and eye shadow.

Once she reached the table, Jim stood up and extended his hand. "You must be Marsha."

"Yes. Pleased to meet you," she replied, meeting his handshake with a friendly grasp.

Immediately after shaking hands, Jim clumsily jockeyed over to the other side of the small table to pull out the chair for her. She thanked him reflexively, and then they both sat down.

Once seated, Jim looked across the table and was startled to notice that her left nostril was abnormally larger than her right and that it was almost perfectly round. It was incredibly distracting, and he felt compelled to fix his gaze straight into her eyes, which was challenging to do given the enormous difference between her nares.

Luckily, the perky blond waitress reappeared quickly with Jim's water. "Good evening. My name is Tammy, and I'll be your waitress this evening," she said, placing Jim's glass on the table. "Can I get you any drinks to get started?"

Jim nodded at Marsha and gestured with his hand for her to go first.

"Yes. I'll have a frozen strawberry margarita."

"And you, sir?" Tammy inquired.

"Gosh," Jim replied indecisively. Although he truly wanted a bourbon, he was concerned that it would give the wrong impression that he was a purveyor of harder whiskey-related alcohol. "I'll have a dirty martini, shaken not stirred." *A safe choice for an aspiring corporate professional,* Jim thought.

"I'll be back shortly with your drinks," Tammy replied as she placed a couple of menus on the table for them to review.

"How long have you been a librarian, Marsha?" Jim asked.

"Assistant librarian. It's been about seven years now, but I hope to be a full librarian someday. It's been my dream ever since I was a little girl. I used to neatly arrange my storybooks well before I could read them," she replied sentimentally.

*What a freak!* Jim thought as he redoubled his efforts to avoid making eye contact with the circular malformation at the base of her nose. "Wow, good for you. You don't see that much anymore—people wanting to be a certain kind of professional as a kid and then seeing it through as an adult."

"I'm lucky, I guess. My grandfather even built me a miniature library for my fifth birthday, instead of a dollhouse. It came complete with an elaborate card catalog based on the Dewey Decimal System for the tiny books that were inside."

"Were the books real?"

"No, they were made from empty matchboxes that Grandpa had painted over to look real. Unfortunately, my stupid older brother got mad one day and stuffed part of one way up my nose—it took the doctor almost an hour to get it all out. That's why my nostrils aren't symmetrical, in case you were wondering."

Stunned by this bizarre revelation, Jim purposely began coughing and took a swig of ice water to buy some more time. "Oh, gosh. I'm so sorry to hear that."

"It's all right. I'm used to people stiffening their necks so as not to look down their noses at mine."

Immediately, Jim felt ashamed by her remark, as that was pretty much what he had been doing since they sat down. *God, is this what it was like for Michele dating all these years before she met Stan? Were dates spent avoiding her elongated teeth that resulted in her perpetual Mona Lisa smile?*

Tammy then came to the table with their drinks. "Are you guys ready to order yet?"

"Gosh, I haven't even looked at my menu," Marsha replied.

"Me neither," Jim chimed in.

"Let me tell you about tonight's specials." Tammy then rattled them off with the efficiency and enthusiasm of a new tour guide at a museum.

"I'll have the stuffed mushroom caps over angel hair," Marsha said.

"That sounds good; make it two," Jim responded.

"Great. Do you guys want to put in your dinner orders now or wait until your appetizers get here?"

"What do you think about the twin stuffed lobster special for two?" Marsha asked Jim.

"Great," Jim answered. *Why wouldn't this girl order the most expensive thing on the menu since I am a hotshot executive?* he lamented.

"Say, it's a nice night—would you like to sit out on our patio?" Tammy asked.

"Sure," they both replied almost simultaneously.

Tammy then led them across the room to a narrow walkway adjacent to the bar that led to a quaint and quiet patio. She sat them at one of six empty tables and lit a small citronella candle that had already been on it.

During the next several minutes, Jim and Marsha engaged in clunky and shallow banter about music, clothing, and other safe subjects. All the while, Jim was physically tormented about where to keep his eyes. *Keep your neck loose, man! Don't keep staring at her eyes—she'll know you're only avoiding her nose. Don't look away too much. Don't look at her subtle cleavage. Good God, I wish I'd ordered the bourbon!*

"So, what did you do in the service that you couldn't send me your picture?" Marsha asked pointedly.

"I was assigned to a military intelligence unit as their medic," Jim replied, knowing that he'd only spent a brief stint with them and the bulk of his time assigned to an airborne infantry company.

After an awkward pause, she then said, "Well, you look just like you described in your email."

*Is that good or bad? What do I say about her looking as she described? Oh, don't look at that nostril! Is it pulsating now? Is it getting bigger?* "I like your pearl necklace—are they real?" Jim replied. *Damn, what a dumbass remark! Is she going to think that I think that she's cheap?*

"Why, yes. I got them from my Aunt Millie. She's a retired Boston librarian, originally from Salem, but now she lives with me."

Tammy's presence then interrupted their conversation as she placed the appetizers on the table. "Do you guys want another round?" she asked, noticing that Jim's glass was empty and that Marsha's was nearly empty.

"No, thanks," Marsha replied.

"I'll have another when you bring dinner, please," Jim indicated, hoping not to convey the impression that he was a heavy drinker.

They both began eating the delectable morsels, which were meticulously presented on small, oval-shaped pewter plates. As they ate, Marsha continued to talk about her Aunt Millie, library books, and their black cat named Dewey.

*Oh, man, this is painful!* Jim thought as Marsha droned on. Suddenly, Jim looked down at the last mushroom on his plate and began to wonder if it would fit snugly up in her left nostril. He found the thought cruel yet irresistibly amusing. And much like not looking at her nose, not thinking about seeing that mushroom crammed up her snout was almost impossible. *Dammit, Jim, stop thinking about it! What if she was your sister?*

"Have you ever had lobster from Boston?" Marsha asked.

"No, but I hear it's pretty good."

Marsha nodded vaguely, evincing her disinterest with the course of the conversation.

"Speak of the devil," Jim said as Tammy appeared at the table with their moderately sized lobsters, containers of melted butter, and Jim's martini.

As they ate dinner, their conversation devolved into sporadic and polite topics of no particular importance or controversy to either of them.

When they finished their food, Marsha looked over at Jim and asked, "Do you mind if I let my hair down and smoke?"

"That's fine. Mind if I join you?"

"Not at all," she replied.

To Jim's surprise, she then reached both hands behind her head, released her bun, and gently shook her head back and forth, letting her luxurious brunette hair tumble down to her shoulders. *Wow, I didn't think she'd literally let her hair down.*

"How long have you smoked?" Marsha queried, putting an unlit cigarette to her mouth.

"Since high school," Jim said as he quickly pulled out his lighter and ignited their cigarettes.

They both took a few drags, and Jim was now horrified to see that her left nostril was indeed pulsating with each deep drag that she took. To make matters worse, the flickering citronella candle on their table was casting aberrant shadows up that quivering, cavernous hole. He quickly distracted himself by finishing off his second martini in one large gulp.

"So, how long have you been a nurse?"

"About five years now."

"How is that corporate?"

"Well, it is—I do some quality assurance, in addition to treating patients clinically," Jim replied, stretching the truth a bit, as the only part of his job description that could be construed as quality assurance would be making sure that the right pills made it into the right envelopes.

"What type of patients do you see clinically?" she asked in a curious tone.

"Mostly psychiatric," Jim responded.

Marsha nodded with interest, then said matter-of-factly, "I tell you; the best sex of my life was in Harvard's library when I was on Prozac. It turned me into a real nympho."

Jim was completely taken aback by her erotic revelation and unsure how to respond. *Oh, my God, why did she tell me that? Does she want to have sex with me? How much more would her nostril quiver if we did it? Would it swallow me whole? Would I enjoy it?* After an awkward interlude of silence, Jim stammered, "Say…I, uh, I know this great Italian place—not too far from here—that has the best pastries and expresso in the world. Would you be interested in heading over there for dessert?"

"Oh, gosh, I'd love to, but I have to take Aunt Millie grocery shopping first thing in the morning—but we could do dessert here."

"That would be okay, too," Jim replied, still unnerved thinking about her undulating nose in the sack.

"I believe that the dessert menu is on the back," she said, simultaneously flipping it over to peruse.

Jim did likewise and contemplated finally having the bourbon that he had been avoiding all night, to get up some liquid courage for exploring romantic possibilities with this self- professed nymphomaniac.

"Are you guys ready for dessert?" Tammy asked as they both had their heads lowered, looking at their menus.

"I'll have the tiramisu and another strawberry margarita, please," Marsha replied.

"Are you Italian?" Jim queried.

"Half Milanese and half Irish."

"I'm half Sicilian and half English." *Maybe opposites do attract?* Jim pondered.

"Are you going to have the same thing?" Tammy asked.

"No, thanks. I'll go with the German chocolate cheesecake and Maker's Mark on the rocks."

Benign chatter again transpired as they waited for Tammy to get back with their drinks and desserts. Soon she returned, but not before Jim had failed several times to divert his glance from

Marsha's candlelit cleavage. It certainly did have much more appeal than her candlelit nostril.

Their dessert conversation remained light and more relaxed than their prior dinner discourse. Soon their glasses and plates were empty, and the sun had completely set.

"Can I get you your check?" Tammy said from the doorway of the bar, which was a couple of tables away from the now packed patio area.

Jim nodded and raised his hand.

"Do you want me to get half?" Marsha politely inquired.

"No, that's fine," Jim answered, feeling like a corporate hotshot, without the corporate part.

Soon they were off the patio and meandered over to Marsha's compact hybrid car.

They chatted comfortably for a few more minutes. Jim noticed how the street light emphasized her modest cleavage and simultaneously minimized her nasal defect. The inevitable lull in the conversation ensued, and Jim decided that it was time to go in for the kill of a sensual good night kiss. With the agility of a panic-stricken quarterback looking for an open receiver, Marsha quickly moved her head at the last second, resulting in Jim's lips barely landing on the corner of hers. Jim then nervously opened her car door (which she had recently unlocked) and mumbled something about having a good time, to which she expressed the obligatory sentiment about going out again in the future.

Jim drove back to his apartment and took some Motrin for his arms, which were sore from punching the bag earlier at the gym. He then settled in for what proved to be a tortured night's sleep.

# CHAPTER TWENTY-ONE

The next day Jim woke up shortly before noon and just moped around before getting ready for work. *I'll let Chief Wahoo do my smiling for me today,* Jim thought as he donned his Cleveland Indians ball cap. Checking his agency voice mail before heading out to work, he heard that Cindy had gotten Wanda a dentist appointment for the following morning.

Once at Wanda's apartment, Jim saw that she was a little less disturbed than previously.

"Hi, Jim. How are you?" she said, opening the door.

"Not bad. How 'bout you?"

"My tooth is feeling a bit better than the last visit," she replied.

"Mind if I take a look?"

"Nope," she said, pulling her lip back for Jim to view her tooth.

Indeed, her tooth did look better than before. "Did you do anything to it?" Jim asked.

"Yeah, I gargled salt and water every couple of hours, and it felt better."

"Well, Cindy got you an appointment at the free dental clinic in Ashford for 9:30 a.m. tomorrow. You should still get it checked out," Jim said.

"Why bother? It's gettin' better."

"You should have a dentist look at it just in case," Jim said softly.

Wanda just shrugged her shoulders, not wanting to offend Jim by her recalcitrance.

Jim, not wanting to get into an argument with her, changed the subject. "Are you still hearing any voices or seeing any strange things?"

"I am still hearing those awful voices sometimes when I hit that tooth, but not as often as before."

"Well, if it gets worse, please let us know," he replied.

After a couple more minutes, their visit was over.

Once in his car, Jim decided to call Cindy and leave her a voice mail asking her to try to coax Wanda to the dentist in the morning. Cindy never picked up the agency phone when she wasn't on duty, but she was religious about checking her voice mail.

When Jim was at Richard's, they went into his laboratory to conduct their clinical transactions. Richard looked very fatigued, as evidenced by the dark circles beneath his eyes.

"Sir Richard, are you getting enough sleep?" Jim asked respectfully.

"Not really. Night is when I work best. Besides, that's when the chances of surveillance by my neighbors are minimal."

"What about now? Aren't you concerned that they'll see the concoction that you're brewing during the daytime?" Jim asked.

"Well, the pot is Teflon-coated lead, so the chances of any infrared surveillance picking up on the simmering Paramatter are slight. But more importantly, during the daytime I can spy on my neighbors to see if they're surveilling me," he said. After a brief pause, Richard then asked, "What do you think of it—this batch?"

Again, Richard invited him over to the Paramatter caldron for his layperson observations. Once at the pot, Richard lifted off a heavy lid for Jim's inspection. This time it looked like green pea soup with fur balls interspersed. It smelled like the nearly rancid bacon that Jim had once encountered in the army.

Not wanting to offend him, Jim responded, "It seems very primordial to me."

Richard smiled, then said, "Ah, I must be getting close!"

"Are you hearing or seeing anything unusual since our last visit?"

"Why, yes, indeed! I noticed some soot on the wall at the far end of my laboratory. Thinking that it was some residue from a batch of potential Paramatter that I was boiling yesterday, I walked across the room to inspect. As I approached, I realized that it was a message written in ash:

*TE*
*MPUS FUGIT*
*PARAMATER EST SIMILIS*
*QUOD LUX VENIO ANTE OBSCURRUM*

"When I grabbed for my cell phone to snap a photo of this amazing sight, the ash blew away, as though it had been from the breath of God. Fortunately, I had the presence of mind to quickly write down this oracle." Richard paused for a moment and then asked, "Do you realize the supreme significance of this message?"

Jim shook his head slightly, indicating polite interest.

"Time flies, and Paramatter is like the light that came before the darkness!"

"Cool. So, then this light existed before the beginning of time?"

"Not just that; this light also opens up a whole new universe of inquiry: What are the colors and properties of its unknown brilliance? Does it have the same characteristics as our current electromagnetic spectrum?"

"Does it travel at the same speed?" Jim ventured to ask. "Good God, man, this truly does change everything! If this ancient light travels at a different speed, then all physical matter and energy could be completely different! It would give $E=MC^2$ an entirely new meaning!"

"Well, keep up the good work and make sure to get some sleep. You don't want to get sick."

"Not to worry, my good man. I believe that I'm finally on the right track! And once I win the zoning appeal next month, then I can accelerate the pace of my research!"

Richard's sugar was only slightly elevated, and soon they were done.

On the way to the YMCA, it started to rain gently. Once inside Phil's corridor, Jim was disappointed that no one answered the door. He discreetly slipped down to the pool area and was not surprised not to find Phil there, as it was a much cooler day. He decided to try Phil back at the end of the shift.

As he headed back to his car, Jim was annoyed to see a faded American flag on top of the YMCA's flagpole on their roof. Flying a flag, and a faded one at that, in the rain truly bothered him. Jim had been imbued with respect for the flag when he'd served as an occasional honor guard for funerals during his time in the Army. He recalled his platoon sergeant telling him that the flag was so important that every flagpole on U.S. military installations had hidden measures to protect it. The ball on top of the flagpole, also known as the truck, contained a hollow chamber in which was hidden a razor blade, a match, and a single bullet. If it ever became apparent that the flag was about to fall into enemy hands, the truck was to be unscrewed and the flag dissected with the razor and burned with the match. The soldier performing that task was then expected to take his life rather than surrender to the enemy.

At Sally's, Jim found Walter puffing a stale cigar and Sally drinking coffee in front of the VCR.

"Hi, Jimmy! How are you?" Sally inquired.

"Good. How are you today?"

"Fantastic! I think I got Jesus' throne idea all worked out!"

"What do you mean?"

"I found a large, empty bucket downstairs and an old piece of plywood."

"What are you going to do with it?"

"I figured that I would tie the board to the bucket, then paint them both yellow to look like gold," she said.

"Why don't you turn the bucket right side up so Christ can use it as a crapper?!" Walter shouted from the other room.

"Why—why don't I turn you right up and crap in your mouth!" she retorted.

"Sally, I've been swallowing your shit my whole life, so it really wouldn't faze me!"

"Hey, Walter, if she wants to do something nice for Jesus, why don't you just leave her alone? She's not hurting anyone," Jim interjected.

"Well, she's hurting my—insulting my intelligence," Walter replied sheepishly.

A few moments of silence passed, and then Sally continued, "Jim, do you really think Jesus will like it?"

"If it comes from your heart, how could he not?"

She smiled, and they finished up their visit.

Jim was alarmed when he arrived at Mike's to discover an ambulance in the driveway with its emergency lights on. Jim carefully parked beside it on the grass. Arriving at the front door, he knocked gently and then entered. Once he entered the living room, he saw Mike laying on the couch with the medics checking his vital signs. Betty and the Greek girl stood nervously nearby but kept a few feet of distance between each other.

"Hey, Betty, what's going on?" Jim discreetly whispered to her.

"Mike had a bad seizure, so I called an ambulance," she replied.

Jim nodded, then went over to Mike and said, "How you feeling, champ?"

"Lousy—one minute I'm watching TV with Penelope, the next I wake up and see her and my mom standing over me, flippin' out."

"You gonna go to the hospital to get checked out?" Jim asked.

"Nah, I'm all right. I'm just tired and wanna sleep," he replied.

"Can you take your pills first?"

"Sure," Mike replied.

"I need you to sign right here that you're refusing to go with us to the hospital," one of the medics said, handing Mike a clipboard with a form on it.

Mike signed over his mother's vehement protests that he should go to the hospital to be more fully evaluated for his seizure.

Times like this demanded good nursing judgment, but Jim was still distracted and demoralized about Paramount Mutual and to a lesser extent about Marsha. Also, he felt physically drained and on the verge of illness, as the lymph glands in his neck were swollen. Still, he quickly intervened. "Mike, if I get you an appointment tomorrow to have your Dilantin level checked, will you go?"

"You bet. Can I get the pills and go to sleep now?"

Jim nodded, then they wrapped up their visit. Jim then left a voice mail for Cindy to get an order in the morning to check Mike's Dilantin level.

Soon, Jim arrived at St. Monica's and was told by June that Lucinda and Rob were both on the boat. Before going out there, he decided to get Nick's visit out of the way.

Nick immediately started with him. "Have you decided to repent yet? Time is short—the ax is already at the root of the tree!"

"I repent on a fairly regular basis. Thank you for asking."

"Repenting to a sinful priest strangled by a white collar will not save you!"

Jim, feeling increasingly exhausted and ill, attempted to change the subject. "Are you still seeing that shuddering man in the corner—I mean, are you still having that prophecy?"

Nick, sensing what Jim was trying to do, refused to relent. "Didn't you hear what I said? Hiding out with a corrupt cleric inside a black box cannot save your soul!"

"I never said anything about going to confession. I said that I repent regularly. I usually prefer to cut out the middleman and ask God to forgive me himself. How often do you think it necessary to repent?" Jim said softly, trying to save his voice, which now felt strained.

Nick seemed surprised by his answer and unsure how to respond. He finally said, "Once you repent and join the ranks of the Lord's army, there's no need for further repentance—only retribution and destruction of stiff-necked heathens and ignorant pagans!"

Jim had enough and shot back, "Well, isn't it possible for those in the Lord's ranks to ever disobey orders or even go AWOL? And why would the Lord take them back without further repentance?"

"Don't make me smite you again, Nurse James! You must repent and join the ranks of the Lord!" Nick shouted angrily.

*Ah, smite makes right,* Jim thought. Then he gently replied, "Look, I don't want to keep arguing with you. I hear and respect what you're saying, and I'll give it some thought, okay?"

"Well, don't think too long! The end of days is rapidly approaching!"

Jim nodded, then the two concluded their transactions, and Jim headed out to the boat in the backyard.

Once onboard, Jim was impressed that the entire deck was just about done being sanded. Rob was working the sander at one end of the deck, and Lucinda was wielding paintbrushes covered with white paint at the other end.

Rob approached Jim wearing a light summer dress, which was covered in sawdust.

"Hey, Rob, looking ship-shape, my man!" Jim said enthusiastically.

"Thanks. I'm hoping this time next year to be on my way back to Ireland. Then I told Lucinda that we could go to the Caribbean during the winter months."

"Where'd you get all the paint for this?" Jim asked.

"I got a small inheritance from my grandmother, Mary Elizabeth, and Vicky's hubby is a contractor who gets me paint wholesale."

"Good for you," Jim said. "Are you having any pain or problems?"

Rob shook his head, and the two finished up their business. Next, the lovely Lucinda, who was wearing a white tankini top, denim cutoffs, and a flimsy painter's cap, jumped in front of Jim.

"Hey, bud! What's cooking?" she shouted playfully.

"What are you today—a white-speckled hen?" Jim said jokingly, pointing to the paint splatters up and down her darkened arms.

"Hey, at least I wore the right colored top for the job," she replied.

"Hearing or seeing anything unusual today?"

"Just a little crying this morning. It seems to be gettin' less frequent."

"Good. Here you go," Jim said, handing Lucinda her pills.

She quickly gulped them down and signed the MAR, then said, "Better get back to work. See ya later Jimbo!"

Before going back to his apartment, Jim stopped at the Y to see if Phil had returned. He was surprised to find that he was there and had been there all day. When Jim had stopped by earlier, Phil had been in a deep sleep and didn't hear him knocking on the door. Again, Phil politely denied being depressed and sent Jim on his way without taking the medication.

On the way back to his apartment, Jim stopped in at the Bacon Alley Pharmacy to get a big bag of echinacea cough drops.

When he returned to his apartment, he poured an extra- strong tumbler of bourbon and even gargled it before swallowing, hoping to numb the sore throat that he was now getting. Jim sorted through the mail and found nothing intriguing, not even a courtesy rejection letter from Mr. Gordon. Other than a brief update on Michele's wedding flower arrangements from Jenny, his email inbox was all spam. He felt listless yet angry because his hopes of working again in the city and getting a girlfriend seemed further away than ever. After finishing the bourbon, he decided to skip the final cigarette of the day to spare his throat. He did, however, leave Rose a message that he wouldn't be coming into work the following evening due to illness.

# CHAPTER TWENTY-TWO

Jim was glad that he had taken the following day off, as he had the next two succeeding days off from work. During his first day off Jim did nothing much other than bemoan to himself about his professional and romantic disappointments. Toward the end of that day, however, Jim kept replaying his dreadful date with Martha in his mind. Thinking about the way he treated her, especially by lingering his eyes over her cleavage and envisioning a sexual liaison, really bothered Jim and made him feel frustrated and ashamed. *Why the hell did she tell me about her heightened sexual appetite and nymphomania when on Prozac? Why the hell didn't she just keep that to herself? It's not as though she really liked me or wanted to keep dating me. Why the hell did she have to mess with my mind like that?*

Waking up the next morning, Jim couldn't shake his guilty conscience about Martha, and he decided to check in for confession despite what he'd recently told Nick about avoiding it.

St. Francis Church was a quaint little stone building, which reportedly had been modeled after a chapel in France that had been destroyed during the Second World War. Soon Jim found himself in a back pew and struggling to examine his conscience. Within minutes the confessional was opened without any other customers waiting in line.

Jim entered the small room and was pleased to see Father Paul sitting on the other side of it. Father Paul had a unique appearance that was somewhat like a cross between Steve Jobs and Harry Potter. His thick salt-and-pepper hair crowned his head and fell comfortably to about his collar line. He sported a five o'clock shadow that appeared to be about the consistency of fifty-grit sandpaper, and poor boy glasses were anchored at the bottom of his slopping nose. Interestingly, he had a jagged, prominent scar about two inches above his left eyebrow.

After a brief exchange of greetings, Jim started, "Bless me, Father, for I have sinned."

"How long has it been since your last confession, my son?"

"About a year," Jim replied with nervousness in his voice.

"And what are your sins, my son?"

"Well, I went on this date recently and couldn't stop thinking about having sex with the woman and couldn't stop staring at her cleavage."

"And what do you mean by you 'couldn't stop'?"

Jim was unprepared for that question and a bit confused about what Father Paul was getting at. "I'm not sure about what you mean by that, Father."

"Well, what I mean is, what tricked you into thinking that you couldn't redirect your mind and eyes on more honorable thoughts and images?"

Jim paused reflectively for a moment and then replied, "This lady had made some sexually charged remarks, and then, I guess, my mind and eyes just took over from there."

"Had you been drinking during this dinner date?" Father Paul gently inquired.

"Yeah, and probably a little too much. But the worse thing was how I kept looking at her as just a collection of different body parts and not as a whole person. She had a profound nasal defect, and when I didn't look at her nose and face, I was looking at her boobs."

"Do you know what the greatest paradox about temptation and sin is, Jim?"

Jim shook his head no, concurrently looking upward as though he was trying to find an answer.

"The greatest paradox of temptation and sin is that it's never too late *NOT* to sin."

"Well, what exactly do you mean by that, Father Paul?" Jim queried in a curious tone of voice.

"That even in our darkest hour of temptation and sin, choosing not to sin is still a lively option."

After a long and thoughtful pause, Jim asked, "Well, what about when you're actually sinning? Isn't it too late then not to sin?"

"That's probably the best time to realize that it is never too late not to sin. It's harder to do then, but still not too late. Don't get me wrong: We should apologize and atone for our sins as soon as possible, but even before we can do that, we can still *choose* not to persist in sin. This is just as the prodigal son did when he came to his senses and *decided* to return to his dad's house."

Jim nodded thoughtfully.

After a prolonged silence, Father Paul asked, "Is there anything else weighing on your soul, my son?"

"Well, I'm totally frustrated about losing a corporate healthcare job in Manhattan, and much like my love life, it seems as though the harder I try to get a good job and girlfriend, the further away God puts it out of my reach."

Father Paul nodded thoughtfully and sympathetically, then said, "For your penance I want you to take some quality time to *taste* and *see* the goodness of the Lord."

After a brief absolution and exchanging goodbyes, Jim found himself back in his sedan feeling emotionally exhausted but less physically ill. As he was driving back to his apartment, Jim realized that it would be easier for him to get some tasty food on the way home rather than having to go back out after getting there. He made a brief detour to a mid-sized gourmet supermarket that wasn't too far from the Bacon Alley Pharmacy.

By the time he arrived home, Jim's physical exhaustion had caught up with his emotional weariness. After putting his groceries away, he plopped on his bed and started watching a *Cheers* marathon that had started at noon. Over the next several hours, Jim remained listless watching TV, and he opted to turn in for an early night's sleep.

Jim woke up the following day feeling a lot better but didn't do anything much 'til it was time to get his supper with God prepared. He had gotten a broad swordfish steak and a full-bodied chardonnay. He decided to cook his fish in a skillet on his stove.

Once his food was plated, Jim looked down on the table and closed his eyes to say grace. He then cut a small piece of fish and began chewing it. *Dang! I can't believe that I overcooked such a great-looking piece of fish.* After chewing a few more bites, Jim decided to check his fridge for anything to make the fish more palatable. *Crap, I totally forget to buy tartar sauce yesterday!* Jim thought with an increasing sense of frustration. After checking his fridge for mayo and relish, all Jim could find was a stick of butter. After buttering the fish and taking a mouthful, Jim was disgusted by the overwhelming flavor of salt.

After finishing the unsavory meal, Jim went to bed and looked up through the skylight, which displayed a clear and moonlit sky strewn with innumerable constellations. Jim began wondering about his future. *Man, I hope Chris comes home safe and Jake keeps his sanity with the triplets. Maybe I'll have a lucrative job in New York by this time next year. Maybe I'll find another normal girlfriend like Maria. Maybe Michele's wedding and marriage will be a huge success, and I could be an uncle in a few years from now. I wonder if there is some other lonely soul in a distant corner of the universe looking up at the same stars, wondering if he'll ever find true love and happiness.* Soon Jim's thoughts became more sporadic and less coherent as he drifted off to sleep.

# CHAPTER TWENTY-THREE

The next day he was looking forward to his fishing trip with Jake that had been confirmed by email late last night. The trip was about a week away. Jim was melancholy as he got ready for work, as it was now August and he had hoped to be returning to life in the city by the end of the summer.

Jim arrived at Wanda's. He learned that she had had her incisor tooth pulled, as the Valley Dental Clinic had rescheduled her quickly after Wanda had missed her initial appointment. Wanda was pain-free and a bit more cheerful. She denied hearing any more derogatory voices but had been hearing some muffled grunting on occasion.

At Richard's, Jim found him unusually anxious, as the zoning appeal hearing was that evening.

"Hello, Sir Richard. How are you?"

"Pensive. Tonight is the big night, and my lawyer had better put an end to this nonsense so I can get on with conducting my research any time that I see fit," he replied.

"Have you been seeing or hearing anything unusual?"

"Not really."

As Jim entered the lab, he was surprised by the lack of Paramatter aroma and by the absence of any Teflon-coated pans.

"Hey, Sir Richard, I don't see any Paramatter prototypes in here. Are you feeling okay?"

"Yes, my friend," he said with a sigh. "Science, like any other profession, sometimes compels hard choices."

"How's that?"

"I simply don't have the time and resources to pursue the necessary pyramid research along with biochemical attempts at Paramatter prototypes. I now must look for the light and not the substance of Paramatter."

"What pyramid research?" Jim queried.

"It is a new line of research based on the pyramid-shaped ashen omen on my wall. Time indeed flies, and I must devote myself exclusively to that avenue of research!"

"Well, best of luck with that and with your hearing tonight."

Richard nodded. Soon they were done, and Jim was on to Phil's.

A short time later, Jim was greeted at Phil's door by a Phil that Jim hardly recognized. Phil was unshaven, unkempt, and unmotivated, as evidenced by his manner in opening the door. His room was likewise messy and looked as though it had been burglarized. Again, Phil flatly refused his pills and insisted that he was just tired, but not depressed.

Jim respected his wishes and ended their visit but was concerned by Phil's continued non-compliance in taking his medication. While on his way to Sally's, Jim decided to call Vicky and see what could be done about Phil. She informed Jim that Phil had done the same thing a while back, and after about a month they had to discharge him from the agency for his non- compliance. He then ended up in the hospital for a short stay in their psych unit, after which he was discharged home and readmitted to the agency for outpatient visits.

Jim consumed a cigarette as he approached Sally's. It was a hotter day, and he wanted to satiate his olfactory receptors before smelling anything that might be stagnating or rotting in Sally's house. Once at Sally's, he found Walter in a rocker on the front porch, fanning himself with a magazine. They perfunctorily exchanged a greeting, and then Jim headed in to tend to Sally.

"Hey, Sally. How ya doin'?" Jim asked.

"Good. Whatcha think of my throne?" she replied, pointed to a stout metal bucket that had a narrow piece of plywood crookedly attached to it by some old twine.

Jim went over to examine the piece and carefully tightened the rope to make the plywood backrest more upright.

"Oh, thank you, Jimmy. That's terrific!"

"Hearing or seeing anything unusual?" Jim asked matter- of- factly.

"Nope, but Jesus told me that he's going away to visit some of his brothers and sisters in Mexico."

"Really? When's he going?"

"He's going soon and said he'd be gone for a few weeks," she replied.

Suddenly, a large chunk of sheetrock collapsed from a wall behind the couch and hit the floor with a dull thud. Jim went over to inspect, and he detected a dank and musty odor.

"Ah, don't worry about that. It happens all the time to the walls upstairs," Sally said nonchalantly.

Jim walked back over to Sally, and then they finished their visit in a routine manner.

When Jim pulled into Mike's driveway, he noticed Mike pushing a lawnmower at the far end of his lawn. Jim soon made his way over to discover that Mike looked somewhat angry as he pushed the mower.

"Hey, Mike. What's goin' on?"

"Same ol' shit," he replied, wiping his sweaty forehead with the back of one hand.

"What happened to your hand?" Jim asked, noticing that Mike had a large bandage stuck to the back of one hand.

"Cut it," Mike tensely replied.

"You okay?"

"I'm fuckin' aggravated."

"Wanna talk about it?"

"Sure," Mike said. "You know that girl Penelope I've been dating, right?"

"Yeah."

"Well, last night we were makin' out in my car outside her house. Man, it was really getting intense. All of a sudden, I hear this loud knocking on my door. I look up, and it was her father. His face started to snarl and turned red. Then he started pounding on the door even harder. When I tried to get my hand out of Penelope's shirt, it got caught on a piece of underwire that was sticking out. Next thing you know, I'm bleeding all over the place as I jumped out of the car to talk to him."

"What did he do then?"

"He jacks me up against the car and says that if I ever see his daughter again, he'll string up my nuts like bundles of old goat cheese. She then ran into the house screaming and crying. I've called her three times today, and she hangs up every time she hears my voice."

Jim was unsure what to say, so he changed the subject. "Is the cut so bad that you needed stitches?"

"Nah, it stopped bleeding after a couple of minutes."

"Hang in there," Jim replied. "If you ever get too mad and need to talk, feel free to give me a call."

Mike nodded, then the visit ended shortly afterward.

Jim was making decent time as he headed toward St. Monica's. Once inside the building, June informed him that Lucinda had been called into work and that the others were in their usual places.

Jim decided to see Nick first after giving June Lucinda's envelope of medication. Nick was in the kitchen awaiting his meds before his AA meeting.

"Hello, Nick. How are you?"

"Saved and delivered. Are you finally prepared to follow Christ and his servant, the Reverend Roberts?"

"Even if I wanted to, I don't have the money for the baptism, as my car is a little older and my mechanic tells me that it's gonna need some expensive repairs soon."

Nick looked confused by Jim's remark and immediately changed the subject. "The man—that man shudderin' in the corner. He's back! His end is near! The ax is at the root of his tree!"

"What about me? What if I can't afford the good Reverend Billy Bob's baptism? Will I be damned to hell?"

"It's the Reverend William Roberts!" Nick retorted angrily. "You must sell all your belongings—if you have to—in order to follow him!"

"Most of my stuff is a bunch of crap; who'd want to buy it? The good Reverend?"

"The Reverend is not running a pawn shop! You must sell your possessions to secure the only true possession. You must sell them as though you were using the proceeds to buy a rare gem or a hidden treasure!"

"Well, would the Reverend at least give me baptism at a discounted rate?"

"You must give up everything for his Kingdom! You must sacrifice your very self! What can you give in exchange for your soul?"

"Well, I'll keep thinking about it—and perhaps start budgeting my money a little bit better."

"Don't think too long! Time is short! The ax is already at the root of the tree!"

"Well, shouldn't I pray more for manure to nourish my roots to avoid getting the ax?" Jim posited metaphorically.

"Prayer won't save you! Only sacrifice! You must sacrifice all and join the Lord's conquerin' ranks with the Reverend Roberts to exact his retribution!"

*It always comes back to the retribution with this guy,* Jim mused with an increasing sense of frustration. After an awkward and prolonged pause, Jim replied, "Well, in the meantime I think I'll just keep praying and saving—all the same."

Nick shook his head skeptically, then the two ended their visit.

Jim was pleased to see Rob was in good spirits. Rob was ecstatic that the sanding of the deck was completed and that it was already nearly half-painted. Jim kept their visit brief to allow Rob to return to his work.

He was relieved that Rob seemed to have a new focus in his life since his near-death beating. Jim truly hoped that Rob would find a way to get the old boat up and running. However, Jim knew that in addition to paint, it would likely take several thousand dollars to properly weatherproof the hull and make it genuinely seaworthy.

Once home, Jim started his usual routine. He was not surprised to discover a rejection letter from the automobile insurance company that he had interviewed with in Ellingford, as he had never sent them a courtesy letter thanking them for the interview. He now felt a bit embarrassed and unprofessional by not sending such a letter. He wondered if the interviewer had felt at all slighted by not having received a thank you letter, in the same way Jim felt slighted by not receiving a rejection letter or return phone call from Mr. Gordon at Paramount Insurance.

Jim received only one email of interest. It was from Jake, suggesting that they go out to dinner because his wife had pressured him into bowing out of the fishing expedition that had been scheduled for the next weekend.

# CHAPTER TWENTY-FOUR

That Friday night, Jim sat in a corner booth of Big Bill's Steakhouse and Barbecue. It was an unusually decorated place, with various steer horns and antlers hanging on the walls and horse saddles mounted on posts that served as bar stools. He started a second cigarette as he anxiously awaited the arrival of Jake Gianni.

Soon Jake appeared and took a seat opposite Jim. Jake stood about six feet tall and had an olive complexion, a high and tight haircut accentuating his black hair, and steely grayish-blue eyes.

"Sorry I'm late, chief," Jake said.

"No problem."

"Hey, sorry again about bailin' on the fishin' trip. Joy's not ready for me to take a weekend furlough from the triplets yet. She said that if I'd gone, she would've changed the locks."

"That's all right. Maybe next year."

Jake nodded at Jim's understanding but looked demoralized nonetheless. "Having triplets is like nothing I imagined. It was kinda fun goin' to the prenatal ultrasounds, but now that they're here and I'm losing sleep hours at a time—that's a real drag."

"How's Joy holdin' up?"

"Man, I tell you, she's not the same girl that I married. I came home from work the other night, and we got into this huge fight. It's like I don't even know her anymore."

"What happened—if you don't mind my askin'?"

"Nah, that's okay. I had just gotten home from workin' a double shift on the ambulance and was full of shit from some ol' gomer I had to catheterize. Soon as the guy drops his pants on the stretcher, his ass explodes with the most foul diarrhea ever. So, what do you think Joy does when I get in?"

"What's that?"

"She asks me to change the triplets' diapers because she's too tired. I told her I was full of shit from work and asked if she could just do it herself."

"Probably not a good move on your part, huh?"

"Yeah, you'd think I'd asked her to give birth all over again."

"So whadshe do?"

"Completely fuckin' flipped. It's like I uncorked an angry Diaper Genie or somethin'. One second she's cryin' and the next she's hittin' me with shitty diapers from the garbage. I guess it would've been easier to just keep my mouth shut and change the little buggers myself."

"Man, sorry to hear it."

Jake nodded again and poured a beer from the pitcher that was on their table.

"How's work going otherwise?" Jim asked.

"Not bad—just busy. I've been doin' a lot of double shifts to try to keep up with the bills," he replied. "You know, sometimes

I regret not going to nursing school with you and Chris. Man, I could be makin' almost double what I'm makin' now."

"You would've been miserable stuck in a classroom all that time. An adrenaline junkie like yourself needs to be jumpin' out of airplanes or screamin' down the highway with lights and sirens blarin'.'"

"Yeah, I guess you're right. Say, how's work goin' for you?"

"I dunno—not bad, I guess. I mean, the job's pretty low-key most of the time, but it's not really what I wanna be doing. I'm kinda bummed that this swank job I interviewed for in Manhattan didn't pan out. Dude, I'm dying to work in the city again."

"You ever do a targeted mail campaign?"

"Nah, what's that?"

"It's when you send out resumes and cover letters to companies that you think you might wanna work for. Joy did one years back and landed a great job with a company in Ellingford. You should give her a call. I'm sure she'll point you in the right direction."

"Thanks, I think I'll give it a shot."

Suddenly an enormous waitress with a giant and outdated bouffant hairdo appeared at their table to take their order. They both ordered Big Bill's famous triple cheeseburger with everything on it and a side order of his lattice-cut sweet potato fries.

"Hey, man, I saw Holly's engagement announcement in the paper last weekend," Jake said.

"No shit. How'd she look?"

"Not bad. I mean, she wasn't lookin' all psycho with black clothes and dark makeup—or anything weird like that."

"Good for her. You know, I never saw her Goth side until after we slept together. I guess you don't know someone's true colors 'til you sleep together."

"Nah, you don't know someone's true colors 'til you marry them and have a buncha kids."

"Great—I'll have to remember that," Jim said jokingly.

Jake laughed, then asked, "You got a smoke?"

"Yeah, but I thought that you quit."

"I did, but it's been so fuckin' stressful—with the lack of sleep and all—that I gotta have some outlet. Some days, it seems like nicotine and caffeine are the only things that get me through the day."

"Yeah, I know whatcha mean—well, except for the lack of sleep from babies."

Jake chuckled, and Jim slid the pack of cigarettes and lighter across the table. As they were enjoying their smokes, the behemoth waitress appeared with their food. At once they began devouring the burgers, which were dripping with hot cheese.

"Man, this is a killer burger!" Jim exclaimed with his mouth loaded with food.

"Betcha never had one this big, not even in Colorado," Jake replied.

"You're probably right," Jim replied, finishing his mouthful. "Hey—speaking of Colorado, I just got an email from Maria's brother."

"How's he doin'?" Jake asked.

"Fuckin' pissed. He just found out their uncle dodged the feds during a drug bust in Colombia. The first solid lead on the whereabouts of this dirtbag since Maria's murder, and he fuckin' gets away."

"I didn't know her uncle was a rapist, killer, *and* a drug dealer."

"They're not sure if he's a dealer, but he has friends who definitely are. Man, it took Maria's family years of beggin' relatives for someone to get the balls to give up his location. So, once Maria's dad called the feds, they raided this cartel's compound and found the scumbag's wallet in a garden near the exit. And you'll never guess what was in it."

"What's that?"

"A picture of Maria in her cheerleading uniform."

"Shit, that sucks!" Jake exclaimed.

"Totally sucks—but at least they had the decency to give the picture back to her folks."

An awkward silence ensued as they ate their burgers and fries. After a couple of minutes, Jake asked Jim if he was all right. Jim said that he was. *Another white lie,* Jim thought while clearing his throat to conceal his true emotions. The remainder of their visit was occupied with small talk about Chris, Michele's wedding, cars, and catching fish at some undetermined time in the future.

Once Jim returned home, he deviated from his usual routine and did something that he occasionally did whenever he was feeling down or depressed: He looked at his photo album. He poured himself a small glass of bourbon on the rocks for his trip down memory lane. The early pictures from his childhood, of which there were three to four dozen, brought back pleasant recollections of a carefree existence in the wide-open spaces of southern Colorado, where time moved at a slower pace than on the East Coast. His high school pictures were likewise memorable, even the bittersweet ones of Maria. Tonight, however, seeing her in her beautiful blue prom dress made him feel sad and old.

*How many more Marshas am I going to have to date before I find another Maria? Will I ever get married? Will I ever have a family of my own?*

The pictures following high school became sparser, as Jim usually did not do his own photography but relied on loved ones to give him their duplicates. He only had about fifteen pictures from his four years in the Army and about two dozen from nursing school (most of which were of Holly and him). Although not the love of his life, Holly Goodwin was a stunningly beautiful girl in her own right, but she was far too emotionally volatile and complex for Jim.

# CHAPTER TWENTY-FIVE

All weekend Joy's concept of a targeted mail campaign intrigued Jim, and he decided that he would launch one of his own for prominent healthcare companies in the city. His self- imposed deadline was to get the letters out by the end of the third quarter, in hopes that some companies might be hiring for the fourth.

Jim started the new workweek with a renewed sense of purpose, as the impending letter campaign was looming large in his thoughts. He arrived at Wanda's to find her a bit in distress.

"Howdy, Wanda. How goes it?"

"No good, Jimmy. No good," she replied.

"What's bothering you?"

"Got pain in my rectum. It's been really sharp."

"How long have you had it?"

"Off and on for a couple of days now."

Jim didn't wish to inspect it, but he did want to explore the subject further. "Do you want me to set you up an appointment to get it checked out?"

"Nah, I'm sure it'll pass."

"You hearing any more voices?" Jim softly inquired.

"Yeah, they keep telling me that I'm a no-good dirty whore and that they're going to get me," she replied nervously.

"How long have you been hearing those voices?"

"For about a couple of days or so."

"Are they getting more or less frequent?"

"They're not constant. Just pretty steady, though."

"Well, please let us know if the voices or rectal pain gets worse."

She nodded, and then they wrapped up their visit.

Soon Jim found himself back in Sir Richard's laboratory. Richard was confident about the way his zoning appeal had gone but anxious to get news from his lawyer about the outcome of the appeal, as they hadn't made a ruling at the hearing. Jim quickly discovered that Sir Richard was also frantic about a strange new turn in his research.

"Say, Sir Richard, what are you doing with all of these transparent pyramids on your tables?"

"Why, these are all prism prototypes that I'm using to transmit light at different angles and intensities to hopefully unlock the secrets of the true light that came before the darkness."

"Have you started doing your experiments yet?"

"Yes, I am about one-quarter of the way through testing them."

"Well, please make sure that there's nothing flammable next to where the light exits the prisms," Jim politely suggested.

"Rubbish. I have never set my lab on fire, and I'm certainly not going to start doing so now!"

Sensing Richard felt insulted, Jim asked a question about the results. "Say, have you come to any conclusions based on your testing so far?"

"Nothing definitive, but I am starting to believe that the original Paramatter pyramid might be the pedestal of the entire universe!"

"What makes you think that, Sir Richard?"

"Because of the evidence gleaned by the very existence of ancient Egyptian pyramids."

"How's that?" Jim queried.

"Gravitational lensing. The Paramatterical pyramid acted like a prism through which the true light passed. Thus, this light, along with an image of the pyramid, could have also been visible in our own atmosphere to the ancient Egyptians. Just as my experimental prisms are designed to unlock the route that allows the true light to flow, the original Paramatterical pyramid broadcasted a large image of itself from the vantage point at the tip of the pyramid looking down. That image must have overshadowed all of the clouds and perhaps even the moon itself! The ancient Pharaohs must have been completely captivated looking up into the sky and viewing the image of something so awesome that they simply had to reproduce it themselves!"

Jim was perplexed by these remarks, and Sir Richard could tell by the look on his face. "I can see that you are skeptical, my young man. Tell me, what are your reservations?"

"Well, if the Earth was so close to the original light flowing through the tip of the Paramatter pyramid, as observed by the ancient Egyptians, wouldn't our planet have been burned up by its intensity?"

"That is the beauty of gravitational lensing! The original and true Paramatterical pyramid could have been billions and billions of light-years away during the dawn of time when the true light was shining through it like a prism. However, another celestial object must have come between the Paramatterical pyramid and our Earth. Therefore, I believe that this intervening celestial body acted like a lens to project an image of the Paramatterical pyramid and its light onto our sky, the image of which would otherwise have been unseen if it were not for that planetary object. Once Mother Nature moved that planetary magnifying glass from between the earth and the Paramatterical pyramid, the awesome image of the pyramid disappeared from our sky. Similar research has been done on gravitational lensing by scientists studying solar eclipses."

After a few more minutes of discussing Sir Richard's theories, their visit ended, and Jim was on his way to Phil's.

Once at the YMCA, Jim was disappointed to see Phil unkempt again and in denial of his depression. He politely refused his medication, and Jim reluctantly accepted his refusal, although he did attempt to cajole him a little bit before accepting it.

On the way to Sally's, Jim decided to call Rose about Phil.

"Hey, Rose, this is Jim. Sorry to bother you, but I got a problem."

"Shoot, what's up?"

"Well, it's Phil. He's been refusing his meds for a while now, and Vicky said that we'll probably have to discharge him," Jim replied.

"Yeah. Actually, Vicky talked to me about it the other day, and she's right. If he goes to the end of this week without taking his meds, we'll have no choice but to cut him loose."

"Isn't there anything else we could do?"

"You know, I don't believe so, but let me think about it, and I'll get back to you."

"Thanks a lot, Rose. I appreciate it."

"No problem. I'll call you later in the week."

At Sally's, Jim found Walter in his recliner and Sally in the living room listening to Christmas Carols. She seemed exceedingly happy, as a menthol cigarette was dangling from her mouth.

"Hey, Sal. How are you?" Jim asked.

"Great! Jesus gave me a pack of menthols before he left for Mexico. He says he's hopin' to bring his brothers and sisters back to the Valley with him!"

Jim smiled and said, "Don't be surprised if it takes some time. You know sometimes it can take a while for a shepherd to round up his flock."

"Well, hopefully, I'll have his throne finished by the time they all get back. That way he can let them sit on it too!"

"I'm not trying to bum you out or anything—it just might take several months for the whole flock to migrate here," Jim said tactfully.

"That's okay. I can wait."

"Are you ready for your pills?"

She nodded enthusiastically, then the two completed their visit.

Jim soon found out that Mike was out at his Uncle Joe's. Betty offered to take the envelope, but given Mike's recent seizure, Jim tactfully insisted on taking it directly to Mike. Betty obliged by giving Jim the address.

Arriving at St. Monica's, Jim was annoyed to find Maureen sleeping in front of the television. He headed directly upstairs.

Nick was agitated and said that he had to get his pills at once, as he was about to be on his way to a special and earlier AA meeting. Jim was more than happy to oblige, and soon he was at Lucinda's door.

Lucinda beckoned Jim to enter, and he did to find her hitting a heavy bag in her gym room. Her body glistened with sweat as she repeatedly and purposefully landed hard punches against the bag.

After Jim was in the room for a moment, she suddenly said, "Put 'em up, pal!"

Jim did, and Lucinda began landing alternate punches against his palms. Her wet face was focused and intense as she berated Jim with repeated punches.

"Not bad. You're a regular Mia St. John," Jim said.

After a few more punches, she stopped and then took a mouthful of water from a nearby water bottle.

"When and where did you get the bag?" Jim asked.

"There's a sporting goods store a few blocks from the Dawg. I got it with the money I made from Boobiepalooza."

"Dare I ask what that is?" Jim said with a hint of sarcasm.

"It's an event held at the Dawg around this time every year. They import dozens of strippers who are DD or better. All those big boobies really command a huge crowd, and with all those *tetas* in one place, it's an unbelievable cash cow! Man, they had this new Greek girl debut, and her bouncy fun bags totally brought down the house!"

Jim coughed for a moment, then asked sarcastically, "And all you got from this big event was a punching bag?"

"Nah, the bag is the only thing that I needed or wanted. I put the rest of the money in a short-term CD."

"Thoughts of saving up for masseuse school?"

"I'd probably hurt someone if I became a masseuse," she replied laughingly. "You know, I'm really not sure what I want to do with it. I'll guess I just save it up for a rainy day in the meantime."

After a few more minutes of banter, they concluded their visit, and Jim found himself next to Rob's ship. Rob was earnestly scraping large patches of old paint from the ship's hull in preparation for sanding and repainting it. He didn't offer any unusual complaints, and Jim was quickly on his way to Mike's Uncle Joe's.

Once there, Jim noticed Mike loading some lumber into his uncle's large pickup truck.

"Hey, Mike. How ya doin'?" Jim asked.

"Just getting Uncle Joe ready for a new job in the morning," Mike replied.

"How are you feeling?"

"Bummed out since Penelope won't talk to me anymore. This was the first girlfriend I've had since losing my apartment after the accident. I thought maybe we had a chance for a future together. Now she won't even talk to me."

"Why'd you lose your apartment?"

"Well, I was laid up for a while after my fall and got behind on my rent. My landlord wouldn't cut me any slack, and my mom wouldn't lend me any rent money—so I moved back home," he said with frustration evident in his voice.

"Have you been going to those TBI support groups still?"

"Yeah, but none of those people lost their housing—their freedom—at a young age because of their brain injuries. They just can't relate."

"Well, if you ever need to talk to someone, please let me know, and I can set something up."

"Nah, but thanks, anyway."

Soon their visit ended, and Jim was back in his apartment, undertaking his typical evening activities. There wasn't any mail other than a quick update from Jenny announcing that professional-grade fireworks would be used at the end of the reception, as Stan had a client in Japan who could get them cheap. *That'll be a nice way to wrap things up,* Jim thought. Soon, his thoughts drifted to his impending letter campaign. He planned on heading into New York the following Monday to kick things off by visiting the public library to research the Fortune 500 healthcare companies that he wished to target. Jim figured he'd probably tool around Greenwich Village afterward before heading home.

# CHAPTER TWENTY-SIX

His trip to the city the following week was quick and exhilarating, but he ended up spending all of the day in the library doing research and never made it to the Village.

Jim checked his voice mail as he got ready for work on Tuesday. There was a message from Rose indicating that Joanne had talked to Phil and that Phil was now ready to take his medications again. Jim later learned that Joanne, a former Harmony nurse, had the same demeanor as Phil's former wife and that Joanne's father had been a veteran agent with the GBI. Phil's family had moved from Georgia when Phil and his brother were toddlers during the early '60s to escape the brutal treatment that their father's generation had suffered. Nonetheless, Phil had always enjoyed talking to Joanne about Georgia, as he did have a few idyllic memories from his toddlerhood and he also enjoyed hearing sleuthing stories about her dad. Jim was impressed that Rose had the shrewdness and insight to enlist the help of a former employee to resolve the matter.

Once at Wanda's apartment, she appeared frazzled to Jim. Wanda continued to complain of rectal pain, as well as hearing derogatory voices. She refused any medical attention for her pain. Before leaving her apartment, Jim discreetly checked the medical tape that he had previously applied over the rat hole to ensure that it was still intact.

At Richard's, Jim found him even more distraught than Wanda had been. He could immediately detect it in Sir Richard's facial expression.

"What's wrong, Sir Richard?"

"I just got word from my lawyer that we lost the appeal."

"Sorry to hear that."

"This ruins everything. He said it will cost at least another two thousand dollars for me to appeal it to the next level. I just don't have the money for the appeal, my research, and then construction costs should I win the appeal. I would have to borrow it from my cousin in Iowa, and that's assuming he would be willing to give it to me. I just can't keep working nights anymore—it's killing me. Besides, I can feel my neighbors' prying infrared eyes spying on me and my research. This is terrible, my boy!"

Jim thought for a few moments. As he peered out of a window in the railcar's laboratory, he noticed several bundles of bricks and large lead sheets lying on Richard's lawn.

"How tall are those lead sheets?"

"I'm not exactly sure. Probably twelve to fifteen feet," he replied.

"You expect to make some money once you discover Paramatter?"

"I'm sure discovering the blueprint of all that *is* will yield tremendous financial gain," Richard replied.

"Why don't you just lean the lead plates against the wall of the laboratory until you complete your research? Then, once you're done, you will acquire the money to pursue an appeal and also to have your wall properly completed."

Richard seemed unfazed by Jim's suggestion, but then replied, "Genius! Sheer genius, my boy! I'll call a contractor today to move the plates into position!"

Jim was happy for Richard, and their visit concluded on an optimistic note.

Soon Jim found himself at Phil's door, and Phil answered still looking messy and unmotivated. True to his promise to Joanne, however, Phil took his pills without any fuss. Their visit was fairly brief and somewhat to the point, and soon Jim was smoking his usual cigarette while driving to Sally's.

Once at Sally's, Jim found her in an agitated mood.

"What's wrong, Sally?"

"That damned Walter spilled beer on the pack of menthols that Jesus gave me. He said it was a mistake, but I know it wasn't."

"It was a mistake, you pathetic moron! I wouldn't waste beer just to spite you!" Walter retorted from the other room.

"Hey, Walter, how 'bout not calling Sally names while I'm here? It doesn't make my job any easier," Jim interjected, appealing to Walter's bureaucratic work ethic.

After an awkward pause, Walter replied, "Sorry, pal. Sometimes it just really pisses me off that she thinks that I'm always out to get her."

*You really are out to get her most of the time,* Jim thought.

"It doesn't matter," Sally said. "Santa says that Jesus will bring me more goodies from Mexico."

"Are you hearing or seeing anything else unusual?"

"Santa's not unusual. He's got elves. Jesus has angels. Angels from Jesus and elves from Santa—they'll bring me menthols. They'll bring me goodies from Mexico. Elves aren't unusual—angels aren't unusual. Are they, Jim?"

"Nope. I'm just wondering if you are hearing or seeing anything other than elves and angels," he sheepishly replied.

"You think I'm crazy, just like Walter, don't you?" she said with tears welling up in her eyes.

"No, no, no. Rose just makes me ask these questions to everyone—because sometimes people need to change their medicine to hear and see the right things."

Sally sobbed heavily, then nodded her head, recognizing that Jim wasn't out to get her like Walter was. Jim quickly ended their visit to avoid any further confrontations with Sally.

Jim's visit with Mike was brief, as Mike was still sullen about his ended relationship with Penelope.

At St. Monica's, Jim found June on the couch doing some knitting.

"Hey June, how are you?"

"Great. How are you?"

"Pretty good. Where's everybody?"

"Upstairs and on the boat," she replied.

"Thanks," Jim responded as he turned to leave the room.

A couple of minutes later, Jim found himself at Nick's table.

"Son, have you finally decided to give up all you have and join the ranks of the Right Reverend Roberts?"

Jim, hoping to completely distract Nick, asked, "Any further prophecies about the man in the corner?"

Strangely, Jim's diversion worked this time.

"He's shudderin'! He's rockin' with fear and regret! His days are numbered!"

"Well, please keep me posted about this prophecy—it's very insightful," Jim said, trying to keep Nick's visit brief.

Nick nodded, and then Jim successfully diverted Nick's attention to taking his medication.

Soon Jim was in the apartment of the lovely Lucinda and much more relaxed because of that.

"Hey Jimmy, my man! What's shakin'?" Lucinda inquired.

"Same ol', same ol'. What's shaking with you?"

"My knockers first thing in the morning without my bra!" she said while vigorously shaking her shoulders and chest.

Jim felt himself getting red with embarrassment as Lucinda laughed loudly. "Any more voices or visions?" he asked.

"None this week. I can usually tell when they're finishing up. No visions. Hopefully, the lullaby of my baby brother won't be back 'til next summer."

"That's great. Please let us know if you hear anything more at any time."

She nodded knowingly, and they finished up their visit with the necessary activities.

Jim's visit with Rob on the boat was brief and without any problems. Shortly afterward, Jim was back home enjoying his bourbon and final cigarette of the day while leisurely surfing the net for more insight on how to improve his resume, cover letters, references, and mission statement. *Now, this is the type of ammunition I need to win this campaign,* Jim mused with the determination of a young Patton. After printing out the best articles, Jim quickly fell asleep.

# CHAPTER TWENTY-SEVEN

The remainder of the workweek sailed by without any hassles or complications. Jim looked forward to continuing preparations for his letter campaign during his upcoming two days off. On his first day off, he met with a career counselor recommended by Jake's wife to tweak his cover letters, resume, and mission statement. He felt a new sense of empowerment and optimism after the meeting.

During his second day off, he began printing some new resumes, as well as specifically addressing some cover letters for the Fortune 50 companies that he was targeting. He planned his campaign in three phases: the first batch of cover letters and resumes would be sent to Fortune 50 companies; then the second batch to Fortune 100 companies; and the final batch to Fortune 500 companies. He had several companies that he had researched at the New York Public Library that were to his liking. As it was already the middle of August, Jim was a bit concerned that he wouldn't be able to complete the entire campaign by the end of the third quarter. He figured that he'd be in good shape if at least he could get the Fortune 50 companies done by the end of the month.

After his days off, Jim's shift began at Wanda's, where he found her shaking, disheveled, and frantic.

"What's wrong, Wanda?" Jim nervously inquired.

"Fat, little gnomes are trying to get me!"

"What do you mean?"

"Every time I start fallin' asleep, they creep up on me and say that I'm a 'no-good dirty whore!' Then, they tell me if I fall asleep, they're gonna get me in the ass! They say they're gonna get me in the ass until my guts spill out! I'm a filthy, no-good dirty whore, and they're gonna get me in the ass until my guts spill out!" She screamed hysterically.

"Wanda, please, try to calm down. When was the last time that you got some sleep?"

"I dunno. The pain in my rectum—it's fuckin' unbearable! The evil gnomes are gonna get me in the ass until my guts spill out!" she wailed again.

Suddenly, Bubba started to screech incoherently, mimicking the screaming coming from Wanda. The cacophony was horrific. Wanda then sat down, barely making the chair, and continued screaming and crying to the point of near hyperventilation.

Jim quickly took out his agency cell phone and called for an ambulance. Wanda grew pale and tired, and her screaming and crying became more intermittent while the ambulance was en route. Once there, the paramedics started an IV and then rushed her off to the hospital.

Jim was unnerved as he made his way to Richard's. He devoured a couple of cigarettes during his ride, trying to refocus for the rest of his shift.

Richard's mood also was a bit frenetic, and he eagerly invited Jim into the laboratory.

"I'm getting close. I can feel it!" Sir Richard said jubilantly.

*The Paramatter*, Jim presumed to himself. He then asked, "Sir Richard, are you seeing or hearing anything unusual today?"

"I saw another microcosmic universe last night shortly after sunset!"

"Was it inside your hedges again?"

"No, my boy, I saw it inside my heart! It was the most vibrant microcosmic universe that I've seen to date. It was aqua-colored with the most sensational golden constellations swirling inside of it in perfect harmony. And with each passing beat of my heart, it shined brighter and spun faster!"

"Are you having any chest pain or shortness of breath?" "No, it's nothing like that. This is the universe's way of telling me that my heart is now pure to receive the secrets of Paramatter!"

Jim hesitated before speaking and then gently asked, "Sir Richard, would you mind if I checked your pulse and blood pressure?"

Richard immediately grimaced with annoyance but acquiesced to Jim's request.

After checking Richard's vital signs, Jim said, "They're perfectly normal. Hey, I hope that you weren't offended by my checking your heart. It's just that your story was so unusual that I wanted to make sure that you were okay."

Richard nodded sympathetically and said, "I know that you're just looking out for my well-being, so no offense taken, my good man."

"Well, if you ever do experience any chest pain or shortness of breath that doesn't go away quickly, please call an ambulance."

Richard agreed, and they concluded their visit shortly afterward.

At Phil's, Jim found Phil watching a culinary program in which the host was baking an assortment of Italian pastries.

"Hi, Phil. How are you?"

"Not bad. And yourself, boy?"

"Pretty good. You like baking?"

"Nah, I just like consuming the final product," Phil replied.

"Me too," Jim said. "What's your favorite?"

"Anything from Mario's."

"Mario's off the Parkway?" Jim asked.

"Yeah. You've heard of it?"

"Who hasn't?"

"I love that place! Debbie and I went there a few times when we were dating. It's a beautiful ride in the fall when all the leaves are changing colors, and the Sicilian owner seems so friendly— he treats everyone like family."

"Yeah, and his cannoli are out of this world!" Jim exclaimed.

Phil nodded with a nostalgic smile on his face, then they ended their visit after he took his meds and they had a few more minutes of idle chatter.

As he entered Sally's usually malodorous home, the smell of wet paint permeated Jim's nostrils as he made his way toward the living room. Walter was conspicuously absent. When Jim entered the living room, he found Sally splattered with fresh yellow paint and her makeshift throne dripping with the same.

"Looking good, Sally."

"Thanks, Jimmy," she replied.

Jim peered at the closed windows at the end of the room, then said, "Sally, you probably should open some windows so the paint fumes can escape."

"The windows are swelled up from the summer heat."

"Do you mind if I try to open them?"

"Nope."

Jim went to the first window and tried his best to open it. It was immovable and felt like it hadn't been opened in years. He experienced the same result upon attempting to open the other windows.

"Say, Sally, where's Walter?" Jim inquired.

"Went to the pub with some friends or something," she replied.

"What do you say we move the throne to the back porch to let it dry out before Walter returns?"

"That's a great idea. Can you move it for me?"

Jim looked at it for a moment, then replied, "You bet."

He then donned a pair of non-sterile medical gloves, carefully picked up the piece, and headed toward the back porch, where he placed it in a sunny corner.

"Thanks, Jimmy, you're the best. Santa, Jesus, and Jimmy!" she shouted gleefully.

"I'm not quite in their league, but thanks, anyway," Jim replied.

They then re-entered the house and concluded their visit with the usual blessing of the pills and signing of the MAR.

Jim was running a bit behind schedule between helping Sally, and he was hoping to make it to St. Monica's on time to avoid an argument with Nick.

At Betty's house, he found Mike in the backyard chopping some wood.

"A little early to be chopping firewood, don't you think?" Jim said jokingly.

Mike stopped, glanced up at him with a look of annoyance, and then replied, "This is the only thing that keeps me sane sometimes. Just splitting these stupid logs into pieces."

"What's bugging you?" Jim asked in a gentle yet serious tone of voice.

"Same old stuff. I hate living here. Got no girlfriend. Got no money for an apartment, and I can barely afford my car."

"You don't make that much working for Uncle Joe?" Jim asked.

"Like I said, it makes me enough money to pay for my car, and that's about it."

"Is there any better job that you could get?"

"Who knows. I've got no focus and little thinking skills left since my accident, so it's not like anyone is going to offer me any high-paying job without any higher brain power between my ears."

"What about starting that landscaping business that you told me about before? Couldn't your Uncle Joe help you get set up?"

"Nah, he barely makes enough money to pay his own bills. My mother has enough money, but God forbid that she should lend me any—because then I'd be able to get out from under her thumb and out of her house."

Jim nodded sympathetically, and then they finished up their business.

Arriving at St. Monica's, June greeted Jim and informed him that Lucinda had gone out with Rita and Nick had gone to an impromptu church meeting. Jim was pleased to hear that. He gave her their envelopes and then exited to see Rob.

Jim found him on the boat. Once onboard, he discovered Rob sitting on a folding chair in his boxer shorts. A crumpled summer dress and several crumpled beer cans lay scattered in the immediate vicinity.

"Shane?" Jim quietly inquired as he approached the chair.

"Yes, me lad."

"Where's Rob?" Jim politely queried.

"He's too much of a pantywaist to mount such a majestic vessel."

With such clear evidence of Shane's intoxication, Jim didn't even dare offer Shane Rob's medications. He chatted nonchalantly for a few minutes, then departed without Shane ever questioning why Jim was visiting the boat in the first place.

With Lucinda and Nick being absent, Jim finished his shift more or less on schedule. He savored a cigarette as the full moon shone brightly on the quiet country road that he routinely took as a shortcut back to his apartment. It wasn't shorter, but it was usually quieter and more scenic than the city streets or highway routes that he could have taken.

Once home, Jim deviated slightly from his usual routine in that he printed out a few more cover letters before having his bourbon and final cigarette of the day.

# CHAPTER TWENTY-EIGHT

The remainder of Jim's workweek was uneventful, and his attention and efforts were largely distracted by the fledgling letter campaign.

Another scorching August day was underway as Jim got ready for his shift with a large cup of iced coffee.

Before arriving at Wanda's, he learned in a voice mail from Cindy that Wanda had just been released from the hospital after nearly a week. She had undergone a hemorrhoidectomy in addition to being observed for her worsening psychosis. They had discharged her with a new order for an increased amount of clozapine. Jim was able to simply split a 50-milligram pill of clozapine taken from the supply in Wanda's medicine drawer to add to her existing dose to equal the newly ordered amount. The new dose wouldn't be available from the pharmacy until the next day.

The visit with Wanda was brief, and she denied any rectal pain or problems, as well as denying any voices. She was profusely thankful for Cindy feeding Bubba every day while she'd been in the hospital. It was the type of situation that justified Rose's copying nearly every patient's house key to be kept by the agency.

Jim entered the lab and to his surprise saw several glass pyramids affixed to the ceiling with the tips pointing down. He also noticed numerous prisms laid out on the lab tables.

Sir Richard immediately began, "Measuring all angles of my prisms and intensities of different wavelengths of light flowing through those angles has gotten me no closer to finding the true light. If only I could see all that *is* from the tip of the pyramid, then all my equations would balance out! Then, the ancient secrets of the universe would be revealed to me, and I could help save our world! My equations and experiments are simply not adding up. There must be some angle that I'm missing!" After a brief pause, the expression on Sir Richard's face changed from frustration to excitement. "You!" Richard exclaimed. "I need your opinion! You rightly figured out the solution to hiding my research by positioning the lead shields against my windows. Now, I would be most honored and grateful if you would take a look through my best prism to see what angle I am missing."

Jim asked if he could pick it up, to which Richard responded yes. After picking up the prism, Jim held it up to the light and began twirling it around like a Rubik's Cube. "So, you've passed light through every angle?" he asked inquisitively.

"By God, yes, my good man!"

"Well, the only thing that I can think of is that, maybe, the true light didn't pass through the pyramid but rather escaped from the pyramid itself."

"Brilliant, my young man! Simply brilliant! I shall thoroughly explore this new angle!"

After a few more minutes of chatter, Jim was on his way to his next visit.

Once at Phil's, Jim found him watching a documentary about racism while he sat in front of a small fan that circulated the lukewarm air generated by his secondhand air conditioner.

"Hey, Phil. How come you're not down at the pool today?" Jim queried.

"It's busted. Something about the filter not working and the chlorine levels being too high."

"Whatcha watchin'?"

"Some docudrama about racism in America. Sadly, there's still so much of it around. You think folks would've learned something from the civil rights pioneers of the '50s and '60s."

"Yeah, and it's not just neo-Nazis promulgating this crap, either."

"You bet. I mean, just look at the upper tiers of every major institution—politics, business, education, and even sports—and people of color are still in the minority."

"Just take sports alone. Look how long it took for black quarterbacks, managers, and executives to get widespread acceptance," Jim said.

"Man, when I was growing up quarterbacks were pretty much all white."

Jim nodded his head with interest.

Phil continued, "What's flat-out sad is the blatant racism that some trailblazers still face today as they break into the upper ranks. Look at Colin Powell and Michael Steele, two public figures who have been berated by many Uncle Tom slurs during their long careers—and some of those slurs, sadly enough, coming from other people of color. With the way those statesmen are being treated, I don't know if we'll ever see a black president in our lifetime."

"So, what do you think can be done about it?" Jim asked.

"I don't think there are any easy answers, but an honest dialogue and education would be refreshing."

"Okay, but how can you teach about moral judgments in the current climate of political correctness?" Jim posed.

"What do you mean?" Phil asked.

"Dr. King said that he hoped his kids would be *judged* on the content of their character—how can we teach in school about any kind of judgment, much less character judgment, when tolerance is the mantra of the day?"

"But isn't the opposite true?" Phil quipped.

"How's that?"

"I don't think that Dr. King would want our teachers to be conveying the message that we should merely tolerate others. Tolerance is a poor substitute for love and respect. Regardless, in my experience, I believe that people judge and tolerate all of the time."

"How so?" Jim asked.

"Well, take my work as a trooper, for example. I had a matter of seconds, sometimes split seconds, to *judge* whether or not someone I pulled over posed a threat to me. After meeting the person, I then usually had several minutes to decide whether or not I could *tolerate* their attitude enough not to give them a ticket. I tell you, one thing that I never did was to accept any driver's personal interpretation of the speed limit," Phil replied with a brief chuckle.

"Well, I guess some things, like the speed limits, just aren't open to debate," Jim replied jokingly.

They bantered for a couple more minutes before their visit came to an end.

Sally's house reeked of cat urine, rotting food, and a noticeably musty scent wafting throughout all the rooms. Jim wished that he could smoke right then and there to overpower the foul stench that he was enduring, which was magnified by the summer's heat. The closest that Jim came to doing that was passing Walter, who was puffing on a cheap cigar in his recliner.

"Hey, Sally, how are you?" Jim asked.

"No good. Walter says Jesus is never coming back."

"What do you mean?"

"He got pinched by the friggin' feds, trying to smuggle drugs back into America!" Walter bellowed from the other room.

"No, he didn't—Jesus didn't get pinched for nothin'!" she shouted back.

"He's a no-good fuckin' mule! Instead of riding a mule—your savior became one himself! They found thirty packets of heroin inside his filthy intestines at JFK! It's true! Tony the barber told me, and that guy knows everything that goes on in this town!"

"Jesus ain't no mule! Jesus don't get pinched—he saves people!"

"Hey, Walter—" Jim began.

"Ah, don't bother, Jim. I'm not trying to tease her, but someone should tell her the truth about her so-called savior. I don't know why I bother, though. She'll just start believing in some other fairy-tale."

Sally got red with anger, but Jim managed to calm her down by reassuring her of the validity of her beliefs.

Jim's visit with Mike was brief, as Mike was still somewhat sullen and quiet about losing his girlfriend and living at home.

Once back in his car, Jim noticed he had received a voice mail from Stella asking him to meet her at the Silver Street Apartments so the two of them could then go to see a new patient in Ellingford. The new patient was being discharged from a nursing home with terminal cancer, and Stella wanted to pick up all of the patient's medications that she had been sent home with to take them back to the agency's office. The pills would then be doled out to her daily according to her doctor's instructions by Harmony's nurses. The Silver Street projects had been the hub of many gang-related crimes, including three murders in the past two years. The area was so bad that Rose refused to send any nurses out there during the evening shift.

After a fairly brief ride to the address that Stella had left on his voicemail, Jim met her at the multi-apartment complex. Jim's senses were heightened as they cautiously made their way to the new patient's place. After Stella did an initial nursing assessment, she gathered all of the patient's medications into a nondescript shopping bag. Jim was particularly nervous, as there were ten blister packs of Percocet, which totaled three hundred individual pills. Their street value was not insignificant.

As they left her apartment, Jim stuffed his right hand deep into his pocket to project the appearance of being sufficiently armed and ready to defend himself and Stella. Although he tightly gripped the handle of his .380 caliber pistol, he was careful not to have his finger anywhere near the trigger.

Soon they were back at their cars, and Stella thanked him for his escort. Jim was running only slightly behind schedule as he headed to St. Monica's.

After talking with June for a couple of minutes in the living room, Jim headed upstairs to see Nick.

"Hello, Nick, how are you?" Jim asked.

"Saved and delivered."

"Are you ready for your pills?"

"Are you ready to accept Christ as your Lord and Avenger?"

"My car's on the brink of falling apart, so I've gotta conserve my cash to fix it or get a new one."

"I think you have a demon."

"What do you mean?"

"A demon. A big, fat demon. Reluctance is his name."

"Are you having prophecies about demons now?"

"No, no, no! This is about you—you have a demon, and Reluctance is his name! He's a big, fat, lazy demon keeping you from Christ!" Nick replied with more animation now.

"Well, what would you suggest I do about it?"

"Deliverance! The Right Reverend Roberts can perform a cursory deliverance service for only $49.99!"

"How much is the complete package?" Jim inquired with a hint of sarcasm in his voice.

"Well, that would be a total of three sessions at $49.99 apiece."

*Great, I hope he doesn't go back to trying to convince me to give up all that I have for this charlatan,* Jim thought. "What kind of guarantee or warranty does the good reverend provide if Mr. Big, Fat, Lazy Demon returns?" Jim asked.

Nick looked flummoxed, then defensively replied, "If Reverend Roberts does it, there's no chance of it returning!"

"Just the same, I'd rather get my car situation squared away first before making any other monetary commitments," Jim replied. "Are you still having any prophecies about the shuddering man in the corner?"

"Yes, he's cold and shudderin'! He's rockin' back and forth on his buttocks! He's chantin' somethin', over and over and over again! His end is near! The ax is at the root of his tree!"

"How often are you having this prophecy?"

"Daily, but his days are numbered!"

"Well, please let me know if you have any changes with this prophecy, okay?"

Nick nodded, then they proceeded to finish their visit.

Soon Jim was in Lucinda's kitchen and watching her primp her makeup in front of a large hand mirror. She was wearing a florescent pink summer dress that tightly hugged every curve of her body.

"Going dancing with Rita?" Jim casually inquired.

"Nope. I've got a hot date!"

"Really? Good for you! What's his name?"

"Chad. He goes to the law school near New Haven," she replied.

"Yale?"

"Nah, he goes to Quackipiac or something like that. His friends told me the school's mascot is a Fighting Duck. Anyhow, it's in the next town over from Yale."

"Where did you meet him?"

"He was at the Dawg a few days ago for a bachelor party with one of his friends. They kept sending him up to the bar to get drinks. After a few rounds, he asked me for my number."

"Wow, that's great. I hope you have a fun time."

"Thanks, Jimmy. I'll try my best."

After a couple more minutes, Jim finished and was in the backyard with Rob. He was pleased to see that Shane was absent and that Rob was again focused on more productive endeavors. Jim was impressed that most of the bottom of the hull was now sanded. Rob didn't offer any complaints, and Jim cautioned him to keep well-hydrated while working on hot summer days.

Soon Jim was back in his car and enjoying a new cigarette with his air conditioner cranking at full blast. He decided to stop at Sully's for a cold beer and chili dog before going home.

# CHAPTER TWENTY-NINE

The rest of Jim's week unfolded without any major difficulties or problems. He was now facing the final days of August and was ready to launch the first wave of his letter campaign. To do so he decided to head down to the post office in the Village where he had rented a PO box earlier in the summer. He'd done so intending to use the PO box address on his resume rather than his less glamorous street address in the Valley. He hoped that prospective employers would gloss over the fact that it was a PO box and be more impressed that it was a Village address with a New York City postmark on the envelope. Besides, it was possible to live in the city and work in the Valley, as those locales were within driving distance of each other.

Since Wanda's hemorrhoidectomy, her voices had gradually returned, first as background chatter, then as full-fledged derogatory statements. As Jim pulled up to her curb, he noticed her sitting on it, wearing loose-fitting sweat clothes.

"Hey, Wanda, what's going on?" Jim asked.

"They're gone! I beat them! They're finally gone!"

"What do you mean?"

"I saw a big, bald gray man. He had black eyes and teeth. He was skulkin' around in the corners of my room. So, I say, 'Who the hell are you, and whaddya want?' Then, he says, 'I'm the master of your voices! You are a no-good, dirty, fuckin' whore who will never beat me!' So, I say, 'Fuck you! I'm not a dirty whore! Get the fuck outta here!' So, then I throw my cigarette at his face, and he starts screaming in agony!"

"You did what?"

"I threw my cigarette right at his ugly face!"

Jim paused to think for a moment when suddenly Wanda's front window shattered, and large flames leaped skyward.

*Oh, shit!* Jim then frantically scrambled for his cell phone to dial 911. "Say, Wanda, why don't we get across the street to get out of the way for the firemen?"

"Nah, I'm pretty comfortable," she replied, reaching into her sweatshirt pocket for another cigarette to light.

A couple of minutes transpired, and no fire trucks appeared yet. Even though they were about twenty feet away, Jim could feel the heat wafting from the growing inferno. A small crowd of neighbors began to congregate. One of the neighbors, a retired cop, speculated that as Wanda's apartment was right near the town line, the two towns' fire departments were probably bickering over whose department should respond.

Suddenly, a police cruiser arrived, and Jim began telling the officer what was happening. Next, an ambulance arrived, and then the faint wail of fire trucks could be heard in the distance.

Jim returned to Wanda as paramedics were taking her vital signs and starting an IV line. They picked her up off the curb and began escorting her to the ambulance.

Without thinking, Jim asked, "Hey Wanda, where's Bubba?"

"What? Oh, God, no! Bubba! Bubba!" she began screaming and flailing against the paramedics, who were still escorting her to the ambulance.

Several fire trucks soon pulled up, and Jim rushed over to a fireman and begged him to search for Bubba. By this time the ambulance had departed, and the fire crew was rapidly engaging a structure that was fully engulfed by flames. Taking a second look at the building, Jim was certain of Bubba's fate.

Again, Jim quickly consumed a couple of cigarettes on the way to Richard's.

After a brief jaunt through Sir Richard's rotunda, they arrived at his laboratory.

"So, have you had any luck researching to see if Paramatter flowed from inside the celestial pyramid?" Jim asked.

"Well, my mathematical equations aren't quite panning out yet, but I have a new theory about how the Paramatter came out of the pyramid. I've been thinking that since Paramatter is similar to light, it should also additionally have some properties of both mass and energy."

"How could that be?" Jim asked.

"It should be a plasmatic substance akin to lava, according to my preliminary calculations. Just as lava is the center of our earth, this prehistoric Paramatterical lava should likely be the center of our universe from which all celestial bodies sprung forth."

"Interesting. So, the Big Bang sounds a lot like a volcano," Jim remarked.

"Oh, my, yes! And once this celestial pyramid became too engorged with primordial plasmatic mass, it was ejaculated into the darkness. It was much more like a volcanic eruption than an atomic explosion. This Big Bang event created the dawn of time!"

"How did it do that?"

"As the plasmatic mass escaped from the pyramid, it did so at a predetermined rate, necessarily implicating time. This rate is represented by speed, and all speed requires time as part of its divisor, whether it's demonstrated in seconds, minutes, or hours. Even the speed of light is determined with an equation that requires time. That is, it's calculated at 186,000 miles *per second*."

"Wow, Sir Richard! Sounds like you're on to something!"

"I certainly hope so. All I need now is the math to prove it."

Jim wished him well and was soon en route to Phil's. On the way, Jim toyed with Richard's latest theory and thought to himself with amusement, *Maybe the speed limit is debatable sometimes.*

Inside Phil's room, Jim found him watching a cable news program. Nothing special, just news.

"Hey there, Phil. How ya doin' today?"

"Not bad, Jimmy. Just watching some news. It's so damn depressing, it makes me feel better about my situation."

"You know, Phil, I was runnin' some errands yesterday, and I just couldn't resist taking a short detour off the Parkway to Mario's."

"Really?"

"And once I was there, I had to buy something," Jim said as he reached into his book bag to retrieve a cellophane-wrapped, quarter-pound tray of cannoli and assorted pastries.

Phil immediately recognized the distinctive Mario's logo as Jim handed him the tray. Tears began filling up in Phil's eyes as he unwrapped it. He quickly popped a miniature cheesecake with blueberry topping into his mouth and closed his eyes, savoring the morsel with the intensity of a Yogi slipping into a karmic trance. "Oh, God, Jim. Thank you so much. Do you want some?"

"Nah, I had my fill yesterday. Thanks, though."

After Phil greedily consumed a tightly packed cannolo, they went on to finish their visit. Jim was pleased that the pastries had remained fresh in the cooler, which had been in his trunk.

Jim sucked down another cigarette, feeling a little bit better about his shift as he headed toward Walter's and Sally's.

Jim found Sally somewhat out of sorts. She seemed to be realizing that perhaps Walter was correct about her messiah's fate. Her homemade throne now sat in the corner, gathering dust and starting to show signs of feline abuse, as it appeared that the yellow backrest was being used as a scratching post. Their visit was brief, and soon Jim was on his way to Mike's.

Betty was home, but not Mike. When Jim arrived, she said Mike was still sulking about losing his Greek whore and that he was spending more time with Betty's brother, Joe. Jim thought better about giving Betty Mike's meds and instead told her that they would be given to him at Uncle Joe's. Jim's chat with Betty was short, as he was now catching up on the time that he'd lost with Wanda.

Within minutes Jim was at St. Monica's. June was working, and Nick and Rob were waiting for him in the kitchen. Nick was wearing a white T-shirt with blood-red initials that read,

"WWRRD?" He immediately stood up and approached Jim as he entered the kitchen.

"Hello, Nick, how are you?"

"Blessed and delivered, thank you."

"What does your T-shirt stand for?"

"'What would Reverend Roberts do?'"

"Any more prophecies about that man in the corner?" Jim quickly inquired.

"Oh, yes. It seems like it's gettin' clearer every day. He's shudderin' and cryin' while rockin' on his buttocks in the corner. There is distinct darkness around his eyes. He's chantin' something incoherently. His days are numbered! The ax is already at the root of his tree! He shall be smitten and stricken down for the heathen that he is!"

Jim nodded, feigning interest, hoping that Nick wouldn't segue into berating him for not being baptized and delivered by the Reverend Billy Bob. Luckily, his silence worked. As soon as Nick finished conveying his latest prophecy, he glanced down at his watch and demanded his pills so that he wouldn't be late to his AA meeting.

Rob then took his medication in turn and headed back to the boat in the yard to continue his work. Jim was glad that June had rounded up most of the patients in one place, as she had been lax in doing so for most of the summer. Even on a bad day, though, she was still preferable over the slothful Maureen. Jim thanked June, then headed upstairs to see Lucinda.

"Hey, chief! How ya doing?" Lucinda shouted playfully as Jim appeared at her screen door.

"Not bad. How 'bout you?"

"Fantastic!"

"Really? How come?"

"Chad. Man, he's really a terrific guy. He's the first one in a long time that doesn't see me like a piece of meat or a whack job."

"Wow, good for you!"

"Yeah, we've only been out a few times, but I've got a great feelin' about this guy."

"How far along is he with law school?"

"He's going into his fourth year. It's a part-time, evening program. Full-time law school is three years, but he works during the day in Manhattan as an investment banker and goes to school at night."

"It's amazing that he has time for anything else besides school and work," Jim said.

"He's a real go-getter and multitasker. I can't wait—he's coming up to Ellingford to stay with a buddy over Labor Day weekend. He's driving his BMW motorcycle here and said that we'd go for a nice long, romantic ride during his visit."

"Hopefully you'll get good weather for it."

"Geez, I sure hope so."

They chatted for a few more minutes, then finished up their visit.

Soon Jim was at Mike's Uncle Joe's, where he found Mike still in a funk. He denied any seizure activity or any new complaints, and Jim was quickly on his way home.

Before arriving at his apartment, he stopped in at Sully's for a quick black and tan to end his day.

# CHAPTER THIRTY

The remaining days of August passed quickly, and Jim was scheduled to work Labor Day weekend. Most of his patients were status quo, with the noticeable exception of Wanda, who was now committed to a locked-down and short-term care facility. It was Southbridge Manor. It did not have the frivolous frat house atmosphere of St. Monica's.

The first two days of Jim's weekend passed without any major problems, and Monday looked just as promising. Jim intended to mail out the second wave of letters for his campaign after the holiday weekend was over. He decided, however, not to mail them from New York and would take his chances at prospective employers viewing a Valley postmark on his correspondence.

Jim's visit with Wanda was stark, brief, and without complications. She remained heavily sedated and borderline catatonic. He thought about telling her that Bubba had escaped, that he'd flown away to heaven before the house went up in flames. On second thought, he decided not to. Wanda never talked about religion, and any fib Jim could say about Bubba's fate wouldn't bring him back. Although Jim did not enjoy being in a quasi-prison type facility, most of their staff seemed very pleasant, and they were accommodating to visiting nurses.

Soon, Jim arrived at Sir Richard's. As they entered the lab, Jim didn't see any pyramids whatsoever.

"Hey, Sir Richard, are you feeling okay today?"

"Why, goodness, yes! I'm more than okay! I believe that I discovered what has to be the tip of the pyramid last night!"

"Was it in your bushes or inside your body?"

"Not at all, my boy! I saw it within the dusky sky. What the biochemical prototypes and prisms couldn't reveal, the heavens did!"

"What exactly did you see, Sir Richard?"

"A galaxy that was almost overflowing with a spectacular garden of resplendent and never-ending colors. These colors were far beyond the visible spectrum of the rainbow! And as this uber kaleidoscopic cosmos was twirling around with a brilliant array of stars, asteroids, and comets, I noticed a pale rose star in the middle, and it was completely motionless. It was an unwobbling pivot. These colors were so mesmerizing that neither Monet nor any other Impressionist master could ever capture their beauty! The image was so astonishing that I just had to take a closer look. However, when I adjusted my telescope to zoom in, it completely disappeared! I searched the entire sky for hours, but it didn't return."

"I didn't know that you had a telescope," Jim said in a surprised tone of voice

"Yesterday after working on the prisms for hours, I decided to unpack my old telescope. I had been hoping to clear my mind by gazing at the night sky, and that's when I spotted it."

"Did the cosmos tell you anything, or did it touch you at all?"

"No, but it did make me realize that I now must look to the stars to unlock the secrets of Paramatter!"

Shortly afterward at Phil's, Jim found him watching ongoing cable news coverage of the Hurricane Katrina disaster. The two sat in front of the set, mesmerized by a group of hapless civilians stranded on a highway overpass.

"Who'd think that we'd see a bunch of Americans looking like ragged refugees again, after 9/11?" Phil remarked.

"Wow, talk about a massive failure of government response."

"Yessir, and at all levels, too. You'd think that after nearly three years of having a Department of Homeland Security that such a lackluster response to a catastrophe wouldn't've been possible."

"No kidding. And what the hell would've happened if it had been a dirty bomb instead of a natural disaster?"

"Those poor people would be completely screwed," Phil flatly replied.

After a few moments, Phil began the microwave ritual with the MAR before the visit concluded.

Soon Jim was in his car and inhaling a cigarette as he headed over to Sally's. Walter was out at the local pub, and Sally was in her usual spot on the couch watching another Christmas video.

"Hey, Sally, how are you?" Jim gently inquired.

"I miss my Jesus," she said in a strained tone of voice.

"Ah, try not to think about it. I'm sure he'll be back someday, Sal."

"But I don't think I'll ever get to see him sit on his throne," she said, pointing to the bucket and board structure that was now showing even more signs of deterioration.

"Well, you can repaint it before Christmas, can't you?"

"Nope. Walter threw my yellow paint out. He said it stunk too much."

*Shit, that paint was probably the freshest aroma around this place,* Jim thought.

"Well, let me tighten up the ropes in the meantime, Sally," Jim said and then went over to the structure to untie the knots, pull the ropes taut, and retie them.

"Wow, thanks, Jimmy! I love you! Santa loves you too!"

"Thanks, Sally, you, too."

Soon their visit was over, and Jim was on his way to St. Monica's, as Mike had received his envelope of evening medication in advance due to his sleeping overnight at his Uncle Joe's.

Upon arriving at St. Monica's, Jim discovered from June that Nick had gone to an AA picnic and that Rob had gone to a party at the recreation center. Jim left their envelopes with her, then headed up to Lucinda's.

Jim gently rapped on her screen door once there. Lucinda was heard from the living room laughing and telling him to "Hold on a minute." She arrived at the door wearing a black skirt and a white blouse that had its top three or four buttons undone. Her hair was completely disheveled, and her lipstick was askew.

"Hey, Jimmy! Come on in, pal!"

"Hey there, Lucinda. What's going on?"

"Not much. Me and Chad are just relaxing after taking a spin on his BMW motorcycle. I'd like you to meet him," she said as she turned and started walking toward the living room.

Jim followed and found a pale, wiry, blond-haired man sitting on her couch.

"Chad, this is my friend Jim," Lucinda said enthusiastically as she and Jim entered the living room.

"You must be the Quackipiac legal eagle. Pleased to meet you," Jim said, extending his hand to be shaken.

"That's *Quinnipiac*, pal," Chad replied with a strong tone of annoyance in his voice.

"Geez, I'm sorry—I didn't know how to—"

"Don't worry about it. People mispronounce it all the time," Chad interrupted while perfunctorily grasping and shaking Jim's hand.

"So, what do you do when you're not in school?" Jim asked.

"I'm an investment banker on Wall Street."

"Why the interest in going from the boardroom to the courtroom?"

"None. I just want the law degree to get further ahead in business."

"I used to work not too far from there last year as a case manager for a large insurance company," Jim said, hoping to get the guy to warm up to him.

"Why did you leave?" Chad asked with suspicion in his voice.

*Dammit! Why the hell did I bring that up?* Jim thought. He paused, then replied sheepishly, "I just missed working with patients."

Chad nodded vaguely, then subtly redirected his gaze toward the TV in the corner that was playing softly. Jim took the hint at Chad's disinterest in engaging him in anything but brief and superficial conversation. This was fine with Jim. During this brief and awkward pause, Lucinda suggested that she and Jim go to the kitchen to do their business. Jim and Chad exchanged an obligatory "nice to meet you" and "goodbye."

Once in the kitchen, Lucinda said, "Isn't he great, Jimmy?"

Jim nodded and smiled.

"He treats me so good, too. More like a Bond babe than a biker chick!"

"You wear a helmet when you ride with him?" Jim inquired, spying a dark helmet on her table.

"Nah, why bother when you're young and free?" she said laughingly.

They chatted for another minute or so before Jim noticed that she was intentionally gravitating back toward the living room.

On his way home, Jim was glad to find Taco at the bar, ready for another bitch session about the absence of Jim's love life. After a couple of beers, Jim headed back to his apartment to settle in for the night.

# CHAPTER THIRTY-ONE

The following day Jim mailed out the second wave of his letter campaign. He started specifically addressing the letters for the third wave. Optimistically, he looked at the template for the letter:


Dear Sir or Ma'am:

I am writing to be considered for a position with your prestigious company.

For the past several years I have worked in a variety of clinical settings at different tertiary care centers and also for a major corporate client dealing with the evaluation and administration of workers' compensation claims. My ability to understand medical records, coupled with my industry knowledge of healthcare, makes me particularly well-suited to work for your company. Further, my military experience has taught me to work well with a diverse range of people, often under adverse circumstances.

I am available to meet with you at your earliest convenience to discuss how my skills and experience can be used to assist you in the achievement of your vision and objectives.

Very truly yours,
James Greene, RN

During the week Jim was able to fill in most of the particular addresses for the third wave and figured he would finish them up over the weekend.

Friday, September 9th was a beautiful late summer day, and Jim was hoping for an easy shift, as he wanted to be focused and well-rested to finish up the third wave of his letter campaign over the weekend. Thus far, Jim hadn't received any responses or rejections from the prior letters that he had sent out.

Jim's visit with Wanda was brief, as she remained somewhat catatonic and disengaged.

Shortly afterward, he arrived at Richard's and found him again at the drawing board.

"Sir Richard, how are you today?"

"Aggravated. My calculations seem to be going nowhere, and I just found out that the court hasn't scheduled my case to be heard until next January."

"Sorry to hear it."

"January is simply too late. I've been told that the secrets of Paramatter shall be revealed to me this year. So, I think I shall fire my attorney and use the money I'll save to buy a newer and better telescope."

"Best of luck with that."

Richard nodded, then checked his sugar level. It was slightly elevated, and their visit ended within a few more minutes.

Once at the Y, Jim found Phil glued to the TV watching another documentary about 9/11.

"Phil, do you mind if I ask you a personal question?" Jim gently asked.

"Go ahead."

"How can you watch this stuff, after all that you've been through?"

"I guess it's like driving by a bad accident—you just can't help but look." After an awkward silence, Phil continued, "Do you mind if I ask *you* a personal question?"

"Shoot."

"What were you doing that day?"

Jim paused for a moment, then answered, "It was my day off, and I was making breakfast and having a cup of coffee. I heard some DJ on the radio talking about a plane that had crashed into one of the towers, and he compared it to an aircraft that had crashed into the Empire State Building during the '40s. About twenty minutes later, they announced that a second plane had struck the South Tower. Seconds after that, my phone rang, and my supervisor told me to get into work immediately. I had been working at Valley Hospital at the time and got to work within fifteen minutes. All clinical staff got called in, elective surgeries were canceled, and trauma teams were standing by, expecting to be slammed with mass casualties. Well, by the end of the day we all were depressed when we realized the worst— that no casualties would be arriving," Jim replied. "Where were you, if you don't mind my asking?"

"It was my day off, too. After the second plane hit, I got the call to report to the barracks. They then deployed us to strategic locations in and around the city to maintain order over the several thousand people who were leaving New York. I tried calling Debbie countless times, but all circuits were busy. She was in the South Tower on the ninety-third floor," Phil said as his voice started to crackle. "I still don't know if she burned, jumped, or suffocated from the smoke."

An uncomfortable silence ensued. The documentary commentator could be heard talking about the war on terror that commenced following the 9/11 attacks.

"'The war on terror'—what the hell does that mean?" Phil queried.

"What are you saying?"

"It's a confusing concept. Just look at the wars on poverty and drugs, and you tell me how successful they've been."

"Yeah, I guess it's kinda hard to be victorious over an idea or substance," Jim pondered.

"Exactly! When the hell can we expect to see General Heroin or Admiral Impoverishment signing documents of unconditional surrender on the majestic deck of some austere battleship?"

"Doesn't seem to make much sense," Jim replied.

"You know what? The 'war on terror' makes even less sense than the wars on poverty and drugs—it's the mother of all misnomers!"

"Why's that?"

"How can you win a war *on* terror, when war *is* terror?"

"Maybe we should've declared war on just Al Qaeda or all international terrorist organizations?"

Phil looked distant, then replied with tears running down his cheeks, "All I know is that I lost my war on terror that awful morning Debbie died."

Jim now felt very uncomfortable with the conversation. He stood there for about ten seconds, then asked, "Can I do anything for you?"

Phil shook his head but remained silent. The two then completed their visit without much more being said.

Jim was soon in his car and nervously smoking a cigarette on his way to Sally's.

Once there, he found Walter sitting in his usual chair but hunched over an all-too-familiar yellow bucket.

"Hey Jimmy, guess what I'm doing?" Walter said as he spat a large hawker into the receptacle.

Jim was so appalled that he was at a loss for words.

Walter then exclaimed, "I'm doing what the mule messiah should've done before getting on the plane!"

Jim shrugged his shoulders nonchalantly, trying to conceal his disgust. He then went into the living room to find an irate Sally restless on the couch.

"That damned Walter! He ruined Jesus' throne! Now I'll never see him in his glory!"

"When you want to see him, why don't you just close your eyes and picture him?"

Sally closed her eyes momentarily, then opened them, looking even angrier. "I can't see him! It's all Walter's fault!"

Jim kept trying to reassure her, but she remained agitated for the remainder of their visit. Jim was truly relieved that she was not scheduled to receive her haloperidol shot that evening, as he would've had a difficult time trying to give it to her.

Shortly afterward, Jim went to Mike's and found him likewise in an aggravated state. He was upset that his Uncle Joe was mad at him for forgetting to secure a load of wood on the back of his pickup. Mike was being hard on himself and was angry at having a traumatic brain injury that caused him to forget things that he otherwise wouldn't have forgotten.

Their visit was brief, and Jim smoked a cigarette more leisurely as he made his way to St. Monica's.

After his arrival, he was informed by Maureen that Lucinda had gone to visit a relative in New York City. Maureen denied knowing where the other clients were.

Jim then made his way up to Nick's. Nick was in an even more aggressive mood about religion than usual, as the Right Reverend Roberts was promoting a new membership drive for his flock. With the deftness of a young boxer, Jim managed to bob and weave his way out of Nick's recruiting conversation and quickly arrived in the backyard with Rob. He was on the grass and sloppily painting the port side of the boat.

"Hey, Rob. How ya doin'?"

"Not bad, and you?"

"Pretty good. What color are you painting the boat?"

"Well, the guy at the paint store had several gallons of discontinued and unwanted paint, so he sold them to me for a deep discount. I figured that I'd use all of them to make a collage of colors for the sides and top of the boat," Rob replied.

"Do you have a name for her yet?"

"Yeah, I'm gonna go with *Mary Elizabeth*, in honor of my late grandmother who left me the money that I'm buying the paint with."

"Good for you. Are you having any pain or problems?"

"Nope. Just hoping to get this ol' gal done before winter."

Rob and Jim talked for a few more minutes and then went on to complete their visit.

Once at home, Jim engaged in his usual routine but was disappointed to find no responses to his letter campaign as of yet.

Checking his inbox, Jim found an email from the overworked bride-to-be asking that he call her. He was initially a bit nervous, as Jenny had been virtually in total control of all wedding plans, thus allowing Michele to work seventy-plus hours per week at her furniture business. He quickly dialed her number and got her on the second ring.

"Hey, sis, is everything okay?"

"Oh, yeah—I just wanted to tell you something about the wedding before you heard from Jenny."

"What's up?"

"Unfortunately, we've been crunching the numbers, and we don't have enough bridesmaids for you to walk down the aisle with. Stanton thinks that he can't exclude any of his corporate friends who are already ushers, and I don't have enough bridesmaids to match you up."

Jim hesitated for a moment, absorbing the impact of what she had just said. "Gosh, well, it certainly is within Stan's discretion to choose his own people, and I wouldn't want him to lose any business or anything."

"Geez, you're the best, Jimmy! We definitely want you to do the second reading—you know the one about love and patience? It's really very short," Michele said, fully aware of Jim's aversion to public speaking.

After a couple more minutes of idle talk, their call ended, and Jim hung up the phone. He was crestfallen by their decision. *Sure, Stan, it's not okay to offend your corporate pals, but it's okay to offend your future family,* Jim pondered as he entertained the thought of another glass of bourbon.

# CHAPTER THIRTY-TWO

Jim finished addressing all the letters for the third wave of his campaign and dated them September 11, 2005. He hoped using that date would convey to prospective employers that he was unafraid to work on Sundays and that he was unafraid to work again in the city.

Jim mailed the third wave out first thing on Monday the twelfth, and later in the week, he began receiving a couple of responses from the first wave, thanking him for interest but denying him an interview.

He began his shift on Thursday of that week with a large cup of coffee, as he hadn't slept well after receiving his first rejection letter the night before.

Jim found Wanda in her usual listless condition but now noticed that she had developed the habit of cooing quietly at times, perhaps in memory of Bubba.

Once at Richard's, Jim found him in an anxious state of mind.

"Sir Richard, how are you, my good man?"

"Perplexed. I've been told that the secrets of the Paramatter would be revealed to me by the end of the year, but it seems as though the harder I try, the further away the goal is. I haven't seen any more microcosmic activity, nor have I yet seen the new light concerning the original light. It's like I have a valid theory that cannot be validated," he said with a sigh.

"Did you get that new telescope yet?"

"Not yet, but the problem remains that I simply don't know exactly what I'm looking for mathematically. Edison once said that 'Genius is 1 percent inspiration and 99 percent perspiration,' but how do you find inspiration to unlock the correct equations? How do you confirm the hypothesis that you desperately believe is correct? I used to think that I was a superlative research scientist regarding cancer treatment, but then one day what I thought was inspiration turned out to be psychosis."

"What do you mean?"

"When I thought I was on the verge of discovering the cure for cancer, I saw several happy little pills dancing in a conga line. At first, I thought it was inspiration, but then I soon realized that I was going mad. It's the same thing with the cosmoses in the bushes and the light that came before the light. I thought that it was a hypothesis coming together, but it was just another series of mad hallucinations."

Jim was at a loss for words and gently gave Richard an encouraging pat on the back. Richard thanked him for his support, and they finished their visit in the typical manner.

Once at the Y, Jim found Phil watching a documentary about the history of India.

"Hi, Phil. How are you?"

"Okay. Just watching a special on Gandhi."

"Great man."

"Yeah, too bad there aren't more like him."

"Things would probably be a lot different today if the Arabs had had a man like him back in the '60s and '70s," Jim responded.

Jim's remark seemed to sadden Phil, who momentarily blanked out while looking at the TV screen.

Then Phil said, "I worked with some Muslim troopers and they were some of the bravest and best people I had ever met."

Jim nodded, then gently inquired, "Are you having any thoughts of hurting yourself?"

Phil shook his head but remained quiet. They then went on to finish their visit.

Jim nervously smoked a cigarette on the way to Sally's, worried that he had aggravated Phil's depression by the Arabian Gandhi remark. Once inside Sally's, he discovered Walter puffing on another Churchillian stogie, with the yellowed bucket beside him. By this time the bucket had morphed from being just a spittoon into an absolute cesspool for cigar butts, kitty litter, and other debris. The stench made Sir Richard's Paramatter smell appetizing. Sally was still upset about her savior being missing in action and his throne being desecrated. Their visit was short, and soon Jim was at Mike's.

Mike was in a better mood, as his Uncle Joe had forgiven him and gave him another chance to keep working. Mike denied any seizures or other symptoms and acknowledged that he would keep his appointment to have his Dilantin level drawn as previously scheduled.

Soon after arriving at St. Monica's, Jim settled in at the kitchen table, as June had gone to round up the patients.

Suddenly, Nick appeared, and Jim wanted to immediately distract him from any further recruiting conversation.

"Hello, Nick. Are you still having that prophecy about the man in the corner?" Jim quickly inquired.

"Yes. His time is drawin' nearer! The ax is at the root of his tree! His eyes are dark, and he's rockin' on his buttocks—chantin' incessantly!"

"Any other prophecies?"

"No, sir," Nick replied. "Are you ready yet for the deliverance of your demon of reluctance?"

"I still can't afford any of the Right Reverend's programs at this time. My transmission is probably going to need to be replaced soon."

"No excuses, son! You must sacrifice everything to worship Jesus and to follow his servant, the Reverend Roberts!"

"Well, if I sacrificed my car, then I'd lose my job and wouldn't be able to contribute anything to the good Reverend," Jim tactfully replied.

Nick looked confused yet encouraged by Jim's response. Jim adroitly slipped Nick his pills and MAR, then did the same for Rob, who was now standing at the table next to Nick. As Rob starting talking to Jim, Nick took his pills and simply slid the signed MAR across the table and then left out the back. Rob offered no complaints and soon left the kitchen to return to the boat in the backyard.

Within a couple of minutes, Jim was inside Lucinda's kitchen.

"Jimmy, how's it going, buddy boy?"

"Not bad. How was your trip to the city?"

"Just terrific! I looked up my second cousin, Katherine, who's a professional photographer. My mom always said that she was kinda snooty, but, man, was Mom wrong! She gave me a cool tour of her neighborhood, and then we hooked up with Chad for dinner and dancing. It was the best time, and she lives only a few miles away from Chad."

"Sounds like fun."

"It sure was. And the best part is that she invited me down to stay overnight next weekend. So, I'll get to have fun with both her and Chad again!"

Jim nodded and smiled, hoping to conceal his envy that she was seemingly falling in love with such an arrogant jerk, particularly one in a locale that Jim desperately hoped to return.

Once home, Jim engaged in his usual constitutional and received an awkward email from Jenny about Stanton's failure to pick Jim as one of the ushers. She indicated that she knew how disappointed he must feel and that she would see if there was any way she could discreetly persuade Stan and Michele to pick Jim. *Maybe if I got a solid six-figure corporate job, then Stan would find me qualified to walk back and forth in a straight line wearing a monkey suit,* Jim cynically thought.

# CHAPTER THIRTY-THREE

The remaining days of September were drifting by as inevitably as autumn leaves falling from bright deciduous trees on a breezy afternoon. And like the falling of leaves, a steady stream of polite rejection letters began wafting into Jim's mailbox. He remained optimistic, however, as there were still many companies who hadn't yet replied.

Jim's shift began uneventfully, as his visit with Wanda was brief and awkward due to her heavily sedated state of mind. He hoped that she would make a comeback and get another apartment in the community, but clinically she was barely capable of doing anything at all.

Within minutes Jim reached Sir Richard's house.

"Say, have you found the tip of the Paramatter pyramid yet, Richard?"

"Despite looking for it every night in the sky, it has eluded me. I'm trying to calculate its location on this map, but that's hard to do, as I truly saw the pale rose star for only a matter of seconds. However, I've been doing more theorizing and crunching the numbers. I believe that the pale rose star represents the tip of the pyramid through which the dawn of time occurred!"

"Why do you think that, Sir Richard?"

"Well, the pale rose star was the only thing in that galaxy that was remotely red like lava, and also it was the only thing that was not moving whatsoever. This leads me to believe more than ever that the Paramatterical pyramid is the pedestal of the universe!"

"How's the number crunching going?" Jim cautiously inquired.

"I'm not quite there yet. Nonetheless, the laws of the universe are just, and the secrets of Paramatter shall be revealed to me as promised!"

After a few more minutes of conversation about the pale rose star and its relationship to the celestial map, their visit ended.

At Phil's Jim found him watching a TV show about hot rods. Phil reminisced about the 1966 Chevy that he had owned as a teenager. It was a muscle car that was built like a Sherman tank. Although Jim had a preference for pickups (like the badass F - 150 that he'd had as a teenager), he did admire and respect a good American muscle car. He regretted getting the Ford sedan that he currently had, and he'd only purchased it because it seemed like an acceptable choice for an aspiring young executive.

Once at Sally's, he found her door unlocked and nothing but a dim kitchen light on. Walter was absent, and Sally was nowhere to be found in the living room. Suddenly, Jim heard a vague mumbling coming from upstairs.

The stairs were completely dark, and Jim cautiously made his way up them.

Soon he was at the landing of the second floor, and he could hear that the mumbling was Sally, who was behind a closed door facing him that was missing a knob. He tried to turn the metal post upon which the knob had previously been attached, but it did nothing to open the door. Then he tried to push firmly against the door, also without any success. Finally, he warned Sally to back away from the door, and he kicked it open with one hard thrust.

As she left the dark bathroom, they cautiously made their way back to the kitchen. She thanked him profusely for saving her and was praising Jesus for sending her an angel.

"What happened to your eye?" Jim inquired, noticing that she had a large bruise over her right eye.

"What?"

"Your eye, what happened to it?"

"Nothing—Jesus loves me. He sends me angels!"

"Did you fall down in the bathroom?"

"He loves me and sends me angels! He's gonna come back to me!"

"Where's Walter?"

"Angels! Angels! Angels! He loves me and brings me angels!"

"Did Walter do this to you?"

"Angels! He loves me and brings me angels! I love him, too! I wish I could send him angels!"

Jim then gently asked, "Do you want me to take you to the hospital?"

Her eyes became glassy with tears as she replied, "No, please—no. Jesus and will take care of me."

Jim was hesitant to leave her alone but felt that he was unable to do anything, as she was denying treatment and her brother and conservator, Walter, was nowhere to be found. They finished their visit, and Jim left a voice mail with Vicky reporting what had happened, as he knew that she was a fearless champion for their patients and would figure out a way to do something.

Jim's visit with Mike transpired without any problems, but Jim was bothered by the image of poor Sally and her black eye.

Following a brief and uneventful ride, Jim made it to St. Monica's and found Maureen asleep on the couch. He made his way upstairs to see Nick. Thankfully, Nick was in a hurry to attend a special church meeting that was being convened by the Reverend Roberts, and the visit was brief.

Jim then headed up to see Lucinda, who was luckily alone.

"Hi, Lucinda. How's it going?"

"Wonderfully!" she gleefully replied while twirling a long strand of her hair.

"How was your stay with Katherine?"

"Fantastic! The three of us went to Central Park to have a picnic, and she shot the most magnificent pictures of the leaves there."

"Sounds like fun."

"I know it sounds crazy, but I think Chad could be the one. I've never dated anyone for as long, and he really seems to respect and understand me. And by this time next year, he'll be a lawyer! I can't wait—he's coming up to the Valley to stay with his friend this weekend but said that we'll go for another nice long ride on his bike to enjoy the fall colors."

"You really should wear a helmet, you know," Jim said.

"Ah, c'mon, Jimmy, don't be such a stiff!" she replied with her iridescent eyes flashing defiantly.

Jim didn't push the subject, and they wrapped up their visit with the typical exchanges.

In the backyard, Jim found Rob hard at work painting the outside of the behemoth boat. Rob's painting seemed almost purposefully sloppy yet intriguing. It was as though Jackson Pollock was guiding his efforts. Rob offered no complaints and seemed eager to get back to work. After Jim gave him the pills and received back the signed MAR, he cautioned Rob to remain well-hydrated and even gave Rob a couple of bottles of water that Jim had in his bag.

Jim then returned to his apartment and began to wind down his day. He received two rejection letters, one of which promised to keep his resume on file for a year, should any "appropriate openings" occur.

# CHAPTER THIRTY-FOUR

October began, and the influx of rejection letters increased slightly. Jim remained positive and even planned on taking a day trip to Boston over the weekend for no particular reason. He had only been there once before when Holly had surprised him with tickets to a Red Sox-Indians game. Other than being at Fenway, he hadn't gotten out to see the town. Also, Jim looked forward to what was supposed to be prime-time viewing for autumn foliage on the train ride.

Jim began his shift at Southbridge Manor, where Wanda was still incoherent. He had learned that her social worker, Maggie, had arranged for her to stay there another ninety days. If she didn't recover, she'd likely be transferred to VMI permanently.

While at Southbridge Manor, Jim also met with their newest patient, Sally. Jim's faith in Vicky had not proven to be groundless. When Jim reported to Vicky his concern that Sally was being abused by Walter, Vicky immediately contacted one of her friends who worked for the government. Within hours they had initiated a more aggressive investigation as the first step in condemnation proceedings. Vicky's actions had the effect that she had intended: Walter at once resigned his conservatorship of Sally, citing the fact that he was relocating to Florida with a friend and former colleague, Mitch.

Within a few days, Walter and his filthy belongings were nowhere to be found, and Sally was transferred to Southbridge Manor. She seemed to take to institutional life much better than Wanda. Sally enjoyed her new surroundings, had three square meals a day, and was befriended by one of the workers there who gave her a menthol every morning.

Arriving at Sir Richard's, Jim found him absolutely ecstatic. Richard informed him that his voices had told him that the secrets of Paramatter would be revealed to him within the next forty days. Genuine relief was expressed, as well as sheer jubilation. He assured Jim that he would reward him for his continued support, but Jim politely informed Richard that gratuities were not acceptable due to agency rules.

Soon Jim arrived at the Y and found Phil in good spirits. His room was swept clean and put in order. An enormous black suitcase occupied the middle of it.

"Hey, Phil, how are you?"

"Great. How you doin' Jimmy?"

"Not bad. Goin' somewhere for the weekend?" Jim asked.

"Yes, sir. I'm goin' to rediscover myself in the Adirondacks!"

"Good for you. I hope you enjoy the ride up. The colors should be terrific."

Phil nodded enthusiastically, then took his pills and signed the MAR retrieved from the baggie.

Shortly after Phil's visit, Jim pulled up to St. Monica's and found June doing some needlework on the sofa.

"Hey, how are you, June?" Jim asked.

"Pretty good, and you?"

"Good. Where's everyone?"

"Rob went to a movie at the recreation center. Lucinda and Nick are upstairs."

Jim nodded thankfully as he reached into his bag to hand her Rob's envelope.

"Be careful with Nick. He's been drinking, and he's mad."

"I thought he gave it up a long time ago."

"Yeah, but it seems like every other year he falls off the wagon when his AA group expels him."

"How can they do that?"

"Well, AA is non-denominational, and when Nick gets too opinionated with his religious views, they ask him to leave," she replied.

"Thanks for the warning."

Arriving at Nick's, Jim found the main door open and the screen door shut. He rapped gently, hoping that Nick wouldn't appear.

He did. Stumbling across the kitchen, he opened the door without comment. The pungent stench of alcohol and urea from Nick's oozing pores immediately insulted Jim's nostrils.

"Are you okay?" Jim asked.

"Magnificent and delivered, but everybody else is an evil heathen!"

"What are you talking about?"

"Those goddamn losers at AA! They pretend to rely on a higher power, but they have no fuckin' clue! Jesus Christ and his faithful servant—the Most Reverend William Roberts—is the only higher power! There is no other! They're all a bunch of fuckin' heathens! I'm surrounded by goddamn heathens! It's bad enough that they're at my meetings, but I have to live with them too! That cocksucker Reilly and that no-good whore upstairs! I'm surrounded! And now I have to listen to that vulgar slut moan all night while gettin' wildly fucked by some godless pig! 'Vengeance will be mine,' sayeth the Lord!"

*Great! That pasty jackass Chad is doing a total hottie, and I can't even make out with a horny librarian!* Jim thought with an immediate sense of frustration. He quickly refocused on the problem at hand. He knew that he couldn't give Nick his pills when he was in such an intoxicated state and began thinking of a discreet way to get the hell out of there. *Maybe I could just take his vital signs, then excuse myself,* he thought.

He decided to give it a shot. "Can I take your vital signs, Nick?"

He nodded, then continued his tirade in a heavily slurred voice, "'Vengeance is mine,' sayeth the Lord! 'Vengeance is mine!' The ax is already at the root of the tree! The man with the dark eyes in the dark corner is rockin' hard! 'His days will end soon,' sayeth the Lord!"

Other than a mildly elevated pulse, Nick's vitals were normal. Jim politely excused himself and was grateful that Nick hadn't asked for his medications.

Seconds later he arrived at Lucinda's door to the sounds of giggling from the living room. She entered the kitchen in response to Jim's knocking and was wearing a stunning black cocktail dress. She still retained most of her tan from the summertime and looked radiant with her dark hair pulled up off the smooth skin of her neck and shoulders.

"Whatcha all dolled up for?" Jim inquired as he entered the kitchen.

"Chad and I just got back from the most terrific Law Review luncheon at Quinnipiac."

Jim nodded and feigned a smile.

"Come on in, bud, and say hi to Chad!"

Jim again remained speechless and tried to muster another polite smile. "Hey, Chad, how's it going?" he asked as they entered her living room.

Chad nodded slightly while looking somewhat in Jim's direction but remained seated on the couch with the top few buttons of his tuxedo undone.

"So, how does Quinnipiac compare to Yale?" Jim queried matter-of-factly, trying to conceal his jealousy.

Lucinda interrupted, "Oh—it's much better! Vanessa dated a law student when she was at Yale, and I went to visit them once near the school. Yale is just a bunch of dingy gray buildings surrounded by beggars and deadbeats—but Quinnipiac is beautiful! It's a newer brick building, surrounded by fresh green grass on all sides. And a beautiful mountain overlooks the entire campus! Man, it's so pretty!"

*Dammit! Doesn't she know that Yale is the cornerstone of the Ivy League*, Jim thought with a sense of green-eyed frustration.

Chad cracked a slight but vindictive smile, realizing that Jim had failed at what he was trying to do.

Recognizing his defeat, Jim proceeded to quickly wrap up the visit.

Jim angrily smoked a new cigarette on the way to Mike's Uncle Joe's.

He found Mike in a good mood, as his Uncle Joe had told him that he could stay over for the entire weekend. Joe's business had been booming lately, which was also good for Mike, as he was now working nearly full-time for him.

Jim was on the way back to his apartment when his phone rang.

"Hi Jim. This is Rose."

"Hey Rose. What's up?"

"Did you notice anything unusual about Phil tonight?"

"Nah, he was in a great mood. Said he was going to his family's cabin in the Adirondacks for the weekend."

There was a long silence.

"What's goin' on?" Jim nervously inquired.

"Phil hanged himself from the Y's flagpole."

"Is he going to be all right?"

"I'm sorry, Jim. He didn't make it."

Their conversation ended shortly afterward, with more sympathy from Rose rather than recriminations. He would find out later that Phil had had a token grave for Debbie near the cabin, where he was soon to be interred. Jim drove home in disbelief as he smoked several more cigarettes.

Arriving at the large vestibule of his apartment, Jim threw his bag against the far wall. Reaching into his right pocket, he retrieved his chrome pistol and plopped it onto the steamer chest in the center of the room. The room was not completely dark, as copious moonlight poured through a stained-glass window at the far side of the foyer. He stared at the gun glistening in the moonlight for a few minutes while feeling numb about Phil's suicide. He berated himself and couldn't believe that he had missed Phil's suicidal cues, such as signing the MAR without putting it in the microwave. An increasing wave of anger and guilt overcame him. *Oh, God, I can see why you let me screw up my whole life, but couldn't you help me save Phil's?*

Then, Jim violently flipped over the large trunk and collapsed onto the floor, where he cried for several minutes until sleep overtook him.

# CHAPTER THIRTY-FIVE

Rather than going into Boston that weekend, Jim mainly stayed in bed. The following days were gray, bleak, and cold. Jim lost interest in almost everything, including his ambitious letter campaign. Most days he slept until noon, and then he would just bum around until going to work.

Another mundane shift started with a large cup of coffee and a slightly crumpled cigarette. The ladies of Southbridge Manor were status quo—although Sally seemed to be doing better than when she'd been living with Walter. She had actually lost about fifteen pounds from receiving a better-balanced diet.

After a couple of cigarettes, Jim arrived at Richard's. He was greeted by Sir Richard, who was decked out in full Maltese regalia.

"Trick or treat," Jim said jokingly, although Halloween wasn't until the following evening.

"It's neither, my good man! Tonight's the night! Come on in, my boy!"

"Tonight's the night for your Paramatter revelation?" Jim asked cautiously.

"By God, yes! And it shall be revealed at the stroke of midnight! Then we both shall be handsomely rewarded!"

"Thank you, anyway, Sir Richard, but I told you we can't accept any gifts."

Richard seemed unmoved by Jim's answer as he led the way into the laboratory. Once there, Jim saw a plethora of

Bunsen burners neatly arranged in the shape of a star on a table.

"This is it! I can't believe that the time is finally at hand!"

"Well, you'll have to tell me all about it next time," Jim politely replied.

Richard looked disappointed but understood that Jim had to move on. He departed after a few more minutes of chatter.

After a couple more cigarettes, Jim arrived at Mike's and was informed by Betty that he was working late with Joe.

After coming to St. Monica's, Jim discovered June working. She informed him that Rob was out back, Lucinda was upstairs, and Nick had gone to an early AA meeting.

Once at the boat's side, Jim was impressed that Rob had just about finished painting the outside of the boat. If the Loch Ness Monster ever puked, he imagined that it would probably look a lot like the color scheme of the *Mary Elizabeth*. Jim was glad for him. Rob was elated that he would have all winter to work below deck on restoring the cabins. Jim's visit was fairly brief, as Rob was in a hurry to put the finishing touches on the exterior.

A short time later Jim arrived at Lucinda's to find her surprisingly alone, yet with her bags packed. The image made Jim shudder as he thought of his final visit with Phil.

"Hey, honey. Where ya goin'?"

"Gonna spend the weekend at Rita's to help her recover from surgery," she replied.

"Is she okay?"

"Yeah. Just a little swollen."

"Where?"

"South of the border," Lucinda replied. "Her boobs look so young and perky that she wanted her private parts to be nipped and tucked a bit. She's kinda vain about her appearance."

"Do you have meds for your trip?"

"Yeah, Cindy gave them to me this morning."

"Are you hearing any more voices?"

"Nope. Chad's so understanding—his is the only voice that I'm hearing in my head. I'm kinda hoping that Rita will be feeling up to going out Saturday night with me, Chad, and his friend, Todd. I think that Rita and him might hit it off. But if she's not, I'll guess I'll see Chad later—because I did promise Rita I'd take care of her."

"Have you ever stopped your medications after the voices of summer are gone?"

She paused to think, then replied, "I did try once or twice, but the voices came back—just not as bad as in the summer."

Jim wished her a good trip, and then they completed their visit.

Afterward, Jim stopped at Joe's, which wasn't too far from St. Monica's. Joe and Mike had just returned from building a patio. Mike was exhausted but seemed happy to be working so much.

After seeing Mike, Jim's shift ended, and he popped in at Sully's for a quick beer and smoke on the way home, then went back to his apartment. Three more rejection letters, a benign wedding update from Jenny, and a couple of bills were awaiting him. Except for the bills, the others were perfunctorily deleted or discarded.

# CHAPTER THIRTY-SIX

Halloween was upon the Valley, and mischief was in the air. Jim didn't wear any kind of costume, as he thought it would be unprofessional. He did hear, however, that Vicky had dressed as a witch last Halloween, as she professed to be one.

At the manor, the residents were having a little Halloween bash. Sally was dressed as an angel, but Wanda was in regular clothes and seemed oblivious to the party going on around her.

Jim looked forward to seeing what Sir Richard discovered once he arrived at his steel castle.

When Richard answered the door, he looked completely peaceful and serene. "Follow me, my boy."

Jim followed him into the laboratory, where he discovered that Richard's equipment was completely bundled up. "Where's the Paramatter?"

"It doesn't exist!"

"Are you serious?"

"Absolutely. The voices whispered to me, 'Paramatter exists only within the castle of the sky. Tear down your walls and build something beautiful.'"

"Wow."

"I tell you, I'm glad that's all over and done with. Perhaps now I can retire from the rigors of scientific pursuit."

Jim smiled and nodded encouragingly. They then bantered for a few more minutes before Jim left Richard's.

Mike had received his meds in advance, so Jim headed over to St. Monica's.

There he found Maureen snoring on the couch with her mouth gaping wide open, which revealed several yellowed and crooked teeth. He was disgusted by her appearance and headed up to Nick's. He knocked, but no one answered. Seeing that the door was ajar, he entered.

After entering, Jim heard mumbling emanating from the living room. He cautiously entered that room to discover a most appalling sight: Rob was sitting in the corner wearing pink silk underwear, with black eye shadow and mascara running down his cheeks. He was crying and mumbling loudly and incoherently. His fingers were interlocked beneath his knees, and he was rocking back and forth on his buttocks.

Jim was truly amazed and horrified that Nick's prophecy had come true. However, Jim later found out from Stella that Rob reverted to this particular defense mechanism whenever he was acutely distraught.

Suddenly, Nick appeared at the threshold of the room and exclaimed, "'Vengeance is mine,' sayeth the Lord! 'Vengeance is mine!' He hath struck down the heathen, homosexual enemy!"

Jim was outraged at Nick's remarks but refocused on the issue at hand. Realizing that Rob was having a total meltdown, Jim rapidly dialed 911. While he waited for the paramedics, Nick was completely smug as he quickly took his medication, then departed for his AA meeting. His AA group had taken him back on the condition that he didn't mention Christ or Roberts or wear any offensive T- shirts.

After the paramedics left, Jim went upstairs for Lucinda. She greeted him dressed as a huge emerald-colored Playboy bunny.

Her body was dark and devastating. Hefner would've signed her up on the spot.

"Hey, Lucinda, got a new job?"

"Nah, waiting for Chad to pick me up. We're going to a party at Rita's spa."

"Did you and she end up going out with Chad and his buddy last week?"

"Nah. She was still pretty swollen, but she's okay now. Maybe they'll hit it off tonight because Chad is bringing Todd to Rita's party," Lucinda replied. "Did you hear what happened out back?"

"No, what?"

"The boat burned down."

"Really?"

"Yep, went up in seconds. Cindy thought it was arson because it went up so quickly. Her dad was an arson investigator for the county."

"Did they investigate?"

"Nope. Cindy overheard one of the firemen saying that since it was abandoned property and nobody was hurt, there'd be no investigation."

They talked for a couple more minutes, and then Jim departed, glad that he had missed Chad. Before heading home, he stopped at Sully's for a drink. He was hoping to talk with Taco, who was working that evening, but music from the band prevented him from doing so. After two beers, he went home to sleep.

# CHAPTER THIRTY-SEVEN

The dark days of November began with Jim feeling miserable with just about everything. He was now completely disinterested and unmotivated by his failing letter campaign. He hadn't received a rejection letter in days, and many of his letters simply went unanswered, as though he didn't exist.

However, he did manage to get to Mass on All Saints' Day, which was a Holy Day of Obligation.

When he got to the church, he went into a small chapel room behind the main church. This was used for daily services, as that crowd was usually significantly smaller than those on the weekends. An older priest who had a reassuring tone of voice began the service. As Jim focused more on the cadence of the liturgy rather than the content, he began thinking that this service felt more like another boring day of repetition rather than anything remotely holy or inspirational. As the priest segued into the sermon, he mentioned that every person has the potential and obligation to become a saint. Jim began wondering if he had a greater potential to be abducted by aliens rather than become a saint. He then started wondering if aliens could become saints, if extra-terrestrials did indeed exist.

Jim soon found himself inexplicably resenting the idea of sainthood as the sermon dragged on. *Yeah, it must be easy to become a saint when God gives you a profound revelation and the virtue to live up to it. How the hell can I ever become a saint when God hasn't even revealed anything to me about how to become a healthcare executive? How can I hope to aspire to sainthood when I can't even get a job that would make the most of my talents?*

After the Mass was over, Jim plodded his way back to his apartment to rest up before work.

His visit to Southbridge Manor was brief and uneventful, and Jim made it to Sir Richard's in record time. Luckily, Sir Richard was still in a good mood about discovering that Paramatter did not exist. He was browsing a gardening magazine and plotting out a design to put new hedges along the route of where his walls would have been built. Also, he was enthusiastically planning an elaborate flower garden for the spring. After talking about Richard's plans for a few minutes and then medicating him, Jim was on his way to see Mike.

As he pulled into Mike's driveway, Jim was nervous because of the two police cruisers that were parked there. Arriving at the porch, he noticed the door open and walked inside.

Betty was being interviewed by a couple of cops, and Jim could hear a couple more talking near the rear of the kitchen.

Betty interrupted herself to talk with Jim. "Hey, Jim. Mike's at Joe's."

"Is everything okay?"

"Mike got super mad at me, and he stormed out of here to go to Joe's. On his way out, he shattered the back door window by slamming it. If he's going to act like a criminal, then I'm going to treat him like one."

"Do you mind if I talk to the police for a minute?"

"Yeah, go ahead," she replied.

Jim explained Mike's medical situation to one of the officers and asked if he could give Mike his medicine before Mike went to the police station. The officer told him that they would pick up Mike for processing at their convenience but that Jim could give him his pills at the station if necessary. Jim thanked him, then headed out to St. Monica's.

Once there, Jim found June again knitting on the couch. She told him that Nick had gone to a church meeting and that it was unclear as to if and when Rob might return. After his breakdown, Rob had been admitted to the Valley Mental Institute. As the VMI was an inpatient psychiatric facility with twenty-four-hour licensed staff, Jim would not be visiting him.

Upon arriving at Lucinda's, he found her elated from the fun of Rita's party the night before. She was disappointed that Rita wasn't interested in Todd, as he was very interested in her. Lucinda was looking forward to spending the upcoming weekend at Katherine's in the city. Also, she was flattered that Katherine had offered her a part-time job as her photographer assistant. Nonetheless, Lucinda didn't think that she would take it, as she made a lot more money working at the Dawg, which was much closer to home.

After leaving St. Monica's and arriving at Joe's, Jim was informed by Joe that Mike had been recently taken into custody.

Jim then left to go to police headquarters. Once at the police station, a sergeant allowed Jim to meet with Mike in a secured holding area. Mike looked defeated.

"What's up, Mike?"

"Got into a big fight with Mom. She made some stupid comment about my still moping around about that 'Greek bimbo.' I meant to slam the door—I didn't mean to break it."

"Well, it doesn't sound like the crime of the century."

Mike cracked a smile and chuckled. They ended their visit with the usual exchange of pills and paperwork.

Soon Jim was at Sully's and glad that Taco was there to serve him a cold black and tan.

"Hey, my friend. How are you?" Taco inquired.

"Okay."

A brief interlude of silence unfolded as Jim lit a new cigarette and sipped his beer.

"Have you found your happiness yet?"

"Nah, it keeps ducking me," Jim replied.

"Do you want to talk about it?"

"Sure. It just seems like I'm going nowhere in life. I used to have a much better sense of direction. Now I just don't know where the hell I'm going. I've got no girl, I can't get a job I want, I suck at the job I do have, and I can't even get invited to usher at my own sister's wedding."

"What do you plan on doing about it?"

"I really don't know anymore. I don't even have a good Plan B."

"Plan B?" Taco inquired.

"Yeah, a contingency plan. Plan B," Jim replied, as though Taco had asked him to define what it was. "When I was in the Army, they always taught us to have a backup plan if something went wrong—like if we ran out of medication or if a buddy got killed by the enemy," Jim replied. "After I left the military, I was still able to formulate a good Plan B—an idea of what I'd do if what I wanted to do didn't work out. But this year just seems like a huge waste of time."

"Ah, Plan B or no Plan B, that is the question," Taco said wryly.

Jim rolled his eyes at Taco's bad pun, then took a large sip of beer.

"Do you like what you're doing now?" Taco asked.

"Sometimes, but I don't see myself doing it forever."

"Do you feel like you're making a positive difference in your patients' lives?"

"I used to, but...the one person I thought I was getting through to...killed himself," Jim replied in a strained tone of voice.

"Do you want to know why they call me Taco?"

Jim nodded with interest.

"Years ago, when I was about your age, I was going through a really tough time. Back then, I was living out west. I had a lousy job and no girl and felt like I was goin' nowhere. So, I decided to take a trip into the mountains to get a better sense of direction. Up until that point in my life, I had been a big fan of the outdoors. I packed enough provisions for about a couple of weeks.

About three-quarters of the way through my trip, I twisted my knee. Bad, really bad. It was late fall and getting cold—

downright freezing at night. I tried making a splint with a couple of branches and some cravats, hoping that I'd be able to keep up my pace. Well, I didn't, and at best I was walking only two to five hundred yards per day.

Most of the remaining canned food went quickly. The only food I had left was a few soft taco shells, and by that time I still had at least a couple of days back to the village where I started. Like a knucklehead, I'd forgotten to check the batteries on my walkie-talkie before I left. The reception was lousy, and the battery had died a couple of days before I hurt my knee. To make matters worse, only one person knew that I was out there. He was a crazy ol' hippie named Lazy Luke who sold me some supplies before I left. He had a lousy memory, probably from smoking too much dope as a kid. I began thinking that I was the only person on Earth and that nobody would ever find me."

"Yeah, I know the feeling," Jim interjected.

"I knew I had to make those taco shells last, as I was too feeble to bag any small game. I started eating bits of taco shells and was lucky enough to find some insects to put on top of them. I was also lucky enough to find a tender branch of an agave plant so I could use its nectar as a condiment.

Well, a couple of days had passed, and I was cold, tired, and down to only a few shreds of tortilla. The village still seemed a long way off. That night I looked up at the stars for hours. I thought it might be my last night. Then it hit me—what I had been doing wrong my whole life. It became as clear as the North Star. I realized that if I don't enjoy who I am and what I'm doing, then I'll never be satisfied with who I'll become or what I'll be doing. So, I decided to fight. I fought hard as hell to get back. About a day later I was found, half-conscious, by some college kids hiking."

Jim nodded thoughtfully as Taco segued into discussing the NFL playoffs and whether or not the Steelers would go all the way. After his beer was finished, Jim thanked Taco and went home.

# CHAPTER THIRTY-EIGHT

Over the next week, Jim thought often about what Taco had told him. Jim decided to take a break from trying to scale the corporate ladder and focused on more attainable goals, like becoming a non-smoker. He also began exploring other non- corporate opportunities in the nursing field. That Monday he woke up at about 10:00 a.m. and did something that he hadn't done in a while: He went to the gym and church.

His shift began uneventfully that afternoon, as the ladies of Southbridge Manor were doing fairly well.

Upon arriving at Sir Richard's, Jim found him literally at the drawing board. Glancing over Richard's shoulder, Jim discovered that he was mapping out his spring flower garden on the same type of blueprint paper that he had used to previously plot the coordinates of his lead and brick wall. Not wanting to distract Richard from his delicate floral endeavors, Jim kept their visit quick and to the point.

Mike was not home, as he hadn't returned there since Betty had called the police on him.

When at St. Monica's, Jim was met by the dull Maureen, who denied knowing the whereabouts of any of the residents. Jim went upstairs and soon was at Nick's door.

"Come on in, my son," Nick responded to Jim's knocking at the door.

"How are you today, Nick?"

"Motivated and delivered."

"Ready for your pills?"

"Can I tell you something in confidence—you know, like nurse-patient privileged information?"

"Go ahead."

"I want to reveal to you the meaning behind my prophecy."

"I get it—Rob was the man in the corner."

"No, no, no. That's not the meaning of the prophecy—that's just its outcome. The prophecy is meant for you and all other unbelievers. You must repent and change your ways. If you don't, you will suffer a similar fate."

"What, are you going to set fire to my dreams, too?!"

"I didn't light Rob's boat on fire! That was ordained by the Most Reverend Roberts! He doesn't just sit back and wait for Christ's will to happen—he brings it about! You should join us! Recant your popish ways and join his ranks! Young and powerful *white* men like you are exactly the type of followers that the Reverend Roberts seeks!"

Jim was immediately angered and appalled by his remarks. He was so angry he could feel his teeth and fists beginning to clench. He knew he had to get the hell out of there before he did something stupid. "Look, I'm really running late tonight—just take your pills."

"How dare you talk to me that way! I'm tryin' to do you a favor, and you treat me like the bad guy! I will not take my pills! I smite you mightily, Nurse James! Mightily and forever and ever! I shall not take anything from your heathen hands ever again!"

"Fine, have it your way!" Jim replied as he stood up and left the kitchen.

Before knocking on Lucinda's door, Jim broke down and had his first cigarette of the day. He then took a deep breath and knocked on her door.

"Come on in."

Jim opened the unlocked door and then went into the gym room. He found her wearing a cherry-red tank top and repeatedly hitting the bag with much zeal.

"You okay, Lucinda?"

"I'm pissed at Chad!" she said as she landed another punch against the bag.

"What did he do to you?"

"He blew me off when I was down at Katherine's this weekend. Said he had to study for exams. Who the fuck studies for exams on a Saturday night?" she replied, giving the bag a muscular right hook.

"Maybe he's a real study hound when it comes to exams. I heard you have to be to make Law Review."

"Well, it's not just that. He's hardly talked to me since last week. After a couple of minutes, he can't get off the phone fast enough. Something's wrong; I know it. I just don't know what."

Jim tried to reassure her some more but to no avail. She remained agitated but took her pills nonetheless.

Soon Jim was on to Joe's. Once there, he found Mike near the garage tinkering with a lawnmower.

"Hey, Mike. What's going on?"

"Just trying to fix up this old thing. Uncle Joe says if I fix it, I can keep it."

"Cool."

"You know what else he said?"

"No, what?" Jim asked.

"He says I can live here with him and keep the money that I was giving Mom for rent to buy my own landscaping equipment."

"Wow, that's great! What's going on with your criminal case?"

"I got a court date later this week, but I already talked to a family counselor there who thinks that I can get probation."

"Well, you certainly don't deserve the chair or anything," Jim said jokingly.

Mike laughed, and then they went on to complete their visit.

Jim popped a piece of nicotine gum into his mouth for the ride home and put on his favorite CD. Once at his apartment, he engaged in his normal activities and was looking forward to having the next couple of days off to relax and maybe do some shopping.

Checking his inbox, he spied an update from Jenny regarding a first draft of the wedding program, which was attached as a PDF. Jim opened it and noticed that this particular correspondence was sent to him only. Again, Jenny agonized that Jim had been overlooked as an usher and indicated that she was going to enlist the help of their salesman father to try to persuade Stan and Michele to do the right thing. He then opened the attachment, which revealed a very elegantly scripted and tasteful program. Seeing his name as the lector for the second reading of 1 Corinthians 13 motivated him to find his old Army Bible to see what he had gotten volunteered for:

> Love is patient, love is kind. It does not envy, it does not boast, it is not proud. It is not rude, it is not self-seeking, it is not easily angered, it keeps no record of wrongs. Love does not delight in evil but rejoices in the truth. It always protects, always trusts, always hopes, always perseveres. Love never fails.

Jim read it aloud, softly, two or three times. *This isn't so bad; it'll be over before I know it. Cheaper than renting a tux, too,* he thought. He promptly sent Jenny a reply indicating that he was happy to do the reading and that she need not try to persuade anyone to do anything else to make him an usher. Afterward, he settled in with an ice-cold tumbler of bourbon and began watching an old episode of the *Odd Couple. Maybe I could afford to live in New York if I got a roommate,* Jim pondered as he began falling asleep.

# CHAPTER THIRTY-NINE

Jim began his shift that cold November Thursday with another chalky piece of nicotine gum. He tried to squelch the taste of the gum with a cup of a large coffee.

Jim arrived at Southbridge Manor and was greeted by Sally's new caretaker, Lianna. She had long blonde hair, a roundish face with nearly symmetrical eyebrows, which overlooked her placid, China blue eyes, and her well-sculpted cheekbones.

"You must be Jim," she said as Jim entered the manor's large kitchen.

"Yep, how'd you know?"

"Sally's described you to a T."

"Are Sally and Wanda around?"

"Sally's in the ladies' room, and Wanda's in the hospital."

"What happened?"

"Severe dehydration."

"From what?"

"*Failure to thrive*. I heard that if she doesn't start eating and drinking better, she'll probably get a feeding tube inserted and be transferred to a nursing home."

Jim nodded sadly, knowing from his experience that patients who had been diagnosed with *failure to thrive* did not live long after getting that diagnosis.

Suddenly, Sally appeared at the threshold of the room, grinning widely. "Look at this; my two favorite people in the same room!" she exclaimed.

"Hey, how you doing?" Jim asked.

"Terrific! Lianna gives me coffee and menthols and watches Christmas movies with me!"

"Sounds like you like it here."

"I love it! Especially my good friend, Lianna. She loves Jesus, too!"

Seemingly embarrassed by this remark, Lianna said to her, "Honey, why don't you take your pills and let this good man be on his way?"

Sally obliged, and soon Jim was on his way to Richard's.

He found Richard still in a chipper mood. He denied any visual hallucinations but did admit to a new onset of auditory hallucinations. He claimed that after sundown he would hear voices singing something like Billy Joel's "*We Didn't Start the Fire*" from his laboratory; however, the version that he was hearing seemed a bit quicker in tempo. Richard's sugar was only slightly elevated, and soon Jim was on his way.

After leaving Richard's but before going to St. Monica's, Jim stopped across the street from the YMCA. Before getting out of his car, Jim grabbed a small parcel wrapped in plastic from his passenger seat. Once inside the lobby, he asked to see the facility's manager.

She came up to him. "Hi, I'm Barbara. How can I help you?"

"Hi, I'm Jim Greene. I knew Phil Morgan."

"I'm so sorry for your loss."

"Thanks. I couldn't help but notice that your flag here is all faded and torn, so I wanted to give you this new one," Jim said, handing her the new flag, which was wrapped in plastic.

"Why, thank you. I think Phil would've liked that. You know, the people who knew him around here think that he was a true hero with all that he did on 9/11 and afterward at Ground Zero."

"Yeah, he was one of the best."

Following a brief ride, Jim arrived at St. Monica's. Jim had heard from Vicky in the morning that Nick had been missing for two days. The last time he'd been seen was leaving his AA meeting on Tuesday night. The police had officially commenced an investigation but had absolutely no leads. Jim was relieved not to have to see him.

Soon he was outside Lucinda's door and knocking on it for a while, growing concerned, as she usually answered the door immediately. After a minute the door swung wide open, and Jim was shocked by what he saw. Lucinda was wearing faded and baggy sweat clothes. Her normally electrifying eyes were severely reddened and bordered by noticeably swollen lids.

"Lucinda, are you okay?"

"No—it's just awful," she said, starting to cry.

"What's wrong?"

"Me and Chad broke up!"

"Do you want to talk about it?"

"I feel like such a jerk! I thought he was gonna be the one!" she shouted angrily. "You know how he's been blowin' me off lately, right?"

"Yeah."

"Well, it made me really sad, so I decided to go over to Rita's last night to vent. I got onto the porch of her condo and saw the TV playing through the blinds, so I took a peek inside. On the screen, I saw this hot blond dancer swinging around a pole. At first, I thought maybe it was an old video of Rita from when she was dancing. So, this blonde finished her routine, and then like half a dozen guys jumped up onto the stage. Two of them tied her to the pole, then they all started viciously beating her. It was awful! I looked over to the other side of the living room and saw Rita on the couch. Then—like, after a minute—it happened!" she said, starting to sob again.

"What—what happened?"

"His head popped up! It was Chad—he had no shirt on! Oh, I feel so fuckin' stupid! I thought she was my best friend! I thought he was the one! He said he'd wait for me! He said he'd wait 'til I was ready!" She cried, then collapsed against Jim's body.

Instinctively, he put his arms around her. Then another instinct kicked in: one to avoid taking advantage of this vulnerable young lady. He immediately employed a mental tactic that he had cultivated in the military. When getting screamed at in the face by angry drill sergeants, Jim would simply put his mind in a different place, a serene place, and completely block out the angry barrage of expletives. Now he deployed the same tactic to avoid getting aroused by this sensuous woman whose firm body was now trembling in his arms uncontrollably.

After a couple of minutes, he walked her over to the couch and laid her down. She was still heaving and sobbing but now more intermittently. He got her a glass of water from the kitchen and brought it to her for her pills. She appeared thoroughly demoralized and physically exhausted. He grabbed a blanket from the back of the couch and draped it over her. Within seconds she was asleep.

Jim let himself out and immediately smoked his first cigarette of the day as he headed over to see Mike.

Mike was in a great mood because the prosecutor had given him probation earlier in the day. He was looking forward to moving his stuff into Uncle Joe's, which Mike planned to do over the weekend.

On the way home, Jim popped into Sully's for a quick beer. It was days before Thanksgiving, and Jim wasn't particularly looking forward to it, as he was scheduled to work Wednesday through Sunday. He really couldn't complain, however, as he was taking nearly a week off for Christmas to go visit his family at his younger aunt's home in Garfield Heights.

Back at his apartment, Jim breezed through his mail and email and settled in with a TV dinner followed by an unsavory piece of nicotine gum for his dessert.

# CHAPTER FORTY

The following days of November seemed shorter, quicker, and colder. It was now the day before Thanksgiving, and Jim was getting ready to start his long holiday work stint. He was pleased to discover that some of his patients would be away because of the holiday. Jim also knew, though, that the following week would be more challenging as he was scheduled to get two new patients.

Stopping in at Southbridge Manor, Jim learned that Wanda was still in the hospital and had received the implantation of an artificial feeding tube. She was not yet stable enough to be transferred to any other facility. He also learned that Sally had gone out shopping with Lianna, so he'd have to stop back later on his way home.

Because Richard had gone away for the weekend to see his cousin in Iowa, Jim went directly to St. Monica's Apartments.

Jim found June working in St. Monica's small office and learned from her that Nick was still missing in action. The police still had no solid leads, but that did not prevent the plethora of rumors that swirled around his disappearance. Some said that he had been taken out by an angry mob of lesbian and atheist strippers. Others said that it was a plot hatched by the Vatican. But the explanation that Jim liked the best came from Vicky. She claimed that Mother Earth simply grew too tired of him, opened herself up, and then let hell swallow him whole. Jim hoped that Maria's uncle would end up spending eternity with Nick in everlasting annoyance.

Jim had been concerned about Lucinda's mental health ever since she'd found out that Chad had been cheating on her. He'd recently asked Vicky if there was any counselor whom she could think of that might be acceptable to Lucinda. He was saddened to learn from Vicky that Lucinda had been molested by her therapist when she was only thirteen years old. It was shortly after Vincente's death, during the time when she first started having hallucinations. Her parents hadn't pressed charges, though, as they did not want any more publicity for the family because her father had just resigned his seat in Congress. Ever since this incident, Lucinda did not cooperate with any counselors whatsoever. Jim couldn't stand the thought of Lucinda being abused, as it evoked painful images of Maria's lifeless, violated body.

Jim wished June a Happy Thanksgiving and then headed up to see Lucinda.

After he knocked on the door a couple of times, she appeared wearing faded jeans and a navy sweatshirt.

"Hey, Jimmy. Howya doin', pal?"

"Not bad. Yourself?"

"Pretty good. Headin' down to visit with Katherine tomorrow."

"How come you didn't leave today?"

"Are you kidding? Call me chicken, but I just don't like the thought of going into the city during the busiest travel day of the year. Anyway, Cindy already gave me meds to cover me for the whole weekend. Whatcha doin' for Turkey Day?"

"I'll be working with whoever hasn't gone away."

A brief pause followed, and then Lucinda said, "Hey, Jimmy, I just want to say thank you."

"No thanks needed, Lucy."

"You're the only guy who ever treated me right," she replied. "Guess what I'm doing next week?"

"What's that?"

"Starting work as Katherine's photo assistant. She says if I like it, then she'll help me buy my own camera and equipment someday."

"Fantastic! I'm sure you'll do great!"

"Know what else?"

"What?"

"I met a friend of Katherine's last weekend. She was really cool. She's traveled all over the world and met all kinds of wild people. After we went out with her, Katherine tells me that she's a therapist. So, then I ask Katherine if—maybe—I could see her sometime. She was thrilled to call her for me and set it up. I got an appointment to see her next week."

"Does that mean we can't talk anymore?"

"Nah, you know that I'll always talk to you, bud!"

"Well, I hope you have a great Thanksgiving."

"Thanks. You, too," Lucinda replied, then she took her pills and signed the MAR.

Soon Jim was back in his car and heading to Uncle Joe's. When he got there, he learned that only Joe was home

.

"You must be Jim. Mike's told me a lot about you," Joe said.

"Yeah, you, too. Is Mike around?"

"Nope. He went to a Thanksgiving party with his TBI group."

"Can you make sure that he gets these?" Jim said, handing Joe the small coin envelope with Mike's medication.

"No problem. I'll tape it to the remote control."

"Is Mike gonna be around tomorrow?"

"Should be. I'm taking him and his mom out for lunch at about two, so we should be home by this time. They haven't talked much since Mike got arrested. Sometimes I think that woman's just wound too tight. I know she means well, but she's way overprotective and as cheap as they come. Man, she could squeeze the buffalo off a nickel. Mickey just doesn't respond well to all of that, but she is his mom, and they really should get along."

"Well, I hope it works out for them. He's been through a lot."

"Yeah, I know."

After a pleasant trip in the car, Jim stopped at Bacon Alley Pharmacy to pick up some nicotine patches and his brand-new prescription of antidepressants. Although Jim had worked with countless psychiatrists, he thought it was strange yet intriguing that he was now on one of their couches. Nonetheless, Jim liked his new doctor (whom Stella had recommended) and the fact that he was a psychiatrist as well as a licensed therapist.

Soon Jim made his way to Southbridge Manor. He found Sally in the large day room, drinking a cup of dark coffee.

"Hey, Sally, how are you?"

"Excellent! Me and Lianna went shoppin'!"

"Whadya get?"

"We got some food for tomorrow. We also got some canned food for a package that she's sending to Jesus' brothers and sisters in Africa for Christmas! She said that I could make the Christmas card all by myself!"

"Excellent!"

"Jesus must have a really big family if he's got brothers and sisters in Africa *and* Mexico," she said. "Do you think they'll get some of the food to him?"

"I'm sure they will."

She smiled and nodded; then the two of them finished their visit in the usual fashion.

Jim was driving down the street when he spied a young lady in pajamas walking through a puddle at the edge of the road. She was somewhat heavyset, and had spooky pale skin that seemed especially eerie in the moonlight. She also had gnarly, knotted, dark hair that roughly cascaded to her shoulder blades. She had an overcoat on but otherwise looked completely odd for one taking a walk at night in November.

Jim pulled his car to the curb, turned his hazard lights on and engine off, and got out of the car to go after her.

"Miss, are you okay?"

"Leave me alone!" she exclaimed and walked off the sidewalk into the woods.

Jim followed, then said again, "Miss, are you from Southbridge Manor?"

"Just leave me alone! I want to be dead!"

*Not on my shift, sister!* Jim thought. "Maybe I can help you. My name is Jim—what's yours?"

"It's Lilith. Just leave me alone and let me be dead!"

"I really can't do that. Why don't we talk?" Jim said as he quickly overtook her and began walking backward, with Lilith facing his front.

"I just want to be dead! Amanda thinks I don't have to wear makeup to look good! Even with all the makeup in the world, I'll never look as good as Amanda! I'm just a fuckin' fat pig who deserves to be dead!"

"I think you look just fine. Why don't we go back to the manor and talk?"

"I don't wanna talk—I wanna be dead!"

It got increasingly darker and dangerous as they headed deep into the woods. Jim continued to traverse backward on a soggy layer of wet leaves. Also, a cold and steady rain began falling, which quickly soaked both of them.

"Look, just leave me alone and let me be dead!"

"I can't do that! If we don't start heading back, you'll leave me no choice but to call the police!"

"Good! Call the police! Let them take me to the station and euthanize me!"

He got more nervous, as he could now hear the sound of rushing water approaching from his back.

"Look...please...let's just turn around and head back to the manor. I can get you some help."

"You don't understand. I don't want help! I want to be dead! Let the police take me away to get euthanized!"

"I really can't do that. Please, let's just go back."

"I'm just a big, fat loser! I'll never be smart and pretty like Amanda! Just let me be dead!"

Jim quickly glanced over his shoulder and realized that they were now dangerously close to a cliff. The sound of rushing water became so loud that he had to shout over it. "Look, I can't do that! If you don't turn around now, I'm gonna call the police!" Jim shouted while pulling his cell phone from his left pocket.

"Just let me jump into the river and be dead!"

Suddenly, she ran forward to Jim's right. He quickly turned to grab her but slipped on the wet leaves beneath his feet. She was now running straight toward the cliff when Jim adroitly rebounded and pounced on her like a linebacker.

"Oh, please—just let me jump and be dead!"

"Nope, I can't do that!" Jim exclaimed as he increased his grip around her midsection. He tackled her in such a way that his arms were wrapped around her large belly and forearms. His head, which was turned to one side, was directly against her abdomen. The two of them were now perpendicular and very close to the cliff. Jim was afraid that if he tried to move at all, he'd lose his balance on wet leaves, and Lilith would squirm over the cliff like a fish jumping out of a boat.

Surprisingly, she did not squirm much in the position that Jim had her, but she begged for death nonetheless. "Get off me and let me be dead!"

"Look, we're just gonna wait here quietly until they find us. It shouldn't be too long."

She continued to implore Jim for death over the next half hour or so, which felt like a lot longer since they were both totally cold and soaked. Jim wished that he could get one hand free to call for help, but he knew he'd be risking her life if he tried. So, they waited. After another long half hour, they started hearing voices. Soon a few police officers were surrounding them with flashlights and guns drawn.

"I'm a nurse from Harmony Healthcare. I'm trying to keep this girl from killing herself!" Jim said, glancing over his shoulder and seeing their weapons pointed at him.

Immediately, they put their guns away and approached Jim and Lilith. They carefully restrained Lilith's arms while Jim stood up. Soon she was safely in custody, and they were all making their way back to the street.

Lilith seemed to get a sudden burst of energy being on her feet and started to scream, "Take me in! Euthanize me! Euthanize me!"

Undeterred, two police officers kept her on the wet and slippery path back to the street; however, they did stop to handcuff her after her first outburst.

Soon they were back at Jim's car, and she was safely deposited in a waiting ambulance. Jim stayed for a few minutes to give the police information for their report, and then he headed home. He decided it was best not to tell Rose, as he didn't wish to explain why he was wrestling a patient who wasn't theirs.

A short time later, Jim was back at his apartment but deviated slightly from his usual routine. As soon as he got in, he took a short, hot shower. Once done, he went into the kitchen and poured a tall glass of milk. He thought it was a good idea to avoid bourbon, given the Motrin that he was about to take. After swallowing the pills, Jim briefly reopened the fridge again to explore his meal options. It didn't take long, as it didn't contain much.

Due to his hip pain and fatigue, Jim opted for something quick and easy to make: a couple of leftover buttermilk pancakes with some organic maple syrup that Rose had recommended. Although he ate standing up with his weight shifted mostly to his right leg, he nonetheless took his time and delighted in every succulent mouthful.

After dinner, Jim settled into the cushy futon and prepared to engage in his usual mail sorting routine except for getting his computer out to check his email. He closed his eyes for a bit and felt his hip throbbing with excruciating pain despite his fatigue. He hoped that the full effect of the Motrin would soon afford him a decent night's sleep. Although Jim's hip had hurt less after his trip to Yankee Stadium in the spring, tonight's pain was different. It didn't bother him as much because he knew that it was the best kind of pain. Not wanting to fall asleep on the less supportive futon, Jim abruptly grabbed the pile of mail that he had previously put on the steamer chest before work. After quickly perusing nearly a half dozen polite yet impersonal rejection letters, Jim then turned his attention to the three remaining pieces of mail. He eagerly opened the first one. It was from the Veterans' Administration and contained information and an employment application. The second was from one of the state's universities. That letter contained information and an application to the school's psychiatric nurse practitioner program. The third one was from the car salesman with whom Jim had taken a test drive during the summer. Jim opened the large envelope, which contained the latest brochure of new and powerful Ford trucks. He then began enthusiastically flipping through the glossy photos in the colorful brochure.